# Let N

(McClain Brothers: Book 2)

Alexandria House

Pink Cashmere Publishing, LLC
Arkansas, USA

Pink Cashmere Publishing, LLC
pinkcashmerepub@gmail.com
http://pinkcashmerepublishing.webs.com/

# Let Me Hold You

NBA player, Leland McClain, the baby of the McClain family, is tall, handsome, talented…and spoiled. He's a man who gets what he wants, and what he wants is the lovely Kimberly Hampton.

Kim Hampton is the director of a community center, a woman who lives to help others while trying to forget a troubling past. As far as she's concerned, a relationship with any man is a horrible idea. But a relationship with Leland McClain? That's just out of the question.

He has to have her.

She is undeniably attracted to him.

But will she lower her guard and let him hold her?

*For all the Kims in this world. May you find your Leland.*

# 1

# Leland

I rolled over in bed, felt the heavy gold chain around my neck shift as I slid the soft hand from my chest and reached for my phone on the night table. Easing out of bed, I swiped my underwear from the floor as I stretched my body and headed into the suite's bathroom, phone in hand. I missed the call, but after I emptied my bladder, redialed the number and leaned over the sink as I waited for her to answer.

Instead of a hello, she drawled, "I didn't wake you up, did I?" Her voice was that familiar combination of gruffness and comfort that I loved hearing.

"Yeah, but it's cool. You the only somebody who's allowed to wake me up."

She chuckled. "Well, I'm glad to know I got that kinda pull with you. How you doing?"

"Good. How are you, Auntie? Your blood pressure okay? You had that test for your heart that your doctor recommended yet?"

"I'm fine, boy. What I tell you about worrying about me?"

Staring at myself in the bathroom mirror and stretching my tired eyes, I said, "Can't help it. You the only mama I got left besides Kat."

She laughed. "That girl always did think she could boss you around."

"Think? She did a good job of it! And she look so much like Mama that half the time I thought she was her!"

There was silence from Aunt Ever. I was sure she was trying not to cry, probably thinking about her baby sister, my sweet mother. I had cried all the tears I had for her when I was a kid and held on to the good of the fact that she'd ever lived rather than mourning her loss now.

"You getting settled in St. Louis? Liking it so far?" she asked, redirecting the conversation.

"Yeah, it's cool," I lied. I hated the move, was accustomed to living between LA and Miami. St. Louis was slower than both, in some ways even slower than Houston to me. I preferred a faster pace.

"Made any new friends?"

Before I could answer, I felt her wrap her arms around my waist and press her breasts against my bare back. That irritated the shit out of me. Not that I couldn't go for some more of what she gave me the night before, but I was on the phone with my aunt. The last thing I wanted was a hard dick while talking to her, so I said, "Hey, let me call you back, Auntie."

"Mm-hmm, tell whoever she is I said hi."

I shook my head as I ended the call. "Good morning," I said, covering her hands with mine.

"Good morning to you," she said, sliding her hand down my stomach to my groin, then adding, "and to you, too."

I turned my head toward her a little and smiled. "You tryna get something started that I can't finish. I got places to be, shit I gotta do."

I heard her sigh, felt her warm breath on my back. "So, I'm being dismissed?"

Moving her hands, I spun around to face her. She was pretty, *fine*, and I'd enjoyed her the night before, but I really did have a packed schedule. I had to work out, had houses to look at, calls to make, and a prior commitment I didn't want to be late for. "You ain't gotta take it that way. I had fun with you, but like I said, I got shit to do."

"You gonna call me later? Maybe we can have drinks…or something?"

I left the bathroom, re-entering the bedroom of the suite in search of the rest of my clothes. "Or something, huh? My schedule is packed, but I'ma hit you up as soon as I can, a'ight?"

"Okay, because I want you to meet my brother and my son. They're both huge fans. And maybe we could catch a movie or something?"

It was my turn to sigh. What part of "my schedule is packed" did she not get? And damn, why was she trying to introduce me to her folks when I just met her ass last night? I swear, you'd think a forty-seven-year-old woman wouldn't be trying to move so fast. Shit!

I didn't answer her in the affirmative or negative, just finished getting dressed, gave her a kiss, and left her in my suite hoping she'd be gone when I got back, because like I said, I had shit to do.

*****

I stood on the sideline and watched the hoard of twelve and thirteen-year-olds dribble balls, joke around, and mostly gawk at me despite the fact that I was standing right next to my boy, Polo, who was damn near seven feet tall, a big Shaquille O'Neal-built nigga who was always wearing a mug although he wouldn't hurt a fly. I guess it was because I was new to the area and my team, or maybe because—

"Daaaaaamn, she fine!" Polo muttered under his breath. "Look at her booty!"

I followed his line of sight to her—tight beige skirt that fit her wide hips perfectly and stopped just above her knees so that those big legs of hers were on display. Sleeveless red blouse, huge layered pearl necklace, hair in some kind of fancy cornrowed pattern, smooth chocolate skin. Yeah, she was undoubtedly fine. No, bump that. She was sexy as hell.

Nevertheless, I turned to him and shrugged. "She a'ight. A little too young for me, though. You know how I do."

Polo shook his head. "Yeah, I remember back in college while the rest of us was trying to get with the cheerleaders and those fine-ass sprinters, your ass was always sniffing in behind some professor."

"Or one of those cheerleaders' mamas. They were all fine!"

Polo laughed. "I will never understand you. And her? She older than us, ain't she? I mean, she don't look it, but she gotta be."

"Like I said, she ain't old enough for me. I like my women seasoned. She's salt and pepper, maybe a dash of paprika. I like 'em with salt, pepper, paprika, Old Bay, garlic powder, Goya, muh-fuckin' lemon pepper, cayenne pepper, *and* some Mrs. Dash. And she ain't thick enough, either. Plus, you already know—"

"Mr. Logan, I'm so glad you could help us out with the program," her voice interrupted me. I didn't realize she'd made it over to us. Damn, she smelled good.

Polo nodded, licked his lips, and gave her a smile that I guess was supposed to be seductive but definitely wasn't. "Call me Polo, and it's no problem. I love the kids."

She returned his smile, and I couldn't take my eyes off her mouth. Her lower lip was bigger than her top lip. *I bet they taste good as hell.*

"And Mr. McClain, I want to especially thank you for agreeing to help us out. I know you had every reason to back out of this commitment, and no one would blame you if you did," she said.

I raised my eyes from her lips to her up-turned, black-brown eyes. "It's all good. I made a promise and I don't break promises, Ms. Hampton. I'm looking forward to working with these kids, and I'm honored to get a personal thank you from the center's director."

She blinked, and her eyes softened a little, losing the apprehension I'd initially seen in them. "I figured it was the least I could do since you are volunteering your time here. Well, let me introduce you gentlemen to our boys and then you two can get to it. Thanks again, Mr. McClain, Polo."

"No problem, Ms. Hampton," I said.

"You got it," was Polo's response.

I watched as she walked away—okay, I actually watched her ass walk away from me. Damn! She was fine, like…for real. But anyway, she approached the thirty or so young men scattered on the basketball court then turned and shot another smile at me. "All right, I'm sure you boys know these gentlemen, or at least know *of* them, but I'd like to give you all a formal introduction to them. For the basketball camp portion of our summer program, you'll be learning skills from some NBA players, including these two players from our own St. Louis Cyclones basketball team! First, we have Mr. Paul "Polo" Logan. Let's welcome him!"

The boys clapped and yelled for my current teammate and old college classmate and teammate.

"And," Kimberly Hampton continued, "a new Cyclone, formerly with the Heat, Mr. Leland McClain…let's welcome him, too!"

More applause and louder yells, or maybe that was what my ego heard, but anyway, it was a nice reception, and a minute or so later, when Polo and I separated the boys into two groups to begin teaching them the principals of basketball, I was wearing a smile.

# 2

# Kimberly

I made my way back to my office, fell into the chair behind my desk, and stared at the mountain of papers and folders and phone message slips that were cluttering nearly every surface around me. Rihanna's *Work* played in my head as I tried to decide what to tackle first—the grant proposal the fundraising consultant I'd hired had submitted for my review or the missed calls from the community center's main—i.e., *only*—benefactor. Sighing, I grabbed my phone and dialed our benefactor's number, hoping he was in a better mood than he was during our last conversation. He wasn't, but the conversation wasn't as bad as I anticipated, and after that duty was fulfilled, I dug into the grant proposal, then moved on to some PR stuff I needed to handle, was knee-deep in that paperwork when my cell began to buzz on my desk.

I grinned at the name that danced on the screen. "Hello?"

"Heyyyy! What you up to?"

"Working, what else?"

"Oh, yeah. I forgot you like working there. I mean, you like...actually enjoy your job. You're an anomaly if I ever saw one."

I shook my head, took a sip from the bottle of water that had gone from frigid to tepid over the course of the work day, and said, "My job is my calling just like singing is yours. Who doesn't love their calling? Don't you enjoy singing?"

"I love it, but you should be somewhere sipping tropical drinks on a beach. You damn sure earned the right to take it easy. I don't know why you don't."

"Because, like I said, this is my calling. Now, I know you didn't call me to harass me about my career choices for the millionth time. So, what's up?"

"Oh, yeah! I was calling to see if you needed a ride home from work today. You get off in a couple of hours, right?"

"Uh, why would I need a ride? My car is new, Zabrina."

"I just thought maybe you did. Hey, how about I meet you there? We're still going out for drinks and dinner and stuff tonight, right?"

"Uh-huh, and you think you're slick, don't you? You remembered the NBA guys start helping out today, didn't you?"

"Is that today?! Girl, I got so much on my mind, I forgot all about that!"

"Heifer, please. Your thirsty ass ain't forgot nothing. You probably memorized the damn basketball camp schedule. I bet you know it better than I do."

"Whatever. So…is Leland McClain as fine in person as he is on Instagram and on TV? You know, he likes older women. I could be his sugar mama."

"No, you couldn't with your broke ass, and do you think I have time to check him out like that with all the work I have to do around here?"

"I think your ass is not blind. I mean, shit…as big and tall and fine as he is? Hell, he's finer than Big South, and you know that's a damn accomplishment. How can you possibly not notice how sexy he is?"

"He was wearing basketball shorts and a Romey U t-shirt. He looked…athletic."

"And fine."

*As hell.* "I guess. But, uh…ain't you got a man?"

"Sometimes."

"Sometimes? What kind of answer is that? Don't you live with him?"

"That's debatable. So, did you see a print?"

"Bye, Z."

"Damn, it must've been a *huge* print for you to be trying to hang up without wishing me a happy whatever-random-holiday-today-is. You know how you are about your holidays."

"Oh, yeah…happy Old Maid's Day."

"Fuck you."

"What?! That's an actual holiday!"

"And that was an actual *fuck you*."

"Wow, okay. I love you, too, Z."

"Uh-huh…"

"I do! And I wasn't throwing shade. Hell, I'm older than you and I've never been married, either, and I don't even have a man."

"But you've been engaged before."

"You really wanna take it there?"

"My bad."

"Uh-huh."

"And as far as you not having a man, that's by choice."

"I know."

"Mm-hmm…so, you sure you don't need a ride or something else that will put me in the vicinity of Leland McClain?"

"Bye, Z!"

"Bye, ole cockblocking-ass woman."

I relaxed against the back of my chair and released the giggle I'd been suppressing while on the phone with my first cousin and best friend for life. Zabrina Norris was a nut but spot on with her analysis of Leland McClain. He was fine, extremely so—tall, as fit as any NBA player, gorgeous brown skin, dark eyes, big Colin Kaepernick afro that he kept pulled up in a man bun most of the time, thick mustache and beard. The facial hair made him look older, but he was young, and I was…*me*. The last thing *me* needed to do was get involved with *any* man, especially him. Not that he wanted me anyway.

But whether I was his type or not, I damn sure could enjoy looking at him.

*****

I raised my arms and moved to the beat of Kendrick Lamar's and SZA's *All the Stars*, a song I'd grown obsessed with after watching *Black Panther* three times in the theater. Okay, I actually watched it five times. Anyway, this was my favorite thing to do after a day at a job that both stressed me completely out and satisfied my soul—cut loose with my girls and enjoy the good vibes that always seemed to envelop me when we hung out. And it didn't hurt that Plush-St. Louis was one of my favorite clubs. A new addition to my city's night life offerings and owned by a young black female entrepreneur, Plush was the embodiment of grown folks' fun with a cover charge steep enough to keep the riff-raff out and live entertainment second to none. I loved Plush for the atmosphere and the music. It was nothing for me to hit the dancefloor with my girls and shake my booty, because I had learned years ago that I didn't need a man on my arm to have fun. Zabrina, on the other hand...

"He's looking at you," she whispered, once we returned to our table and all re-upped on our drinks. In attendance with us on this particular night was our cousin, Shelby, and her BFF, Constance. Our usual number five, Merry, had a man now and had basically gone AWOL on us unlike Zabrina, who gladly left her man at home.

Rolling my head around to face the woman who was three years my junior and greatly resembled our grandmother from her smooth pecan skin and big round eyes to her huge breasts and sinfully thick body, I asked, "Who?"

"Zaddy over there in the tailored suit. The one with the salt-and-pepper beard and the nice teeth."

I knew who she was referring to and had felt his eyes on me several times since we'd arrived, but since I had bedroom activities covered, I said, "So?"

"*So*, what do you think?"

I shrugged.

"You are crazy, you know that? How can you be so disinterested in men?"

"How can you be so obsessed with them?"

"Because black men are damn fine and black dick is damn good."

"You need to take your ass home to your black man and his black dick."

She rolled her eyes. "That nigga ain't—oh, shit! Here Zaddy comes!"

My eyes widened as I glanced up to see that he was indeed headed in our direction. My mind raced with thoughts as I tried to think of what to do. Excuse myself to the restroom? Pretend to get a phone call? Take off running out the place? Anything but actually engage in conversation with this man, because that was never a good idea for me. With my track record, I needed to put out a restraining order against every living, breathing man on the planet. Like, for real.

As luck would have it, I didn't have to fake anything. My phone began to buzz in my hand, and as the silver fox approached, I made my escape, saying "Gotta take this," to my tablemates and giving the approaching gentleman a little nod before heading toward the restroom where maybe I'd be able to escape the music thundering from the speakers so that I could hear the voice on the other end.

"Hello?" I said breathily, as I stepped into the ladies' room.

"Hey, what you up to?"

"I'm at Plush, but I'm willing to leave if I have a reason to."

"Is that right? Well, let me give you a reason, then. I'm over here thinking about you."

"Then I better come see exactly what you're thinking about."

"You sure better."

With a grin on my face, I exited the restroom and headed back to my table where *Zaddy* was having an in-depth conversation with Constance. I quickly excused myself and left for what had become as routine in my life as taking a shower—a booty call.

# 3

# Leland

Sitting in my car, my eyes were glued to the brick and stone building in front of me. These two-a-day workouts were kicking my ass, I was tired as hell, and although my heart was in that gym with those kids, I couldn't seem to find the strength to open the door and climb out of the car. I dropped my head and sighed, then lifted it in time to see her walking out the building. She had on jeans and a t-shirt and her ass was *still* fine. I wasn't lying when I said she was smaller and younger than the women I usually got with, but there was something about her that kept catching my attention and wouldn't seem to let it go. There wasn't shit I could or would do about it, though. So, I was relieved when my attention was pulled away from the sway of her hips to my ringing phone.

I answered it with, "Yo!"

"Yo, yourself, knucklehead! What you up to?"

"Nuthin', about to get my volunteer on."

She sighed loudly into the phone. "I still can't believe you're doing this, volunteering at *his* community center when his stupid ass ran you away from Miami? I just don't get it, Leland!"

I knew my big sister had my best interest at heart, and hell, she was kind of right, but I was tired and nowhere near in the mood to explain myself, so I replied with, "I'm doing this for the kids, Kit-Kat. You know that. Plus, I committed to this before all that bullshit went down with dude. And you know I'm a man of my word, just like Daddy and Ev." It was the truth. There wasn't much I wouldn't do for kids, especially these boys who reminded me so much of myself at that age. Life had been good to me despite the bad, and it was almost a compulsion for me to give back.

"A man of your word, huh? I say forget that when your word was given to a horrible person. And you can help kids without doing it through *his* foundation at *his* community center in *his* hometown. You could start your own foundation and center. I told you; I'll help you."

"I know. I just prefer to do it this way. I mean, I donate to a lot of foundations and charities, anyway. Giving my time is taking it to another level."

"But you could take that money and put it into your own charity. Doesn't that make sense to you?"

"Yeah, but…"

"But what?"

Kimberly Hampton finally backed out of her parking spot, and as she passed by my car, gave me a smile and a wave that I quickly returned.

"Leland! But what?" Kat shouted.

"But…I gotta go. Talk to your nagging ass later."

"Whatever. Bye, boy!"

I ended the call and was grinning as I climbed out my car. She was right, though. I really did need to just start my own foundation, but that shit took time and energy and work. And I wasn't down for any of that. I was fine with helping out other outreach programs, even if this one was funded and founded by my stupid-ass former teammate, Armand Daniels.

\*\*\*\*\*

Armand Daniels was a stand-out high school basketball player and a local legend of sorts in St. Louis, was on an NCAA champion team his one and only year of college, was named Most Outstanding Player for that same year, and when he entered the NBA draft, was picked fifth overall in the first round by the Heat. He was talented as hell, on par with some of the greatest shooting guards in league history, but his attitude sucked. He was a hot head with anger issues, loved to fight, and aimed his rage at me toward the middle of his first year with the Heat, which was my fourth year with them. I dealt with that shit the best I could, then decided to take advantage of my free agency and bounce once the season was over. But that honestly had more to do with me knowing my time with that team had drawn to a close than it did with Armand Daniels' ass trying to bully me, because kicking his ass would've been easy. Hell, I itched to do it from the first time he tried to come at me, but I wasn't going to let his young ass mess up my record with the league *or* my money. No, he wasn't the total reason I left. The truth was, I wanted a ring and I wasn't going to get one with the Heat, not even with the addition of that fool to the team.

The St. Louis Cyclones was a new addition to the league, or rather the re-naming and resurrection of a once-defunct team. It was only five years old but full of hungry talent. Shit, we all wanted a ring, and I believed we could win one. That's why I let them court me into a contract. Plus, I was a little closer to Texas now and to Aunt Ever, who I found it hard not to worry about even though she insisted on it. Like I said, she and Kat were the only mothers I had left, and Kat was young and strong. Aunt Ever, the oldest of my mom's siblings, wasn't getting any younger and not in the best of health. It was important to me that I could get to her quickly if I needed to.

Anyway, maybe it was dumb to be volunteering with Daniels' foundation, but I was assured I wouldn't ever be in the same space as him, because his ass couldn't be bothered to make an appearance at his own basketball camp until the final week of it. And standing there watching the boys do the drills Polo and I had taught them a few days earlier, I knew I'd made the right decision in keeping my word. They looked good as they lined up in front of me. Polo had a prior engagement on this particular day, so this one was all on me, but I was good with it.

"A'ight y'all. Good workout today. Y'all will have a couple more of my buddies working with you tomorrow, and I'll be back the day after that. Y'all's layups better be on point when I get back. You heard me?"

"Yes, Coach McClain," they said pretty unenthusiastically. And that's just what I liked to see after a practice session—exhaustion. That proved to me I'd done my job.

"A'ight. Your moms and them are waiting for y'all. Have a good evening," I said, dismissing them.

Thirty minutes later, as I was headed to my car, I noticed a boy sitting on a bench outside the building and recognized him as one of the camp attendees. I thought I'd made sure all the boys had been picked up, even checked the locker room to be sure there were no stragglers. The boys whose parents couldn't pick them up rode the center's van home. I had no idea Lil' Man was left behind.

Moving toward the bench, I said, "Hey, you ain't got a ride, Lil' Man? Why you ain't catch the van?"

His head lifted from where it had been buried in his chest, and he looked up at me. "My mama supposed to be coming."

"You need to call her?" I asked, taking a seat beside him so I could hear him better. He had a soft voice that went along with his shyness. He was one of the quietest boys in the group, but also one of the most talented from what I'd seen. He was shorter than the other boys but got the ball through the hoop every time he took a shot.

"Her phone's off."

"Oh...anyone else you can call?"

He shrugged.

"You're Shemar, right?"

There was a flicker of something in his eyes...surprise, maybe. I guess he thought I didn't know his name, but I was good with names, had a crazy memory. I still remembered the names of every classmate I had in elementary school. Having a memory like that could fuck with you sometimes, though.

He nodded his answer.

"You know your address, right?" He should've, but shit, you

never knew about stuff like that with some kids.

He nodded again.

We sat there in silence as I tried to decide what to do. I could give him a ride home, grab him a burger or something on the way. It was after five, and I knew he had to be hungry. But shit, I wasn't trying to do all that without his parents' permission. That was a recipe for trouble with who I was and what I did for a living. People were always looking for a come-up, and I wasn't trying to be a fresh meal ticket for anyone.

I had decided to take him back inside and see if maybe there was an emergency contact on file for him or something when one of the glass front doors opened, and Kim Hampton walked out. I wasn't surprised to see her since her car was the only one left on the lot besides mine.

She turned to lock the doors, glanced over at us, and jumped a little. "Oh! I thought I was the only one left here."

"Naw, me and Shemar been out here chopping it up. He's-uh-still waiting on his ride," I said. "Says his mom is supposed to be getting him but her phone is off, so he can't call."

She pursed her lips and then started chewing on the bottom one. That was sexy as hell to me.

"Why don't we go in here and see who's on your emergency contact form, okay?" she asked, giving Shemar a smile.

"Can Coach McClain come in with us?"

"Oh, I'm sure he needs to be on his way. He's a busy—"

"Naw, it's all good. I got the time," I cut in.

"Uh…okay. Well, you gentlemen can follow me. I just need to disarm the alarm and—"

The sound of screeching tires snatched all of our heads toward the parking lot where we could see a small Toyota racing toward us and jerking to a stop. A woman hopped out, short and thick and wearing jogging pants and a hoodie in ninety-degree weather. She had a panicked look on her face and a noticeable bruise under her eye.

Rushing toward us, she yanked Shemar into a hug. "I'm so sorry! The time got away from me. You ready to go, baby?"

Shemar nodded, a relieved look on his face.

"Good, I gotta get back and finish dinner. Daddy got off work early."

There was an unmistakable shift in Shemar's demeanor. He almost looked as if he'd changed his mind about being relieved to see his mother. As a matter of fact, as she tried to steer him toward the car, he didn't move but remained glued to the sidewalk.

"Shemar, come on!" she hissed.

"Aye, you good, Lil' Man?" I asked.

He looked up at me and opened his mouth, but his mom preempted him. "He's fine, just don't like my cooking. Always be wanting McDonald's. Come on, boy!"

This time, he followed his mother to the car, climbed inside, and as she gave me and Ms. Hampton a wave and pulled off the lot, he hung his head.

Ms. Hampton and I stood there in silence, both of us staring after the car until I finally said, "Something ain't right with his mom. You see that bruise?"

Turning to face me, she nodded. "Yeah, I did. I'm gonna talk to our onsite social worker in the morning, see if he can look into the situation. Thanks for hanging with him while he waited for her. That was very kind of you."

I gave her a lopsided grin. "It was nothing."

"No, it was definitely something. And I feel like I need to thank you again for still coming to volunteer after all that mess with—"

"It's all good, Ms. Hampton. I don't hold grudges, and I know when someone is just flexing. That's all he was doing."

She shifted her stance, poking a hip out. "Still, thank you. You are truly one of the good guys."

I tipped my Cardinals baseball cap at her. "No problem."

Silence filled the air around us as we both just kind of looked at each other. Then she said, "Um," and I said, "Uh," simultaneously.

Then we both laughed. Well, actually, she giggled.

Looking up at me with wide eyes, her lashes fluttered as she asked, "Why are you so tall?"

Was she flirting with me? Shit, I hoped so, because I had just decided she could have me if she wanted me. On my mama, she could. "Uh, they tell me my dad was real tall, and my mama wasn't exactly short."

She smiled. "No…what I meant to ask was, how tall are you, Mr. McClain?"

I shrugged. "Wikipedia says I'm six-eight."

"Is Wikipedia correct?"

"Naw, I'm six-seven and a half. Just a little taller than my brother."

"Big South?"

I nodded. "Yeah, You a fan of his?"

"Of course, and of you, too!"

"For real? Cool."

She smiled at me, and I smiled at her. It was awkward and kind of nice…really nice.

"Um, so I guess the King's Dream Community Center has taken up more than enough of your time today, huh?"

"Naw, never that. I'm honored to be able to serve the community, but I guess I should head on out. Gotta be up early in the morning. Uh…see you later, Ms. Hampton."

"Goodnight, Mr. McClain."

"Goodnight."

# 4

# Kimberly

*I should've gotten a sandwich, too.*

That thought resonated in my mind as I scarfed down my salad and realized it wasn't really hitting the spot for me. I consciously tried to eat healthier on the days of my Stiletto Step Class, because I guess I wanted to be lighter on my feet, but I also knew expending all that energy after work with only this little salad in my stomach was a recipe for disaster. I was liable to pass the hell out in the middle of class.

I was contemplating leaving my office again to grab a burger when my assistant's voice poured through the intercom speakers of my phone. "Ms. Kim, uh…you have a visitor?"

Was she asking me or informing me?

"Okay…but didn't I tell you I was on my lunch break, Peaches?"

"Oh, I forgot! Want me to tell him to make an appointment?"

I sighed as I closed the top of my dissatisfying salad and grabbed a napkin to wipe my hands. "Well, who is it?"

"Leland McClain."

*Leland McClain?!* "Oh…give me about five minutes and then send him in."

"Okay," she chirped.

Yanking my bottom desk drawer open, I grabbed my purse and dug inside for my lip gloss and mirror. I'd just decided I looked presentable when the door to my office opened and Peaches ushered him inside. All six-foot-seven-and-a-half of his fine-ness waltzed in wearing a purple and gold Cyclones track suit. All I could think was: *wow!* I mean, he was young, but at thirty-five, I wasn't exactly *old* old. Maybe…

"Uh, good afternoon. Sorry to interrupt your lunch," he said, with a nod toward the salad that still held prime real estate on my desk.

"No, no, it's fine. Um, have a seat." I watched him sit in the chair in front of my desk, lean forward, and prop his elbows on his knees. It wasn't like I was hard-up for sex or anything, but damn! Leland McClain was pure sexiness. "What can I help you with, Mr. McClain? I see you're here early today. Want to add to your volunteer hours, maybe teach a STEM class or help out with the garden the boys have been tending?"

He chuckled, cocked his head to the side, and licked his lips. "Naw, I ain't really good with math and science, and I put in more than enough time working my aunt's garden back in the day. I actually wanted to check on Shemar, see what your social worker found out. He's been missing from basketball camp the last couple of days."

It took me a second to realize who and what he was referring to. It'd been a rough week of me putting out various fires since I'd found him and the young man sitting outside the building.

"Um, yes…I talked to my social worker about it, and he's promised to make a home visit," I responded.

Leland gave me a slow nod. "When?"

"When? Uh, when he can. We have thirty boys in this summer program alone, most of whom are living in poverty or single parent homes, and many are experiencing and/or witnessing all types of violence. We also have a girls-only program running simultaneously. We are grossly understaffed for what we're trying to do here, but we're determined to get the job done. Rest assured, Shemar will be taken care of."

"Yeah, well…I know how things like this can slip through the cracks, how kids can end up hurt or forgotten, especially black kids."

Lifting my eyebrows, I leaned forward. "You did notice that I'm black, as well as every single person who works in this building, right?"

"Yeah, and us black people are known for half-stepping when it comes to serving our own."

I tilted my neck back. "And that's what you think we do here at King's Dream? Half-step?"

He shrugged then squared his broad shoulders. "Maybe not everyone."

"So you're insinuating that my social worker is? Or is it me who you think is going to drop the ball with this young man?"

"Honestly, I don't know enough about you or your social worker to insinuate anything. I just know people tend to ignore poor black kids, especially rich black people. And well, it's clear how you got this job, so…"

I chuckled and shook my head. "So you believe I don't take this job seriously because of how you *think* I got it?"

"How I *know* you got it."

"Mr. McClain, I have a degree in social work. This job is my calling, no matter how I got it."

"Then why don't you do the visit yourself? Why you gotta hand it off to someone else?"

"Because I am the director. Someone else gets paid to make the home visits. That's not my job."

"Yeah, I hear you."

I scoffed as I sat up straight and pursed my lips. "You know what? I don't have a damn thing to prove to you. You're temporary, a volunteer who'll go back to his life once this summer program is over and not give a second thought to Shemar or any of the other boys that we'll still be looking out for."

"You don't know me to say some shit like that. How about spending time training these boys is *my* calling? How about I make it my business to volunteer in some capacity year-round, and I know what I see at these community centers. Y'all might be trying to make a difference, but there's always one or two kids that are forgotten. Shemar is smaller and quieter than the other boys and easy to forget.

I'm just making sure y'all got his back. That's all."

I folded my hands in my lap and heaved a sigh. "Look, we're going to take care of Shemar just like we take care of the eight hundred or so children, *black* children, who utilize this center in one way or another year-round. No one is ever forgotten here, because *I* make sure of it. Now, I have work to do, and I'm sure you need to go dribble or jump-shoot or assist or ball-hog or alley-oop or something. So…goodbye, Mr. McClain."

He just sat there and stared at me for a moment before standing from the chair, muttering, "I'll be back soon to see what's going on with him," and leaving without giving me the opportunity to offer a rebuttal.

Once the door closed behind him, I rested my head on my desk and blew out a frustrated breath, because truthfully, I *had* forgotten to tell Elrich, our social worker, about Shemar. Like I said, I had been putting out fires, and Shemar actually *had* slipped through the cracks of my memory. And well…I felt like shit because of it. Total and complete shit.

*****

"So you think there's some abuse going on?" Elrich asked.

I nodded, took a sip of my drink, and sighed. "Unfortunately, yes. All signs point to it; there are red flags flapping all over this situation. If you can find the time, I'd really appreciate you reaching out to his mom, maybe make a home visit?"

He gave me a pensive nod. "You think it's the father?"

"From the way he froze up when she mentioned him? Definitely."

"Okay. I'll try to set something up for when he's not home if he works."

"She mentioned he'd gotten off early that day, so I assume he does."

"Okay, great. I'll try to call the mother's job first thing in the morning since you say her phone is off, see what I can set up. But you know she has to accept any help I offer, and most abuse victims don't initially."

"You know I know that. I also know some women are just waiting for someone to reach out, to show them an escape route."

"True, true. You know, you're good at this job."

"Tell Leland McClain that. He seems to have a problem with how I got this job."

Elrich shrugged. "He doesn't know your whole story. From the outside looking in, it could appear that you're just filling the position in name only, but the community knows better. Everyone knows you've been doing this type of work for years."

"Always the voice of reason. Thank you. Now, on to more pressing matters." I scooted closer to him on the sofa in his small living room, planting a kiss on his lips. When he gently pushed against my chest, I backed away a bit and frowned. "What's wrong?"

"Uh, I'm glad you wanted to come over, because we need to talk…about us."

I looked into his gray eyes, saw how his bushy eyebrows were nearly meeting, and watched as he dragged his fingernails over his low-cut, salt-and-pepper hair. Elrich was twenty years older than me and kind to a fault. He was struggling with something he needed to tell me, and all I could think was…*shit*.

This wasn't going to be good. Not that I was in love with him or anything like that, but at least he'd kept the cobwebs off my vagina and provided a good stress-reliever for me when I needed one since I'd moved back to Da Lou. We usually hooked up only once or twice a month, but the arrangement had been a nice one. No mind-blowing, addictive sex, but decent intimacy that both of us were mature enough not to let interfere with our working relationship, despite the fact that me screwing a subordinate was definitely a reckless thing to do. Yes, I realized that, but I never claimed to be the best decision-maker, and shit, a woman has needs, and Elrich was the safest bet for me. Or at least I thought he was. But I could tell from the look in his eyes that my safe bet was about to let me down.

"Kim, you know I care about you, and I enjoy spending time with you, but I'm…" He paused as if it was killing him to say what he was going to say next.

"You want to end this? Just say it, Elrich."

"I *need* to end it. Me and Adana are trying to work things out, and this—*us*—it's eating at my conscience. I feel like I'm betraying her by continuing with our arrangement."

"Y'all are getting back together? Well, that's great! And I understand. I know you've always wanted your wife back, so I get it. I really do."

"*Ex*-wife. But yeah, putting my family back together is a dream come true. Thanks for understanding."

I nodded as I stood from the sofa and grabbed my purse. "No problem. I wish you nothing but happiness. I truly do."

"Thank you."

Minutes later, I was in my car shaking my head at myself. I wasn't even sad about this. I was just…exhausted. I was *always* exhausted. No matter how I tried to arrange my life for my comfort, it resulted in my discomfort. I was always working or moving around not working, always busy trying not to think about my past, but it was forever chasing me, and I was tired of it. Really, *really* tired of it. It felt like an old record played over and over in my mind, blasting my past mistakes, past hurts, the past hurts I'd inflicted on the people around me, the people I loved most, at top volume. I needed a new tune, something good in my life that wasn't attached to me making a dumb decision to get it like Elrich was. I needed something, period. Shit, anything besides the status quo of work and loneliness and regret.

*Love, that's what you need. Real love. True love. You deserve it and it's time.*

I laughed at the foolishness oozing from my brain, like actually laughed out loud at it. Me falling in love, being in a romantic relationship where I spent time with a man and got to know him and felt things for him? I'd been there and done that with disastrous results for all involved. I brought out the worst in men. That's just what I did. No sense in going down that road again. What I *didn't* need was love. What I *did* need was another booty call prospect.

Yep, that was what I needed.

# 5

# Leland

My phone rang just as I was leaving the men's restroom, making my way through the building. I grinned when I saw the name on the screen and answered the call with, "Yo!" I'd had a good time with the boys at the center that evening and had stayed late to work with a few of the them, giving them some extra pointers. Shemar was in that group. It did my heart good to see him come back after missing a few days. So I was in a decent mood.

"Hey, man. Where you at? Shady Pines?" was my silly-ass brother, Everett's, greeting.

"What the fuck is a Shady Pines?"

"A nursing home. Ain't that where Agnes lives? Y'all be kicking it in her semi-private room?"

"Fuck you. You called to jone me? Ain't you halfway across the world and don't you have a wife, a young one your old ass probably can't even keep up with?"

"Shiiiiiit, she the one who can't keep up. Ain't nothing wrong with my stamina. Just because you can half-fuck Bernice 'nem into satisfaction don't mean you get to hate on me."

"Like you used to half-fuck old Esther? I mean, talk about an old-ass name..."

"Out of bounds, youngin'."

"Naw, that was in bounds like a motherfucker. You don't get to keep fucking with me when your first wife is old enough to be your second wife's mother."

"I see you playing dirty. Don't make me hop on a plane and come kick your ass."

"Bring your ass here if you want, and I'ma break your old-ass hip."

"Fuck you."

"Fuck yourself."

"Eat shit."

"Suck an ass."

"So how's things going? I ain't read about no fights yet."

"Ain't been no fights. Daniels ain't been here."

"Ain't that his program?"

"Yep."

"And the nigga ain't been there?"

"Nope."

"That's fucked up."

"Not really. I mean, it's a bunch of us players in rotation. It's actually a really good program."

"I bet you been putting in more hours than anyone, ain't you?"

"You know how I do it. So what's up with y'all? Where you at now? Germany?"

"Naw, got a few days off so we're in Italy—Venice."

"Nice. How's the wife and new daughter?"

"Good—shit, great. Loving married life."

"Ella?"

"Ella's good. We added a couple of shows in Australia. She's gonna join us there. Aye, I called because me and Jo are planning a party when we get back to LA next month. Trying to give you a heads-up. I need you to be there."

"A party? What kind of party?"

"For Nat's birthday. It's in July. It'll be a few kids there, but Jo wants family there, too."

"Gotcha. Just text me the details. I'll make sure to be there."

"Bet. Now I just gotta track Neil down and hope he's sober that day or ain't got his ass beat over some bet."

By this time, I had checked the locker room and the gym to make sure they were both empty and was heading toward the front doors. "Let me know what's up with him. I ain't heard from him in a minute, and he ain't returning my calls."

"Damn, you too? Shit. I hope his ass is okay."

"Me, too—aye, let me hit you back, Ev."

"A'ight."

I stood just outside the building, letting the doors close behind me as I fixed my eyes on Shemar. He was parked on the same bench he'd been waiting on before, the same dejected look on his face.

"Ride late?" I asked, basically stating the obvious.

Without looking up, he nodded.

"It's your mom again? Or is your dad supposed to be coming?"

Eyes still on the ground, he almost growled, "He ain't my daddy."

I stood there for a second before taking the seat beside him. "Okay…he's your stepdad?"

He shook his head, finally looking up at me. "No, my mom's boyfriend. He my little sister's daddy."

"You got a little sister? Man, I'm jealous. I'm the youngest in my family."

"I know. I know everything about you. Big South's your brother."

I nodded. "Yep. Best big brother in the world. Took care of me when I was a kid. You got any big brothers or sisters?"

"Naw, it's just me and Naheera."

"How old is Naheera?"

"Three."

"You take care of her, watch out for her like my brother did for me?"

"I try, but her dad—"

"Happy No Panty Day, heifer!" followed by laughter cut Shemar off. When she said, "That *is* a real holiday, you trick! We drinking tonight or what? I had a day straight from the rivers of hell," I hopped up.

She damn near jumped out of her skin when she saw me, quickly ended the call, and shrieked, "What are you doing out here?! You almost gave me a heart attack! Look, man, you are entirely too big to be out here lurking around!"

Instead of a verbal response, I moved so that Ms. Hampton could see Shemar sitting on the bench.

Her mouth dropped open, and embarrassment clouded her pretty face. "Uh, what's—sweetie, do you need to call a ride, or do you need me to take you home?"

Before he could answer, a car came screeching into the parking lot. Same car, same worn-out-looking mother. She apologized profusely, snatching Shemar toward her and basically dragging him to the car. For the second time, this woman barely looked at me, which never happened. I mean, I'm not conceited or anything, but women usually stared at me, if not because they thought I was fine, because I was so damn tall. Yeah, something was definitely going on with her.

Movement from the side of me shifted my attention from Shemar and his mom to Kim Hampton. "Wait!" she shouted. "I need to talk to you about something. My social worker has been trying—"

The doors shut, and the car sped away, leaving Ms. Hampton standing on the lot muttering, "…trying to contact you."

My ass stood there for a minute, unsure of what to say, because that was fucked up.

Finally, she turned to me, and said, "I tried, and my social worker's been trying…"

"So y'all done? I mean, that's it? All y'all gonna do is try?"

"I didn't say that. Damn, what is it with you? Do you think I don't want to help him when that's the purpose of this whole program? Or are you on me because of the man who funds this place? If that's it, then you can go and leave us alone. We have plenty of volunteers."

I moved closer to her. "What happened to all that gratitude you were shoving at me before?"

"Shoving? Really?"

"Yes, *shoving*. Not grateful anymore?"

Shaking her head, she said, "You know what? I don't have time for this."

"Got a hot date for No Panty Day you need to get to or

28

something?"

"You had no right to eavesdrop on my phone call."

"I didn't eavesdrop on shit. You were talking loud."

She huffed and rolled her eyes. "Whatever."

"Yeah, whatever. I just hope you aren't giving up on helping that boy and his mom."

"I said I wasn't!" She lowered her voice and shook her head. "Look, I don't have to answer to you when I know I'm doing my job and so is everyone else around here."

"Then why is this the second time I found Shemar out here alone after this place shut down? Shouldn't your staff be making sure the kids get home safely?"

"That—" Her eyes slid from my face to the sky and back. "That's something I need to address. A camp counselor should've been here to make sure Shemar got home. I guess they all…overlooked him."

I could tell it hurt her to say that, so I replied with, "Exactly."

"Look, Mr. McClain. We really are doing our best here. No one is intentionally trying to hurt anyone, least of all that young man."

"That's usually the case, Ms. Hampton, but that doesn't make it any better."

"So what are you going to do? Report us?"

I shook my head. "Naw, I'ma just make sure y'all don't overlook him again."

"*I* didn't overlook him, Mr. McClain. My staff did, and I assure you that will be taken care of."

"It better."

# 6

# Leland

"Hello!" I barked into the phone as I sat up on the side of the bed and rubbed my forehead. I'd woken up with a headache, I was tired of sleeping in a damn hotel, and was basically pissed at the world. I needed to take a trip to LA or Houston so I could spend time with my family, which was the only thing that would lift my mood at this point, but I was training and when I wasn't training, I'd trapped myself in St. Louis by agreeing to volunteer so many hours at King's Dream.

"I see you woke up on the wrong side of the bed this morning." Aunt Ever's voice plowed into my ear. I loved her, but she was as loud as most old country women were.

"The problem is, it ain't my bed. I hate sleeping in hotel beds."

"Then buy a house and put a bed in it, boy!"

I sighed and shook my head. As loud as she was talking, just hearing her voice had eased some of my tension, and I could feel my headache slipping away. "I'm trying. I think I want a condo instead of a house, but I ain't had time to look at much of nothing, Auntie."

"You got one of them real estate ladies helping you?"

"Naw, been trying to do it by myself."

"That has always been your problem, Leland Randall McClain. You always try to do everything yourself, including saving the world. You work hard then spend every break you get volunteering somewhere. You got to learn how to rest. That's probably why you got that headache."

"How you know—"

"Because you used to get them when you were little, and even though they don't really slow you down, they always put you in a bad mood. How long you had this one?"

"Off and on for a couple of weeks."

"Been back to the doctor?"

"No…they all say the same thing, that it's tension and I just need to get more rest, take better care of myself, be intentional about relaxing when I feel the headaches coming on. That same old bull…"

"Like I been telling you for free all these years."

"I know, Auntie. I'ma do better."

"Mm-hmm, and while you're doing better, you better do like every other rich person does: hire someone to find you somewhere to live there in St. Louis and stop being so stubborn. You need you an assistant like Tick got Courtney. You can't do it all, baby. You need to stop trying."

I couldn't help but laugh to myself at her referring to my brother, Everett, by his nickname. No matter that he was a rap legend or I was a supposed NBA star, we were just her nephews as far as she was concerned, and I loved that about her. If no one else did, Aunt Ever was good at reminding us that we were just regular guys. "You're right, Auntie. I'ma call a real estate agent today."

"You still seeing that woman you was with when I talked to you a few weeks back?"

And she *stayed* in my personal business. You'd think she was my actual mom rather than a once-guardian and current aunt the way she rode me about settling down. But at least she didn't judge me for preferring to date older women. "Naw, haven't seen her since that morning."

"Been ignoring her calls?"

"No, ma'am. I told you, I stopped doing that the last time you got on to me about it. I just wasn't feeling her, and I let her know I couldn't see her anymore. And you do know I just turned twenty-seven, right? You don't have to keep questioning me like I'm eighteen and just going off to college."

"I know you grown, just worry about you."

"Don't. I'ma be fine."

"You'll be fine when you get you a wife."

"Neil and Nolan don't have wives, either, and they're older than me. You don't be in their business like this."

"I didn't raise Nolan and Neil. They weren't never…mine. You was, and until you get you a wife, my work with you won't be done."

"Okay, Auntie. I hear you."

"Mm-hmm. Headache better?"

"You know it is, because you know you got the magic touch even through the phone."

"Good. Now all you have to do is apologize to whoever you been taking your frustration out on since you been having these headaches."

"Why you think I been doing that?"

"Like I said, I know you, Leland Randall McClain."

# Kimberly

"What you doing?"

I smiled as I settled in my seat, my phone cradled between my shoulder and ear. He sounded like he was in a good mood, which was a rare and blessed event. "Working. Isn't that what you pay me to do?"

"Just checking, making sure you ain't slacking off."

"No, Mr. Daniels. I am earning every penny you pay me."

"There you go with that Mr. Daniels stuff. A'ight then, *Ms. Hampton*. How are things going at King's Dream?"

"Same old, same old. We're all overworked and underpaid, but we're trying our best to make life better for these kids, nonetheless."

"Y'all want raises? You tryna break me?"

I laughed. "Noooo! We're working on some grants. The last thing I'm tryna do is bust your bank. You know that. This job is just...hard. Serving the public always is."

"Then quit. You know you ain't got to work there or anywhere else if you don't want to."

"Actually, I do. This is my—"

"Calling. Yeah, I know. So, look...I just wanted to see how things were going. Gotta go. You know how it is."

"Yeah, talk to you later, Mr. Daniels—wait, uh..."

"You miss me, don't you? You didn't have to move back there, you know?"

"I did. It was the right thing for me and for you."

"If you say so. Love you."

"Love you, too. Bye."

"Bye, Ms. Hampton."

As soon as the call ended, a text from Zabrina appeared on the screen of my phone: *I hope ur having a good day over there. Mine sucks. Ima kill this nigga.*

I shook my head. Zabrina's boyfriend was a really good guy who took excellent care of her while she pursued a crippled singing career. The issue was that she was spoiled, always had been, and things other women would overlook were major issues for her.

Me: *What is it? Did he forget to cook you breakfast? Refuse to paint your toenails? Only eat your coochie twice last night?*

Z: *Ha, ha, ha. No. He proposed.*

Me: *What?????????? And you wanna kill him for that?*

Z: *No ring. He proposed during sex. Doesn't count.*

Me: *You crazy as hell! Of course it counts! Did you accept?*

Z: *Hell yeah!*

Me: *So it didn't count but you said yes?*

Z: *Yeah.*

Me: *You are insane.*

Z: *Whatever. Anyway, I need to get away from him before I kick his ass. Let's have dinner, celebrate International Caps Lock Day.*

Me: *Wow, I'm impressed. You did your homework. I'm game for Mexican as long as you're paying.*

Z: *Deal. C u at 6.*

Me: *It's a date.*

Virtually the same moment I'd turned from my phone to tackle the mountain of paperwork on my desk, there was a knock at my door. What the hell was going on? A distraction conspiracy? I'd told Peaches that I didn't want to be disturbed, because I *had* to get that paperwork done.

"Come in," I called, without looking up from my paperwork, sure to lace my voice with disdain so Peaches would think twice about bothering me again.

I heard the door ease open and instantly smelled him. His aroma was a distinct combination of expensive cologne and pheromones that seemed to have been specifically designed for my nose. I hadn't seen him in the few days since our confrontation, because he was not scheduled to volunteer again until next week. He wasn't even scheduled to volunteer today. I was sure of that because I had checked the schedule so I could avoid him. I would've insisted he stop volunteering altogether, but he'd offered more of his time than anyone else, so his departure would leave a huge hole in the schedule. Plus, he was good with the boys, and dismissing him would make the whole foundation appear guilty of neglect in his eyes, which we honestly were on some levels, a fact that I was ashamed of since I was the captain of this ship. Hell, his persistent harassment had led to me implementing some needed changes in how things operated at King's Dream, so I should've been expressing gratitude to him, but instead, I leaned back in my chair, laid down my pen, and blew out an audibly frustrated breath.

"Your receptionist isn't at her desk," he said, answering my unspoken question.

"I see. Wish I had been made privy to that information before now. Well, what can I do for you today, Mr. McClain? Here to evaluate my job performance again? Thinking about giving me a raise?"

He smiled, revealing straight white teeth. "You got jokes, huh? See how you're acting with me, and I actually came to apologize to you."

I straightened in my seat as my mouth involuntarily dropped open. "You what?"

He shrugged, looked around my office, then let his eyes land on me again. "Can I sit down?"

"Oh, yes. Sure. Have a seat."

He settled in the chair in front of my desk, stretching his impossibly long legs before him and gripping the arms of the chair with his humongous hands.

Licking my lips, I crossed my legs and tilted my head to the side. "You were saying?"

"Yeah...look, I know I been riding you, and I'm sorry for that. I thought about it and realized you're just one person, the director, and you ain't exactly out in the trenches every day. You hired people to handle certain things and it's not necessarily your fault if they drop the ball."

"Hmm. Well, I appreciate your understanding. I actually inherited the entire staff rather than hired them. This center was already established when I was brought on as director."

He leaned forward. "I thought this place belonged to Daniels."

"His charitable foundation bought it from the city almost a year ago. Otherwise, they were going to shut it down. Anyway, when I took over as director a few months back, I kept most of the employees on. It was already named King's Dream, already in this building. The only thing different is me, but as you have so astutely pointed out to me several times, it might have been a mistake not to hire new people. Nevertheless, I'm working hard to shape things up around here. So honestly, thank you for showing me the holes I needed to repair in our operations, and thanks for your apology."

"You're welcome."

Then we both just kind of sat there, our eyes on each other, as if neither of us knew what to say next, but neither wanted to end the conversation.

"You had lunch?" he asked, breaking the silence.

"Um…no. It's only like ten. So, no," I stammered.

"I was thinking maybe I could buy you lunch, try to make up for harassing you before and for messing with you about No Panty Day. I mean, if you want to celebrate going commando, who am I to judge?"

I grabbed my forehead. "About that…look, I kind of try to celebrate every day, so every morning, I look up what holidays there are and pick a random one to observe, but I wasn't actually celebrating the day in the way you think I was."

"How do you think I think you were celebrating it?"

"By…not wearing panties?"

"I don't see nothing wrong with it if you were. A woman like you can get away with it."

With peaked eyebrows, I asked, "Exactly what kind of woman do you think I am?"

"A beautiful one."

"Uh…"

"I'm just saying, it's cool with me if you *were* celebrating it like that. Shit, when is No Draws Day? I'd love to celebrate that one. Nothing like being free. Know what I mean?" He punctuated his statement by adjusting in his seat and giving me a grin. Did I mention the red jogging pants he was wearing?

Yeah.

"Uh, Mr. Mc—"

"You can call me Leland, or just McClain."

Licking my lips, I ran a finger around the collar of my blue blouse. "Le—McClain…what was the question?"

"Will you have lunch with me?"

*No, no, no. Say no! You can't do this!*

*It's just lunch,* I told myself.

*Yeah, right. Look at him. You go to lunch with him and he'll be the meal. Or you'll be the meal, because he looks like he wants to tear your ass up! Don't do it, sis! You and men don't work! Never did! Never will! And you ain't no cougar. Don't. Do. It.*

*He's like twenty-six and I'm thirty-five. How does that make me a cougar?*

*Whatever. Just don't do it! You know you shouldn't do it!*

I looked up from the spot on my desk I didn't realize I'd been staring at to see him giving me a curious look, and said, "Uh…um, I'm fasting today."

"For real? All day?"

I nodded a little too vigorously. "Yes."

"You gonna be weak as hell, ain't you?"

"I hope not."

"Okay. Raincheck?"

I nodded again, slowly this time, and watched as he stood from the chair, his big, muscular—hell, *fine*—body towering over my desk. "Yes, raincheck. Definitely."

"All right. See you later, Ms. Hampton."

"See you later, Mister—See you later, McClain."

He flashed me another grin before turning to leave my office.

# 7

"Ms. Kim?"

The voice on the intercom jolted me awake, and my mind was so full of the static and fog of a sound slumber that it took more than a couple of minutes for me to realize that for the fiftieth time in the past couple of months, I had fallen asleep at my desk. Checking the time on the office phone's little screen, I was relieved to see it was after hours, so I technically hadn't fallen asleep on the job. Still, this was becoming a problem, an issue that was directly correlated to my inability to get any sleep in my own bed at night. I was really going to have to do something about this. When my eyes finally managed to focus, I could also see that the call was coming from the front desk.

"Ms. Kim?" the voice repeated. I was sure whoever it was had seen my car out on the lot, so there was no sense in me pretending not to be there.

Taking a deep breath, I pressed the intercom button, and replied with, "Yes?"

"Um, this is Pamela, one of the counselors? You wanted us to let you know if there were any issues with Shemar Townsend?"

I sat up straight. "What's going on?"

"Well, we've been rotating making sure the kids get picked up every day like you asked us to, and his ride hasn't shown up yet this evening. He's the last child left here, and he says his mom's phone is still off. I've tried his emergency contact, but they're not answering."

"Uh, okay. I'll be right there. Keep him in the lobby with you. I know he likes to sit on that bench out front, but I don't think he should be out there alone."

"Oh, he's not alone. Mr. McClain is out there with him."

*Shit.* "Okay. On my way."

I hadn't spoken to Mr. McClain since he apologized, had somehow forgotten this was one of his volunteer days, and hated to have to see him on an occasion like this since we were on better terms with each other, because well, no progress had been made in trying to get to the bottom of this child's home situation. Elrich had continued his attempts to get in touch with his mother, which was nearly impossible since her phone was off and she worked at a nursing home where they had something against giving her his messages. He'd even solicited the help of a county case worker. We were trying, really trying, but trying wasn't enough and I knew it.

Still, I had to face the music, and even if I had to take him home and talk to his mother myself, I needed to find out what was going on in her life that she kept picking up her child late or not bringing him at all. There was a van he could ride, but she hadn't signed the transportation permission slip. And besides all that, I could see in the way that young man carried himself that something wasn't right with him. Yeah, something was very wrong.

I grabbed the lanyard that held my King's Dream ID badge from my desk, hung it around my neck, and with my keys in hand and my purse on my shoulder, headed from the area of the huge building where my office was located to the front lobby, informed Pamela she could leave, and stepped outside to find Leland McClain and young Shemar sitting side by side on the bench looking like a giant and an ant—a big, sexy giant and a timid little adorable ant.

"You two out here enjoying the weather?" I asked in the most upbeat, lighthearted voice I could manage.

Mr. McClain's head snapped up and his eyes met mine. The concern in them melted away as he gave me a small smile then nodded toward Shemar. "Naw, waiting with Lil' Man here again. His mom ain't made it yet, so we just out here kicking it."

I nodded and fixed my eyes on Shemar, who was staring out at the parking lot. "Well, how about I just go ahead and give you a ride home, Shemar? I need to talk to your mother anyway."

Shemar gave me his attention, staring at me like he wasn't sure how he should react.

"You can do that? I mean, is that allowed?" Mr. McClain asked.

I nodded. "We can transport the kids in case of emergency. It's after six and I'm sure Shemar is hungry and ready to go home, so I count this as an emergency. Come on, Shemar. My car is right over here."

Shemar hesitantly stood from the bench with Leland McClain mimicking the action. "Hey, wait. I'll drive you two," he offered.

I smiled up at him and shook my head. "No, I got it. We've taken up enough of your time today, but thanks."

"No, I'll drive. I got it," he insisted.

"Mister—"

I heard a series of beeps and watched the headlights of Mr. McClain's SUV pop on. "Aye, Shemar," he said, "go ahead and hop in the backseat. We'll be there in a second." Then he turned to me, lowering his voice as Shemar headed to his vehicle. "Look, something is obviously not right with his home situation. He got a stepdad that I think is terrorizing him and his mom. I'm not letting you drive over there alone when we don't know what you gonna be walking into. Let me drive you. I'll stay in the car once we get there, but just…let me take you there."

His eyes searched mine, and upon seeing that he was sincere and determined in his suggestion, all I could do was give him a slow nod and follow him to his truck.

# Leland

She was quiet on the ride to Shemar's crib. She seemed uncomfortable in the way a lot of independent women tend to be. The look on her face told me she hated receiving help almost as much as she hated asking for it. I swear I'd never dealt with a grown woman who didn't feel this way. It was just as frustrating to me as it was attractive. I loved independent women, but at the same time, I needed to feel like they needed me. It was the magic combination I'd never found in a woman. In the past, I'd heard them say, "I like you, Leland," or "I want you, Leland," shit, even, "I love you, Leland," but never once had a woman told me, "I need you, Leland." I'd never even heard that from family members since my brother, Everett, literally took care of everything and everyone.

"Turn left at the next street," Shemar directed me.

"A'ight," I replied.

A few more directions later, I found myself parking in front of a small, dingy white house with a yard full of brown grass and dirt. Surrounding it up and down the block were other worn-looking houses with old cars and/or toys in the yards—yeah, we were most definitely in the 'hood. The small driveway to what I assumed was Shemar's house was crowded with two cars, including the one I'd seen his mom pick him up in. So his folks were home? Why didn't anyone pick him up? What kind of shit was this?

"This it?" I asked.

"Yeah," Shemar said softly.

"Okay, come on. Let me walk you to the door."

Shemar had hopped out onto the street when Ms. Hampton grabbed my arm before I could climb out my truck. "I thought you were going to stay in the truck. You're not King's Dream staff. You're not authorized to bring him home, so it's not a good idea for you to walk him to his door, and anyway, should you be out here without a bodyguard or something? I'll go. Stay here," she nearly whispered.

I leaned in close to her. "Let me get this straight. You think my big ass needs a bodyguard, but I'm supposed to let you go to that door alone? Naw, *you* stay here."

She shook her head. "I don't like this. It's not…it's not safe."

"For me or for you?"

"For either of us, really."

I stared out at the house and at Shemar who was now waiting for me at the tip end of the driveway. "Okay…if something pops off, I'll give you the signal to call nine-one-one. You got your phone, right?"

"Yeah, what signal?"

"I don't know. I'll hold up a finger, like a number one. You see that, call the cops."

"I still don't think you should go up there."

"Yeah, I know. Just watch for the signal."

She sighed. "Okay."

As I walked Shemar to his door and glanced around, I thought about how Everett was always telling me I needed to hire some security. This was one of those times when I knew I should've listened to him. "You got a key, Lil' Man?"

He shook his head and knocked on the slanted screen door. When there was no answer, I knocked, putting more power into it and rattling the handicapped door on its hinges. I was ready to get myself and Ms. Hampton the hell up out of there before someone recognized me and robbed my ass at gunpoint or something. Almost unconsciously, I tucked my gold rope inside my t-shirt.

A short dude wearing a wife beater and a frown opened the door, then he grinned up at me. He wasn't all that young, but he wasn't exactly old either. He looked like he'd lived a hard life. "Aw, shit! I thought this lil' muh-fucka was lying about knowing you! Fastlane McClain! Wassup, my nigga?"

I couldn't help but smile at him using my nickname, a name given to me because of my speed in getting the ball up and down the court. Then he offered me a hand that I hesitantly took, because flattery didn't change the fact that I was sure this dude was an abuser.

"I'm good," I said.

"Got-damn, you tall, taller than a motherfucker! You brought him home?" he asked, his eyes sliding down to Shemar and the smile on his face quickly fading.

"Uh, yeah. He waited on his mom for like an hour. She here?"

He rubbed the back of his neck. "Yeah…she sleep. Come on in here, boy. Got this man out here fucking around with you. He ain't got time for this shit," he said to Shemar, who dragged himself in the house. "You shoulda let his ass walk," he said to me.

I raked my fingers through my beard, just to keep my hand from involuntarily wrapping itself around this nigga's neck. "Naw, I wanted to make sure he made it safely. Uh, see you later, Lil' Man," I said to Shemar, who I could see standing just behind the dude.

"Okay," he said softly.

"A'ight, y'all take care," I said, then turned to leave.

"Aye, can I get a pic with you, man?" this dude asked.

Was this motherfucker for real?

I was over trying to be cordial with this fool, so I turned back around and fixed my mouth to say, "*Hell, no,*" noticing that Shemar was no longer in the doorway. Then I heard someone scream, "Why you keep letting him do this to you!" It sounded like it came from Shemar, and he sounded upset, maybe even scared. I looked at the dude, and he looked at me.

"Shemar?! That you?!" I yelled through the open door.

The dude moved to close it, but I stuck my foot in the doorway. "What the fuck is going on in there?" I asked.

"None of your damn business! Get yo' foot out my door, man!"

"Shemar!" I yelled again.

He slammed the door against my foot, and the shit hurt, but I didn't move. "Move your muh-fuckin foot, nigga!" dude yelled.

Ignoring him, I thought to hold up a finger, hoping Ms. Hampton would see me. "Shemar! What's going on?!"

"Aye, motherfucker! You trespassing!" dude screamed.

"Call the cops, then!" I said, squaring my shoulders. That's when the door flew open and Shemar appeared beside the dude.

"Get out the damn door, lil' nigga!" dude shouted at Shemar.

"Stop talking to him like that!" I thundered. "Shemar, you okay?"

"It's my mama. She ain't sleep. He beat her up again!"

"Shut the fuck up! This our business! This rich nigga don't care about you *or* your mama!"

"Where your mom at?" I asked Shemar.

"R-right here." His mother stepped up behind her man, her face a canvas of bruises and blood, her bottom lip trembling. She was scared, but something told me she was tired of the way she'd been living, too.

"Bitch, carry your ass back in that bedroom!" the dude spat at her.

She flinched and closed her eyes but didn't move.

"Did you hear me?! Carry your ass back in there before I kick it again!"

"Naw, you ain't kicking shit. Not on my watch," I said.

"You ain't got a damn thing to do with this, McClain. You better take your ass on to wherever you need to be and stay out of grown folks' business!"

I locked eyes with Shemar's mother. "You wanna leave? I can drop you off somewhere if you want."

She nodded, and he flew into her face. "You leave, bitch, and you ain't taking my little girl!"

She flinched again. "You-you can't keep her from me."

"We can take your little girl, too. He can't stop you from taking her," I said. "I won't let him."

"Sh-she at my mama's right now," Shemar's mom said, her voice trembling.

"You talking to this nigga like I ain't even here? You fucking him or something? That why you so damn bold right now?!"

"No! I ain't fucking nobody but you. I just can't take no more. You keep saying you gonna stop hitting on me, but you won't!"

Were they seriously having this conversation in front of Shemar?

"Lil' Man, why don't you go get in my car?" I said.

"Lil' nigga, you better not move! Look, Sheila, I said I'm sorry. You just keep starting shit with me, and you know how stressed I been. You gotta learn when to leave a nigga alone!"

She stared at him, and I knew she was thinking about staying with him. This was probably a cycle with them—he beat her ass, blamed her for it, and she fell for it. Her uncertain eyes shifted to Shemar, who said, "Please, Mama. Let's go."

"You mean it this time? You ain't gon' hit me no more?" she asked dude.

"I told you I ain't! Damn!"

"Okay—"

"Mama, you know he lying! He ain't never gonna stop!"

That's when dude got in Shemar's face. "You need to shut the fuck up before I give you what your little ass *been* needing! Lil' punk ass!"

I stepped forward. "I tell you the-hell what—"

"I'll go! We'll go!" Shemar's mom shrieked. "Just, let me get some stuff and—"

The dude had her yoked up so quick, I almost didn't realize what was going on. Shemar was the first to make a move, grabbing the dude's arm and quickly being flung to the floor. So I grabbed dude by the shoulders and yanked him, making him lose his grip on Shemar's mom. I dragged his little ass outside with him yelling and kicking and screaming the whole way, and all I could think was, where the hell were the cops? Or had she not seen my signal? So I threw my finger up again, keeping a grip on dude's arm as I turned to see if Ms. Hampton was looking. She held up her phone and gave me a nod. With my attention on her, I didn't notice this nigga trying to swing at me, so his fist connected with my jaw, making me stumble a little, more from the shock of it than the actual impact. But not enough to make me release his arm. I punched him back, knocking him to the ground, and as neighbors started stepping out into their yards to see what was going on, the police finally pulled up.

# 8

# Leland

"Are you okay?" she asked softly, her voice shaky, her eyes fixed on the passenger window. "I saw him hit you."

I nodded, my eyes on the road as I drove us back to King's Dream. "Now that dude is in jail and I know Shemar and his mom are safe, yeah. And this ain't nothing but a scratch," I said, rubbing my jaw. "Dude can't hit for shit."

From the corner of my eye, I could see her nod. "That was her mom that picked them up and is taking her to get checked out, right?"

"Yeah, they're gonna stay with her for a while. I just…I hope she doesn't take that man back. The only reason she agreed to leave was because he was trying to jump on Shemar. I mean, you saw her face, and even after he did that to her, she was tryna stay. I just don't understand it. I don't get why women take that kind of abuse off men."

"The women don't know why they take it, either. They just do. Some are groomed to be abused from childhood. For others, it's a learned behavior that's directly tied to low self-esteem."

"I bet you've seen a lot of that as a social worker, huh?"

"Yeah…more than I care to remember. At least she left this time. Some never leave unless they leave in a coffin."

"I know, and I don't want that for Shemar. You can have the greatest family in the world, but no one can take the place of your mother. I know that from experience."

She turned and looked at me. "I'm sorry for your loss."

I shrugged. "It was a long time ago. I'm good with it now."

"Are you really? I know you were young when you lost her."

I shot her a look. "You been researching me, Ms. Hampton?"

She shrugged and averted her gaze from my face. "It's common knowledge."

"I guess it is, but yeah, I'm fine. I mean, I'll always miss her and I wouldn't wish losing a parent on anyone, let alone two, like I did."

She nodded and turned back to the passenger window.

Once we made it back to King's Dream, and I had shut my truck off, she turned to me and gave me a weak smile. "Well, thanks for insisting on driving us there. I definitely wouldn't have handled that situation as well as you did."

"S'all good. Let me get that door for you."

Shaking her head, she said, "I got it. Thanks again."

I nodded and watched her climb out my truck, slowly making her way to her car. When she stumbled a little, I grabbed my door handle, but when she made it to her car, bent over, and started hurling, I jumped out and basically ran over to her. "Ms. Hampton, you okay?"

She shook her head as she continued to empty her stomach onto the pavement. So I just stood there, because I had no idea what the hell else to do.

When she finally stopped and stood upright, she gave me an embarrassed look. "I…I'm sorry. It's my nerves. That whole thing back there at Shemar's—I'm sorry."

"I ain't trippin'. Hey, can you drive? I mean, you need a ride home? I can take you."

"No, I'm fine. I—you know what? I just need to rest for a minute, get a drink of water. I'm gonna go to my office and kick my feet up for a little while, and I'll be fine."

"Okay, let me walk you in there."

"No, you don't have to do that. You've done enough."

"I *want* to do it. So let me do it."

She sighed, let her eyes roam the darkening parking lot, and finally nodded.

I followed her to the building and into her office, watched her collapse into the chair behind her desk and close her eyes. "You got water in here?" I asked.

She shook her head. "I'll get some from the fridge in the breakroom. You can go."

"You sure?"

"Yeah. I'll be fine now."

I said, "Okay," but still just stood there, because leaving her didn't feel right.

"McClain, go home. I'm good."

I nodded, and then realized something. "Uh, the front door is locked, right?"

"Only from the outside, and it'll lock behind you when you leave."

"A'ight. Well, goodnight, Ms. Hampton."

"Call me Kim. I think you've earned the right after tonight, McClain."

"A'ight. Goodnight, Kim."

I left her sitting at her desk, had made it to the door when I recalled she'd reset the alarm when we came in. I guess we'd both forgotten about that. So I turned around and headed back to her office, hoping she'd just give me the code so she wouldn't have to get up. When I made it back, she wasn't there. Frowning, I scratched my eyebrow and then realized she might've been in the restroom, so I waited…and waited…and waited until I finally decided I needed to be sure that was actually where she was and that she hadn't passed out somewhere or something. Before I could leave her office, she walked through the door with a tiny toothbrush and a tube of toothpaste in her hands and tears rolling down her face.

# Kimberly

I jumped when I saw him, wondered what he was doing in my office when I thought he'd left, and then became angry that he'd found me like this, in shambles—*weak*. I hated weakness or being in a weakened state, because at one point in my life, I was so damn weak I believed I didn't deserve to breathe oxygen. And although I was angry at myself, I automatically took it out on him.

"What are you doing in here?" I gritted, tossing my toiletries onto my desk. "I thought you left."

He stretched his eyes in reaction to my tone, I supposed. "I don't know the alarm code, came back to see if you'd give it to me so I *can* leave."

Without a word, I brushed past him, leaving him in my office as I stomped toward the front of the building to the alarm panel next to the front door.

"Aye!" echoed against the walls of the long hall that led from the administrative wing to the lobby.

I didn't stop or even slow my steps. He needed to go. *I* needed him to go so I could be alone and cry and remember and feel sorry for myself and hate myself and shit for a past built on so many bad decisions it was suffocating to even think about. So much so that I avoided thinking about it as much as possible. But tonight, I couldn't. I couldn't fight back the memories, and so, he needed to go!

"Aye! I know you hear me!"

I didn't halt my footsteps until I reached the front of the building, but as I lifted my hand to punch in the security code, a huge warm hand grabbed my wrist. Jerking my arm fruitlessly, I yelled, "Let me go!"

"What the hell is wrong with you? What I do to you?"

"You're here!"

"You're mad 'cause I'm here?" he asked, confusion all over his face.

"Yes! And you need to leave!"

"Naw, you mad 'cause you're embarrassed about throwing up in front of me and crying, ain't you?"

I managed to pull my arm from his grip, but that was probably because he let me. "No, you don't belong here now. We're closed, and you need to go." I stabbed the code in and watched as the words on the panel changed from armed to disarmed. "So go!"

He shook his head. "Bullshit."

I frowned. "What?"

"You ain't acting like this 'cause I'm here after hours. Tell the truth. You mad 'cause I caught you crying, Ain't nothing to be ashamed of. That shit back there at Shemar's house was messed up. It got to me, too. If it made you cry, that's normal."

I scoffed. "Thanks for the permission. Goodnight."

"Damn, really? I ain't do shit to you for you to be acting like this with me, but if that's how you wanna do it, fine. Fuck it and *fuck you.*"

"Fuck you first!" I shrieked. He moved closer, all up in my face, so I pushed against his wide chest and added, "Go! Bye!"

He hadn't moved an inch despite me trying to push his big ass away. Still, he shouted, "I'm going! Good-fucking-night!"

"Whatever!"

"Crazy motherfucker!"

"Asshole!"

"I'm the asshole when you up here having mood swings and shit on GP? Okay, you fucking lunatic!"

"Kiss my ass! You don't know me! You don't know shit about me!"

Somehow, he was even closer, and I hadn't noticed him moving. So I stepped back a little.

"Then fucking tell me!" he shouted. "All I did was make sure you made it in here safe and shit and then I got stuck in here. The hell you acting like this with me for?!"

"Because!"

"Because what?! Shit!"

"It's none of your damn business!"

"You know what?!" he screamed.

I puffed out my chest. "What?!"

His lips were on mine so fast, it took me a full minute to realize what the hell was going on. Then he removed his lips from mine and just stood there and stared at me. I stared back, because I didn't know what the hell else to do.

Finally, he said, "Uh...I-I'm sorr—"

I reached up and grabbed the back of his head, pulling it down to meet mine and pressing my lips against his. A second later, his tongue was invading my mouth, his big hand was on my back pressing my body to his, and I just melted into him, because he felt so...good. Like, really good. Maybe *too* good.

"Mmm," he murmured into my mouth.

Wrapping my arms around his neck, I let my tongue play with his. Then a thought hit me, and I broke our connection. "Wait."

He released a breath and nodded, backing away from me. "I know. We can't do this. It's wrong, and I know it is. I just...I'll go." He turned toward the door, and I panicked.

"No...don't go," I said so softly I wasn't sure he heard me. "I don't want you to go."

He looked at me over his shoulder, his thick eyebrows knitted together, his thick lips slightly separated, dark eyes full of confusion. "You want me to stay?"

"Yes."

He spun around and was back in my face, hands on my arms, lips hovering over mine. "Then why did you stop me?"

I plugged in the numbers to re-arm the alarm without even looking at the keypad. "Because there are cameras out here."

"Oh...any cameras in your office?"

I shook my head, and the next thing I knew, I was being lifted from my feet, tossed over his shoulder, and carried back to my office.

He didn't bother to close the door behind us, but then again, I guess there was no need to. Backing me up against the front of my desk, he held my chin between his thumb and forefinger as he captured my mouth, sliding his tongue inside. I let my tongue caress his as I wrapped my arms around him and felt one of his big hands slide down my back to my butt. Squeezing a handful of it, he moaned into my mouth, which sent a flood to my core and made my mind reel. No, it hadn't been forever since I'd been with a man. Elrich had served a purpose for me as had many men in my past, but none of them had ever made me feel so...*dizzy*, probably because none of them were Leland McClain, since if I were to be brutally honest with myself, I'd have to admit I'd been attracted to him since before I met him. Hell, who wouldn't be? He was a gorgeous man, and it felt like the feeling was mutual.

He ended the kiss and stared down at me before reaching around me, pushing the contents of my desk out of the way, and placing me on top of it. Never taking his eyes off me, he lifted his t-shirt over his head, making me gasp, because I had never seen anything like his tattooed brown skin. He was...beautiful, like a piece of living artwork, and as he stepped out of his jogging pants to reveal black boxer briefs, I decided his beauty extended from his handsome face to his toes. Leland McClain had a body and face that made you take leave of all your senses, which was why I found myself pulling my teal blouse over my head and unbuttoning my brown slacks, hopping down from the desk and letting them pool around my ankles. Then, like we often did when we were in each other's presence, we stood there and stared at each other. Only this time, we were both in our underwear.

"You're gorgeous," he said.

"So are you," I answered truthfully. I saw a flicker of hesitation in his eyes, a look that mirrored what I was feeling, so I said, "We don't have to if you don't want to."

He nodded toward his crotch. "That look like I don't want to?"

I looked down and with wide eyes, asked, "Oh...then what is it?"

He dragged a hand down his face. "I just...I was wondering if I deserve to touch skin like yours, to feel what it's like to be inside you. You're perfect."

"No, I'm not. Not by a longshot."

"To me, you are."

I suddenly wanted to cry again, but not because of my past mistakes or what I'd witnessed at Shemar's house. The tears that were collecting in my eyes were tears of, I don't know…relief? It almost felt like I'd waited my whole life to hear someone say such beautiful words to me, like unbeknownst to me, I'd been anticipating this moment and it was finally here.

"Thank you," I whispered.

"You're welcome," he said, with a smile and then leaned in to kiss me again.

A second or two later, he'd returned me to my perch on the desk, slid my panties to the side, and was stroking my clit, edging me closer and closer to delirium while his tongue explored my mouth. Dragging his mouth to my neck, he suckled on it while sliding a finger inside me, making me take in a breath as he found his way back to my mouth, darting his tongue out to lick my lips. I threw my head back and released a moan as his long fingers eased in and out of me, then felt his free hand on the back of my head, pulling it to his as he kissed me again, much more urgently than before. The movement of his tongue and fingers became almost frenzied as he assaulted me, inching me toward an orgasm more intense than anything I'd ever felt in my life. Seconds later, the pressure swelling in my core reached capacity and shattered me from the inside out.

"Ahhhh!" I breathed into his mouth.

And then he was gone.

Opening my eyes, I watched him reach down on the floor and stand with his wallet in his hand. Then there was a condom in his hand; then he was covering his erection with it. I licked my lips, letting my eyes rise from his groin to his face. He grabbed my hips with both hands and pulled me to the edge of the desk, gently pushed me onto my back, put my legs on his shoulders, and eased inside me with a moan, clutching my thighs. With his eyes clamped shut, he released a groan as he slid out and back inside me. I lay there and watched him, tears spilling from my eyes as I wondered what the hell was happening and how on this earth anything, and I mean *anything*, could feel like this. Because I'd be damned if his dick wasn't made of pixie dust, blood diamonds, that delicious Olive Garden unlimited salad, and childhood dreams or some shit.

Got. Damn.

"Shit, McClain!" I screamed.

Him opening his eyes and staring into mine only added to the intensity of what I was feeling, so I frowned, yelled, "Damn-it!" and reached for his face.

His lips met mine again, and he grunted against my mouth, thrusting in and out of me at a faster pace, finding a rhythm that threatened to drive me completely insane.

"Ohhhh, shit! You feel so good!" I yelled against his lips.

"I ain't never felt no shit like this before in my life," he replied, grabbing my bottom lip with his teeth. "This pussy is—got damn, girl!"

He thrusted and kissed and rolled his hips and yelled my name, and as another orgasm hit me, he screamed, "Ohhhhh, damn!" expanded inside me, and exploded with a grunt.

Resting his head on my chest, through heaving breaths, he asked, "What holiday is today?"

"What?"

"You said you celebrate random holidays every day, right? What's today?"

"Hell, whatever day you want it to be."

He chuckled. "Okay, then it's Got-damn, You Got Some Good Pussy Day."

I smiled and really tried not to giggle like a damn twelve-year-old. "Um, thank you?"

"You welcome, baby."

# 9

# Leland

"Aye, you busy, man?"

"Yeah, busy tryna get some from my wife," my brother said into the phone. In the background, I could hear his wife, Jo, say, "Who are you saying that to?!"

"It's Leland, baby," Everett replied.

"Tell him I said hi, and you need to quit! I just gave you some this morning!"

"Damn, Ev…you tryna wear her out or something?"

"Yeah. So, what's up, man? Trouble with Mildred?"

"Fuck you."

His dumb ass laughed into the phone. "For real, what's up? I know it's early over there in the states, and you never call me early unless you got something on your mind, so what is it?"

"Uh, I ain't on speakerphone, am I?"

"Naw…wait a minute. I'll be right back, Jo." A second or two later, he said, "Okay, shoot."

"So, I fucked someone I probably shouldn't have fucked."

"Probably? You ain't sure about it?"

"I mean, I *know* I shouldn't have fucked her. It just…kind of happened."

"That sounds like the shit niggas say when they cheat on they woman. You cheated on Gertrude?"

"Nigga, will you be serious?"

Through a chuckle, he said, "A'ight, a'ight…so who was it?"

"Kim Hampton."

"Who the hell is that?"

"Armand Daniels' mother."

"Uh, what? Whose mother?"

"Armand Daniels."

Silence.

"Ev, you still there?"

"Um…shit, man. All this traveling and changing time zones and stuff is messing with my head. It sounded like you said you fucked crazy-ass Armand Daniels' mom. Damn, I think I'm losing it."

"You heard right. I had sex with his mother."

More silence.

"Ev?"

"Okay, just tell me this: all the old-ass women in the world and you chose to mess with her? The hell is wrong with you? I mean, what in the LeBron James are you doing?! What you do, make a special trip to Miami to fuck her?"

"She lives here now, in St. Louis. She runs the community center I'm volunteering at."

"But why her? I mean, *why*?"

"I don't know, man. She's fine, but she's young, younger than any woman I've been with in a long time. Shit, she ain't even really my type."

"How the hell she young and got a son in the NBA?"

"Remember when he first got drafted, he was big news and they did that special about him on ESPN? You watched it with me. She was a teenage mother, like fifteen when she had him. He's twenty now."

"Wait, I remember that. Shit, she *is* fine. Pretty, too. She reminds me of that Afro-Latino chick from *Love and Hip Hop: Miami*."

"See, that's what I'm saying."

"Okay, okay. When did this happen?"

"Last night."

"A'ight, so you did it and got it out of your system. You just gotta stay away from her from now on. Act like that shit never happened before some mess pop off with her son, and on the real, man, I wouldn't blame him. That's his mom. That's some ass-kicking shit you did. Actually, niggas get killed over shit like this. That was way out of line. You don't fuck a man's mama. She's off limits like a motherf—"

"I want her."

"Nigga, you done had her!"

"No, I mean…I want to *be* with her."

"Huh?"

"Like, in a relationship."

"Why?"

"I like her."

"No, you like her pussy, but ain't no pussy worth that kind of trouble."

"It ain't? Really?"

"Jo is more than a pussy to me, always has been and you know that."

"Kim is more than that to me, too."

"Man, you don't know her to be saying that…or do you? You wasn't messing with her in Miami, were you? Is that why he was always tryna fight you?"

"No, I mean, I always thought she was pretty, but I wasn't messing with her back then. And how well did you know Jo before you realized she was the one?"

"You saying this woman is the one?! For real, man?!"

"I don't know. I just know I want her. *Bad*."

"Are you doing this just to fuck with Daniels? This some revenge shit for you having to leave Miami?"

"Damn, didn't I already tell you why I left, that it really wasn't about him?"

"But that's what it looks like, man."

"Okay, even if I left because of him, it ain't like my ass is unemployed. Shit, I'm on a better team now with a better contract. And besides all that, you think I'd do some shit like that? Screw her for revenge? You don't know me no better than that, Ev?" It cut me for him to think I was capable of something like that. I wasn't perfect, but I didn't have that kind of heart. I thought my big brother, the one I'd always looked up to and tried to be like, knew that about me.

"Naw, you wouldn't. I just don't understand, though. Why her? You ain't never wanted a real relationship before. Why you gotta want one with *her*?"

"I don't know. Just something about her, man. You know what I mean, right?"

After a few seconds of silence, he admitted, "Yeah, I do. She want you like that, too?"

"I hope so. I mean, I think she likes me, but we didn't do much talking last night. I'ma hit her up later today, though."

He sighed into the phone. "A'ight, look, I got your back if you really got feelings for her. Just...be careful, man. Like I said, a motherfucker will kill over they mama. I know I would."

"I know. I'll be careful."

"Keep me in the loop."

"I will."

# Kimberly

"I thought you said it was gonna be some NBA players here!" Zabrina shouted over the music.

"No, I said they were all invited. I also said I didn't expect any of them to show up."

She huffed before stuffing a piece of a hot dog into her mouth, then garbled, "I don't even know why I'm here."

"To support the center's biggest event thus far this year, maybe? And how you gonna be so disappointed about the ball players not showing up when you got a whole fiancé at home?"

"First of all, he's at work. Second, it don't hurt to look. Third, he ain't my fiancé till he gives me a ring."

I rolled my eyes and scanned the packed parking lot—carnival rides, food trucks, live music from local artists. This Fourth of July block party was proving to be a huge success.

"Armand paid for all this? I can't believe it. He is so cheap—like his mother."

"We're frugal, and yes, he paid for it after I badgered him into it."

"It's nice, be nicer with some NBA players here."

"You know what? I'ma go get me a funnel cake."

I had made exactly two steps in the direction of the Sinthia's Sinful Sweets food truck when yells and squeals made me stop and turn around.

It was him.

And if there was any doubt in my mind that it was him, the look on Zabrina's face and her rallying cry of, "It's that fine-ass Leland McClain!" was confirmation.

My eyes expanded as I watched her and several other people race toward him, and then I looked around the crowded space for an escape route, finally deciding to duck behind one of the other food trucks and head around the back of the stage and into the building. The only part of it that was open to the public was the gym where there were a few activities going on. The rest of the building was empty. I would just close myself up in my office until…when? Until the party was over? That wasn't going to work. At the very least, Zabrina was going to come looking for me and wonder what was wrong, and I was having a hard enough time acting normal around her after what I did, what *we* did.

Although I wanted to forget about it, I couldn't erase the fact that I had sex, really good sex, with Leland McClain, a super-nice, super-hot guy my only child seemed to hate for unknown reasons, from my mind. So I had kind of betrayed my son—I think—and I owed him too much to ever even think about betraying him. Hell, the boy basically took care of me now, and on the most basic of levels, had saved my life. Plus, I promised him long ago I wouldn't make a decision like this anymore, that I wouldn't get involved with the wrong man ever again.

And now look at me.

Different time, same Kim and same dumb-ass thinking when it came to men.

Despite dodging Leland McClain for three straight days—having Peaches take messages when he called and tell him I couldn't be disturbed when he popped up at the office, leaving work early, and missing work altogether yesterday—I wanted him. I wanted all of him, like a crackhead wants that next rock.

Shit.

Fuck it. I was going to my office if for no other reason than to try and get my mind—and vagina—right.

It took forever to get through the crowd to my decided escape route with so many of the adults stopping me to compliment me on the event and the summer camp or some other program we'd been running, but I managed to eventually make it inside the building and was almost home free, inches from my office door, when I heard his voice. "I'm good. How are you?"

I stopped and glanced around before doing a one-eighty, fixing my eyes on him. Tall, almost too handsome, afro up in a bushy ponytail, thick eyebrows lifted, his beard and mustache making him look that much more delicious. He was wearing black basketball shorts, a white t-shirt, and black and white *South* sneakers. I'd always thought it strange that his brother had a sneaker line and he didn't.

"I didn't say anything to you," was my reply.

He took advantage of my stationary position and moved in so close that the heat from his body enveloped mine. "I wasn't talking to you. I was talking to *her*."

I frowned. "Who is her?"

He leaned in, pressing his lips to my ear. "Your pussy."

The floodgates in my yoni opened instantly, more from his proximity than his words, but his words most definitely turned me on, too. "I didn't hear her say anything," I managed to respond.

"You ain't listening. She just said something else."

I turned, continuing my journey into my office on legs that had grown inexplicably weak. "Really? What?"

"She apologized for her owner avoiding me."

"I haven't avoided you," I lied, as I fell into my chair and watched him close the door.

"Yeah, you have, and I wanna know why."

"If you think I've been avoiding you, then you should have an idea why."

He leaned against the door, and I kind of just took him in, all of him. He was so tall, a giant really, not that I wasn't used to tall people. My own child was six-four. Hell, I was five-nine myself. But Leland was a damn skyscraper who made my small office feel like a broom closet.

"Why are you staring at me like that?" I asked, because the intense look in his eyes was making me uncomfortably hornier than I already was.

"Shhhhh, she's saying something else."

I shook my head. "What are you supposed to be? The vagina whisperer? You travel around talking to vaginas or something?"

He shook his head. "Yours is the first one to speak to me like this. It's crazy. It's like we got this special bond."

I fought against smiling, then gave in. "What is she saying now?"

"That she misses me."

*She ain't lying.* "Hmm, I didn't get that memo."

"So you don't miss me?"

"Nope."

"She just called you, and I quote, 'a motherfucking liar.' And your nipples agree with her."

I gasped as I glanced down at my chest. Then I slapped my hands over my snitching-ass breasts. My nipples were hard as hell.

He chuckled and pointed to his groin. "You ain't alone in this, baby."

Licking my lips, I tore my eyes away from his delectable-looking erection. "We can't do this again. It's not right. I'm too old. You're too young. I have a son who's only a few years younger than you. We can't do this."

He pushed himself from the wall and moved toward the desk. "You said that twice."

"Because I meant it."

"Why can't we when we both want to? And you ain't old. Little Kim took offense to that statement."

"Little Kim? You named her?"

"She told me that was her name." He was next to me now, and I could barely breathe.

I glanced up at him, shifted my eyes to the door, and tried to recall if he had locked it, because as hard as I was trying to act, I was exactly a millisecond from giving him some.

"She's real talkative today, huh?" I asked.

"She says she only gets this way around me. Unlike you, she likes me."

"I like you," I confessed.

He crouched down beside my chair. "You do?"

I nodded. "But I shouldn't."

He grabbed the end of one of my braids and twisted it around his finger. "Damn, really?" he asked.

"Yes, really."

"I wasn't talking to you. You interrupted Little Kim." He spun my chair around and opened my legs, brought his face close to my crotch, and said, "Oh…okay."

"What'd she say?"

"For us to stop talking because she wants me to, and I quote again, 'get this pussy.' She nasty."

I was in the middle of laughing when he seized my mouth. I almost involuntarily grabbed the sides of his face, returning the kiss, which was somehow sweet and lava hot at the same time. When we parted, I said, "Lock the door."

"Is that you talking or Little Kim? Y'all sound the same."

"It's both of us."

He stood and pulled me to my feet, burying his face in my neck and suckling on it gently. "I already locked it."

"Good," I said and dropped to a squat.

He looked down at me with wide eyes. "What are you do—"

I snatched his shorts and underwear down and had him in my mouth in seconds. I was so damn hot for him, I think I might've lost my mind in that moment. Either that, or it was just *him*. He made my head spin. Being around him seemed to erase the rational portion of my mind. He was just…too much, but I still wanted more of him—*all* of him.

"Ooooh, shit!" he mumbled. "Motherfuck!"

I popped him out of my mouth to shush him and went back to work, feeling him stumble a little as I lavished him with my tongue and enveloped his erection with the warmth of my mouth, the whole time telling myself that this probably wasn't a good idea. I knew it wasn't, but I honestly did not care.

One of his hands met the back of my head and he released a groan as his hips moved in tandem with my mouth and hand. I took him deeper and deeper in my mouth, moved my hand faster and faster, and when I was sure he was about to meet his happy ending, he pulled back and yanked me to my feet, kissing me with such fervor that it was almost abrasive.

Ending the kiss, he sank his teeth into my bottom lip and tugged on it a bit, then he fixed his eyes on mine. "What you just did…does that mean you're gonna stop avoiding me?" he asked.

I was literally about to have an orgasm from the look in his eyes, so I quickly said, "Uh-huh."

He slid his hand down the front of my shorts. "And give me your number?"

"Yeah…"

"And the next time we do this, it'll be in a bed or at least a bedroom, right?"

"Um…"

He moved his hand and backed away. "*Right*?"

"Okaaay, but before you blackmail me any further, look, I don't want a relationship."

Shaking his head, he said, "I'm not asking for one. I don't want no relationship, either."

"Then what do you want from me?"

This time, he clutched my yoni through my shorts, moved in close, pressed his mouth to my ear again, and said, "This. Now bend over this desk so I can get it."

In case anyone is crazy enough to wonder what I did, I bent my ass over that desk, felt him pull my shorts and underwear down, heard him open the condom wrapper, and as I closed my eyes and rested my forehead on my desk just like I had done so many times before when my chronic insomnia would catch up with me, he thrust so deeply inside me, I thought for sure I would orgasm on contact. I moaned, slapping my hand against the top of the desk, felt him slide my t-shirt up, roll his hand over the three strands of beads I wore around my waist, and kiss my back as he slid out of my saturated core.

"Shit!" he muttered.

"Oooo," I whimpered, as he rhythmically glided in and out of me. The sounds our bodies made as they met, the smell of our sex saturating the air in my office, the way he felt inside me, it all sent me into sort of a euphoric state. It was like a damn out-of-body experience or something.

He slapped me on the ass, bringing me back down to Earth, and said, "Oooo, what?"

"Oooo...ohhhhhh...got-damnit!"

"I wasn't talking to you. Little Kim said *oooo*, too," he said, grabbing one of my butt cheeks with his big hand and jiggling it.

"She...she needs to shut the hell—damn! She needs to shut the hell—oh, my—shit, McClain!"

"You gonna get us caught, baby," he groaned.

"I know...you just feel so good!" I tried to whisper.

"Didn't I feel good the first time?"

I moaned, because I was exactly a second away from a crazy orgasm. Then he stopped and just stood there inside me.

"McClain, please…"

"Your ass better answer me then."

"Yes! You felt good, really good!"

He smacked my ass again and resumed operations. "Yeah, you better recognize who's running shit when I'm in this pussy, you hear me?"

"Y-yes."

"You 'bout to come?"

"Uh-huhhhhh."

"Good. Me, too. Don't scream."

I didn't scream, but I hissed and bit the hell out of my own tongue, was sure I'd given myself a permanent lisp, and just as a knock came at my door and I heard Zabrina calling my name, I felt him grow inside of me, heard him release a soft, tortured grunt, and felt him collapse onto my back.

# 10

# Leland

I stared up at the ceiling, trying to catch my breath and not think about touching her again since I had literally just rolled off of her and we'd been at it damn near all night. I was sure she was tired of me, or just tired in general since she was a working woman, but even after two work-outs in the gym and a whole lot of sex with her, I still couldn't get enough of her. It was the Saturday after The Fourth, and we had seen each other, been with each other, every day since our little reconciliation in her office, if only for a couple of hours at a time. Kim Hampton had quickly become a compulsion, an addiction for me, and I honestly didn't know if that was a good or a bad thing. Sex with Kim Hampton was raw and intense every time, like we were perpetually having makeup sex without the hassle of an actual break-up since we had only known each other for a short time, and according to her, a relationship was off the table, even though that was honestly what I wanted with her. That shocked the shit out of me and confused me at the same time, because that had never been a desire of mine. But hell, I couldn't be bothered to worry about that shit. All I knew was when I was with her, I couldn't get enough of her, and when we were apart, she was all I thought about. And now, with my gaze on the ceiling, my eyes missed seeing her. So I flipped over onto my stomach and turned my head to the side, taking her in and smiling without even trying to.

"You got any brothers and sisters?" I asked, wanting to know as much about her as I could.

"A brother. He's older, lives in DC. He's brilliant, a doctor, but we're not close."

"Why not?"

She shrugged. "We have the same mom and dad but are nothing alike. While he had his nose in the books, I was in the basement of a friend's house getting pregnant with Armand. I was a bit of a disappointment to my family, especially to him."

"You believe that?"

"I believe my family thought I could do better, and I agree with that."

"But you got a degree, raised up a damn NBA player. That's got to count for something."

"Yeah…"

I reached over and rubbed the soft skin of her arm, wiggled a little closer to her to steal a kiss.

"Armand will be in town on Monday," she said, rolling over on her side to look at me. She was naked, wearing only those gold beads that were almost always around her waist and looked so good against her dark skin that was glistening with sweat. She was so beautiful. Every inch of her was beautiful.

"Do those beads have a meaning, or do you just wear them because they turn you on like they turn me on?" I asked.

"I just said something. Did you hear me?"

"Yeah, I heard you. Did you hear me?"

She pulled her bottom lip between her teeth and bit down on it for a second before letting it free. Damn, that was hot. "Um, they've been worn by women in Africa for centuries as a sign of status or as a secret signal to their lover."

"A signal of what?"

"Seduction."

"Shit…"

"Yeah, but they have other uses, too, like for healing."

"So, who were you wearing them for before me?"

"Me."

I smiled and thought, *good answer.* Not that I believed it. Kim was way too sexy to not have had a man before me.

"Back to what you were saying; I know your son is coming to town. It's his week to work with the boys, and they got that intramural game on Friday."

She nodded, dropping her eyes from my face to my chest.

"What? You wanted me to know because I can't see you while he's here or something? That what you're getting at, Kim?"

Her eyelashes fluttered as her eyes met mine. "I…um, I think that would be best. I mean, this…us…our-uh-arrangement is not something I think he should know about."

I nodded. "You're right. He doesn't need to know about all the nasty shit you been doing to me."

Her mouth dropped open. "What? You've been doing stuff to *me*. Smacking my ass—"

"You don't like it when I smack your ass, Kim?"

"Did I say that? And you interrupted me."

"My bad. Please continue."

"Anyway, you smack me on my ass, say all that raunchy stuff while we're doing it, have conversations with my vagina, be talking all kinds of shit about me with her and what do I do? I just take it."

"Yeah, you real good at taking it, too. That's what I like about you. You take it, *all of it*, like a damn G."

As she responded with, "You are so damn nasty," I reached over and gently pushed her on her back, stretching my body over hers.

I kissed her lips, then her cheeks, then her neck, then both her breasts. "But you like it when I do that stuff."

"I guess I do. Been sneaking into your hotel room for the last three nights just so I can take it over and over again."

I kissed her forehead, nose, and lips again. "And you take it so well. Make me wanna give it to you again since I'll be gone all next week."

A combination of shock and relief shadowed her face. "You will?" she asked, as she opened her legs wider for me. "Where you going?"

Settling between them, I said, "LA. Got some business there."

"Oh…"

"Oh? That's it?"

As I slid inside her, she closed her eyes, grabbed my shoulders, and whimpered, "Ohhhhhh, shit!"

"You gonna miss me, Kim?"

She opened her eyes and frowned at me. "Hell, no."

I chuckled, buried my face in her neck, and as I found my rhythm once again, I said, "I bet Little Kim is gonna miss my ass, though."

"Oh, she definitely will."

# Kimberly

Sitting on a pillow on Zabrina's floor, I dug in the plastic bag, unearthing the jewelry I'd just bought at Zumi's Market, a heavenly store that specialized in African and African-themed goodies, everything from clothes to fabric to waist beads to the gorgeous Africa-shaped earrings I'd copped. Plus, they had a wide variety of feminine health and hygiene products.

"Girl, those earrings are the bomb! I can't believe your selfish ass got the last pair. You getting more and more treacherous by the day. And hold your damn head still," Zabrina said.

I rolled my eyes and wondered to myself why I kept paying this nut to braid my hair. She was good at it, really needed her own shop, but she hated braiding hair and only accommodated me because I was her BFF. Hell, she hated working, period. I believed if her singing career ever took off and required her to put in more than a nickel's worth of effort, she'd quit performing altogether.

I heard her rustling through a bag of hair, then felt her yank my damn head to the right, so I turned around and glared at her.

"Wench, I didn't even move my head that time, and you know what? You been acting strange all day. What is your issue?"

"You are foul! That's what my issue is!"

With a deeply furrowed brow, I asked, "The hell are you talking about?"

"That shit you pulled at the block party! You disappeared on me, and when I went looking for you in your office, you wouldn't answer the door, and *I heard y'all!*"

*Oh, shit.* "You heard who? Who is y'all?"

"Don't play with me Kimberly Shay Hampton! Y'all is you and that nerdy-ass Elvis! Y'all were in there screwing and don't try to deny it!"

"Me and *Elrich*? You think I was in there having sex with Elrich?"

"I *know* you were! I saw him at the party, and there was definitely some sex going on in that office, Kim. Don't try to lie to me. I'll know."

"Z, you are tripping." I turned around, because I knew she really could tell when I was lying. She could damn near read my mind. "Wasn't no one in my office doing nothing. You're crazy, thinking I was having sex in my office. Me? Girl, stop."

"Wait a minute. It wasn't Elvis, was it?"

I sighed. "*Elrich, Z.*"

"Uh-huh. So who was it? Let me think…you disappeared right around the time that fine-ass Leland McClain showed up. I was trying to get to him, but everybody and their damn mama had him surrounded, so I grabbed me a lemonade real quick and then I lost sight of him and—Kim?"

*Aw, hell. I should've just tried to lie and say I was screwing Elrich*, I thought to myself as I squeezed my eyes shut and sighed. "Huh?"

"Were you having sex with—"

Before she could say another word, my phone began to ring on the floor beside me. It was Sunday afternoon and I was expecting my son to arrive in a few hours, so I first thought maybe it was him telling me he had arrived earlier than planned, but when I saw the letters *DLS* pop up on my phone's screen, I scrambled to my feet and headed from Zabrina's living room to her bathroom, shouting, "I gotta take this. Be right back!" along the way.

"Hello," I answered, closing the bathroom door and sitting on the side of the tub.

"Hey, what you doing?"

"Getting my hair re-braided. You in LA?"

"Yeah, just calling to let you know I made it."

"You didn't have to do that. It's not like you're my man or anything," I said, trying not to smile. Hearing his voice just made me feel good. *He* made me feel good, but a relationship was a no-no for me no matter what, and he needed to understand that.

"I know that, but I *am* Little Kim's man. Put her on the phone."

I laughed. "I'm not putting the phone to my vagina, McClain."

"You trying to keep us apart? That's wrong, Kim. Put her on. Stop trying to come between us with your jealous ass."

Still laughing, I said, "I'm not doing it! Besides, how will I know when you're done talking to her?"

"Then put me on speakerphone."

"I'm at someone else's house, a nosy someone else who is probably at the door listening right now. I can't put you on speakerphone."

"Then put the phone down there with your hard-headed ass. Damn! I'm tryna talk to my woman."

My stomach was hurting from laughing at that point, but I managed to say, "Fine! I'm putting it down there now." I moved the phone, rubbed it against my shirt, then brought it back to my ear so I could hear him.

"I know you're listening, because I can hear you breathing, so just give her a message for me. Tell her I miss the way she smells and feels and the sound she makes when she gets wet and I slide up inside her, and that I can't wait to come back home so we can talk in person."

"You sound like you're in love with her or something," I said.

71

"Shit, I am. Gotta go. I'll call Little Kim later."

"You are truly crazy. Bye, McClain."

"Bye."

Surprisingly, Zabrina wasn't standing at the door when I opened it. I was back on the floor and she had her hands in my hair when she asked, "Who is DLS?" Evidently, she saw my phone before I grabbed it.

"What?"

"Who is DLS? That someone's initials?"

I remained silent then decided that as ridiculous as she could be and usually was, I knew I could count on her to keep a secret, so I said, "It stands for *Daddy Long Stroke*."

"Damn, really?"

"Yep."

"Somebody got it like that?"

"Uh-huh."

"Is that somebody Leland McClain?"

I didn't respond.

"Kim?"

I sighed and slowly nodded. "Yes, it's Leland McClain."

"You're actually sleeping with Leland McClain?!" she shrieked. I was glad her man was at work.

"We haven't been doing much sleeping," I mumbled.

I expected more shrieking. Instead, the room fell silent as she resumed braiding my hair.

About ten minutes passed before I finally said, "Z? You don't have anything to say? You ain't gonna curse me out for keeping this from you? Call me a ho'? Nothing?"

"I'm jealous as hell and confused and a little happy for you. It's hard to process this, because I almost can't believe it," she admitted. "How? When? Shit, *why?*"

I shrugged. "It just kind of happened in the midst of him volunteering at the center and harassing me over that one kid I was telling you about. He apologized for being mean to me and then that night we took the boy home, it…happened. Then I started avoiding him, but he kinda confronted me about dodging him at the block party and it happened again and it keeps happening because it's the best sex I have ever had in my entire life."

More silence.

"Damn, I'm baring my ho' soul to you and nothing? You got nothing to say?"

"I'm waiting on the why, Kim. After all that shit with him and Armand? I mean, really? You know your son is a little different in the head and downright irrational when it comes to you. Why would you put Leland McClain in that position? Didn't you say he seemed like a good guy?"

"Damn, Z. I didn't *take* the dick from him. *He* initiated things, and I'm not marrying the man. And shit, weren't you the one talking about how fine and fuckable he is?"

"Yeah, but I didn't think your scared of fine men-ass would actually screw him!"

"Me either."

"But you did."

"Uh-huh, and it's good sex, Z. Great sex. OMG, it's sooooo gooooood."

"I get it! He got good dick!"

"Shiiiiiid! He's got excellent, outstanding, preeminent, motherfucking first and foremost dick!"

"Bitch, *okay!* But think about this for a minute: why did he initiate things with you knowing who you are? You need to be careful. He might just be trying to get back at Armand after the way he clowned him, trying to fight him on the court on TV. Hasn't that thought occurred to you? I mean, he left Miami because of beef with your son, Kim. And now he's having sex with you? Could be about revenge for him."

I frowned a little, fixing my eyes on her TV screen, which was playing a bootleg copy of that new *Jumanji* movie. "Honestly, I hadn't thought about that at all."

"You should've! Come on! You're smarter than this, cuz."

"Not when it comes to men and you know it."

"Don't do that."

"It's true. It's *obviously* true. Shit, I gotta stop seeing him before this all blows up."

"Good idea."

"Yeah."

I knew she was right and felt stupid as hell for not realizing McClain's motives could be ill. But even as rational as the idea of breaking off this sexual thing with him was, I felt a little twist in my heart at the mere prospect of it.

"You gonna have to use that yoni egg you got today for someone else, huh?" she quipped.

She was trying to lighten the mood, probably sensing my despair, but it didn't work. I couldn't smile or laugh; all I could do was stare down at the text message that had just popped up on my phone.

DLS: *Damn I miss Little Kim.*

# 11

# Leland

I had to park down that damn boulevard Everett called a driveway and walk to his house, wondering the whole time if they had invited the whole city of Los Angeles to his stepdaughter's birthday party. This shit didn't make no sense! I was in shape and all but was tired as hell once I made it to the front steps and almost fainted when I saw Neil sitting there with his head hanging, arms propped on his knees, a cigarette dangling between the first and second fingers of his right hand. I'd been trying to reach him for over a month and was both shocked and happy that Everett had gotten in touch with him. Shit, I was beginning to think someone had offed him over some owed money or something.

I'd always thought he and Nolan lucked out with being shorter than me and Everett. Not that they were actually short at five-eleven. Anyway, they always had an easier time buying clothes off the rack and fitting in places, didn't have to always be mindful of ceiling heights, stuff like that. But even with what I considered a height advantage, Neil's life was totally fucked up and that really got to me. If I didn't want anything else, I wanted him to get his ass together.

"Damn, man…you done started smoking again?"

His head snapped up and he looked startled, surprised I was even there. Whatever was on his mind must've been heavy as hell for him not to hear me when I walked up on him. "Man, stress. Gotta do something. Ev watching me like a damn hawk. Got me staying here and shit…"

I sat down on the step beside him. "For real? What happened?"

"I got into some shit I don't wanna talk about. Good to see you, man. You liking St. Louis?"

"It's cool. Why you ain't been answering my calls or calling me back, Neil? I was worried about your short ass."

"Like I said, got into some shit."

"Over money?"

He nodded.

"Gambling debt?"

He nodded again.

"You good now?"

"Yeah, I'm straight. Ev took care of it after he cursed me out and threatened to kick my ass. That's why he's holding me hostage now. Talking 'bout I gotta work this shit off."

"What kinda work?"

"I'm his damn assistant while Courtney is on vacation. Ain't that some shit?"

I chuckled. "You a'ight though, other than being on lockdown with Ev?"

"Yeah, yeah, man." He put the cigarette out on the step beside him and stood up, pushing the butt into the dirt of one of the potted plants that flanked the front door. "Let's go on in here so you can check out this extra-ass birthday party Ev hooked Nat up with. You'd think she was turning sixteen instead of three."

"Man, Ev loves that little girl for real," I said, as I followed Neil inside the huge house. I owned a place in LA that had nothing on the palace my brother lived in, but I knew his house was more for Jo than for him. He truly loved his wife, wasn't nothing he wouldn't do for her, and for the first time in my life, I kind of understood what that felt like. I almost got why people decided to get married and have kids and shit.

Almost.

I mean, I liked the hell out of Kimberly Hampton, but it wasn't like I was in love with her after only knowing her a few weeks and having sex with her a few days. I just…I was feeling her like a motherfucker. I was feeling her in a way that if I thought she was with another man, I would have a major problem with it. And shit, I wasn't checking for no other women, either. Her pussy was more than sufficient for my needs.

Neil led me through the foyer, to the kitchen. The sliding wall was open to the massive backyard full of people—Ev's bodyguards, our family, Jo's friends, some kids and other people who weren't familiar to me, and a bouncy castle, some ponies, and a fucking petting zoo, not to mention a hot dog stand. Kiddie music was blaring from huge speakers sitting outside, and not too far from the back of the house, I saw Uncle Lee Chester manning the barbecue grill. *Damn, he flew Uncle Lee in for this party?* Ev was not playing! But we all knew if you were going to have barbecue at a party, couldn't nobody do it right like Uncle Lee.

While Neil walked out into the yard, I snuck up behind Uncle Lee, and yelled, "What-up-there-now, Unc?!"

He jumped, damn near dropped his barbecue mop, and then turned around. Grinning at me, he shouted, "Nephew! You scared the shit outta me! When you get here?"

"A few minutes ago. Aunt Lou here with you?"

"Hell, no. Probably sitting her crazy ass up at home watching *Walker: Texas Ranger* right now. Just crazy as hell. She missing out, though. Tick's ass got all kinds of food here, and you see these sexy-ass friends of Jo out here? Ooowee! Make me wish I'd brought my Viagra stash with me!"

I couldn't do nothing but grin at him. "You crazy, Unc. I'ma go see if I can find Ev and Jo, wish Nat a happy birthday. Can't wait to tear up them ribs. I know they gonna be good."

He laughed, wheezed, coughed, and laughed again. "You-know-how-I-do-this-shit-right-here-don't-you?!"

Chuckling and shaking my head, I said, "Yeah. I don't guess Aunt Ever is here, either, huh?"

"Naw, said her arthritis was acting up too bad to fly or some shit like that. You know she hates planes. Tick had to beg her to fly out here to him and little Jo's wedding."

"Yeah," I said. "Well, Unc…I'ma go see if I can find Ev. I'ma get with you later."

"All right, Nephew!"

It took me a few minutes of wading through people, greeting family and friends, to get to my oldest brother, who gave me a big smile and pulled me into a hug. After his greeting, I bent down and hugged his tiny wife, taking my new niece from her and tossing her up in the air. "Happy birthday, Nat-Nat!"

"Thank you, Uncle Weewin!" she squealed.

I squeezed her to me before setting her back on the ground and watching her take off for the bouncy house.

"Nat, wait!" Jo called after her. Shaking her head, she smiled up at me. "Glad you're here, Leland. Let me go get this girl. It's almost time for her to open her gifts."

Turning back to Everett, I said, "I saw Neil outside looking like a wannabe runaway slave."

"Yeah, he ain't happy with the situation, but I'm out of twenty-damn-thousand dollars because of his stupid ass. He gon' work that shit off this time and maybe he'll think twice before doing that shit again."

"Twenty thousand?! The hell he bet on?"

"A fucking Dodgers game. Dumb ass…"

"The Dodgers? I thought he was an Astros fan. That nigga ain't got no loyalty."

"Not when it comes to that damn gambling. I made him sign the deed to the bookstore over to me before his ass gambles it away, too."

My eyes widened. "You took his store, Ev?"

"Hell, yeah! I'll give it back if he ever gets his self straight, but until then, I gotta look out for him since he ain't got sense enough to do it." Everett sighed and took a sip from a water bottle he'd been holding. "I'm beginning to think I made shit too easy for him, gave him too much."

"Yeah…" I agreed, but I hated to agree. Just like Everett, I only wanted all of us to be happy. Speaking of… "Kat and Wayne here?"

"Yeah, they somewhere around here. Nolan, too." He grinned at me.

"Nolan must have a new girl. I know that look."

Everett chuckled. "Yep. He don't keep 'em long. It's like he gets bored with them after a couple of weeks or something."

"Naw, Nole lowkey like sistas. That's what it is."

Everett raised his eyebrows. "You think?"

"I *know*. I caught him looking at Jo's assistant's ass one time. You know, she tall and slim but she got an ass on her. I even noticed that, and you know she outta my age range."

"Bridgette?" Everett asked. His voice had risen a couple of octaves.

"Yeah."

"You lying."

"Swear to God, man. He was checking her out."

"Daaaaaamn, that's wild, man."

"I know. Shocked the shit outta me, but I know what I saw. I hope he don't do it around Tommy's big ass, though. He still with her, right?"

"Hell, man, who knows? They been into it a lot lately."

"Word? Well, Nolan might be a'ight then."

"I guess, but if he like sistas, why he don't date 'em?"

"Do I look like I know? Hey, is Ella here? I ain't seen my favorite girl in a minute."

He shook his head and his entire facial expression changed. "She was supposed to be here, had been looking forward to it because she and Nat have gotten tight, but Esther popped up at the last minute with some prior engagement she said they had that Ella didn't even know about. I swear she be pulling this shit on purpose."

"But she ain't messing with you and Jo no more, is she?"

"Naw, she done calmed that shit down since her ass got put on probation and lost her show for leaking that video of Jo and Bugz."

"Good. Speaking of Bugz, he ain't here for his little girl's party?"

"Naw, man. That nigga overseas somewhere. He Facetimed her this morning, though."

Before I could respond, little Nat had run up to Ev and was tugging on the bottom of his basketball shorts. "Ebbwitt!!" she screamed. "I wanna open my pwesents!"

"You do? Well, let's get to it!"

*****

"Here you go," Ev said, handing me a glass of some expensive-ass bourbon he'd been telling me I needed to try.

Taking a seat across from him on the huge sectional that occupied the formal living room, I sipped the drink and nodded. It definitely lived up to the hype. "Not bad, Big South," I said.

"I got a bottle for you, too, Fastlane."

"Good looking out, big brother."

"You know it. So, uh, how are things going with...you know?"

"Kim Hampton?"

His eyes darted around the room like someone had it bugged or something. "Yeah," he finally said, in a low voice.

"Nigga, why are you acting all incognito? Everybody's gone except us and Jo and Nat."

"And Neil."

"Who the hell is he gonna tell?"

He shrugged. "I don't know. Look, man...I ain't scared of much of nothing, but this shit makes me nervous as hell. Dude was tryna fight you literally for nothing before. What you think he's gonna do when he finds out about you and his mom?"

"I don't know, and I really don't care."

"You *should* care. Your ass needs some security, but you won't listen to me."

"Because I *don't* need security. What my big ass look like walking around with a bodyguard?"

"The same way I look, nigga. Safe."

"Man, whatever."

"Listen, I'll always have your back, but I ain't taking no bullets for you off some bullshit that could've been avoided, Leland."

"I can't avoid how I feel, Ev. I just...I can't. It's like she's got this pull on me, has for a long time."

"What you mean *a long time*?"

I sighed, dragged my hand down my face, and squeezed my eyes shut. "Uh...the whole thing with Daniels started when he caught me checking his mom out after a game."

"What?!"

I opened my eyes, saw the look he was giving me, and closed them again. "He caught me checking her out—I was looking at her ass—and he confronted me about it a couple of days later, was talking shit about how he heard I like old bitches, as he put it, but that I better stay away from his mom."

"What did you say?"

"I told him to get out my face with that bullshit and walked off."

"No wonder he kept trying to clown you. Why you just now telling me this?"

"Because there wasn't nothing to tell. All I did was look at her. Damn!"

"And you see how he reacted."

"Yeah."

"But you still not gonna stop seeing her?"

"I would if I could, but I can't."

"Man..."

"I know, Ev. I know."

He blew out a breath and then clapped his hands together. "Okay, look...if you gonna do this, you may as well do it right. Do she like pineapples?"

I frowned. "Pineapples?"

"Yeah. Man, let me tell you..."

# 12

# Kimberly

I set my fork down, reclined in my chair at the marble-topped table in my dining room, and smiled. If I was ever unsure of my cooking skills, my boy always made me feel like a culinary genius. There he was, face in his plate, shoveling forkful after forkful of macaroni and cheese, collard greens, and oven-barbecued chicken into his mouth. It was July, too damn hot for food this heavy, but this was the kind of food he loved, so I'd gladly cooked it for him. Plus, spending time with him was rare these days. This was kind of a celebration for me, especially since he was in one of his infrequent good moods.

Probably sensing my inspection of him, he lifted his eyes, but not his head, and cracked a smile. "What?" he asked, before picking up his chicken and biting into it.

"Nothing, just thinking how good it is to get to spend time with you."

He shrugged. "You ain't have to leave Miami."

"Yes, I did. You were terrorizing every guy who even looked in my direction, Boogie. You went off on a waiter one time. You were out of control!"

"That waiter was checking you out. Dudes are always checking you out, and I ain't got time for them to be getting with you and hurting you."

"No one is going to hurt me again. I won't let anyone hurt me again. You gotta let this go."

Shaking his head, he sat upright in his chair and wiped his hands on a napkin. "I *can't* let it go. I had to protect you back then, and I gotta protect you now. You look good. Folks think you're younger than you are. Dudes are always gonna try to take advantage of you."

"Things are not the same as they were back then. *I'm* not the same, and to be honest, I don't relish the thought of being alone for the rest of my life, but that's what's going to happen if you don't stop!"

He sat back and stared at me.

"What?" I said, feeling more than a little frustrated. I loved him, and he had always been my top priority, but he was a grown man now. I'd done my job raising him. And hell, I was lonely unless I was with McClain, and as luck would have it, he hated him. I really needed him to calm down with being so overprotective.

"You tryna get married, Mama?"

"Maybe one day."

With lifted brows, he leaned forward, and said, "To who?" It sounded more like a dare than a question.

"I don't know, but whoever I choose, I'ma need you not to run them away."

A frown appeared on his face. Boogie, AKA Armand, looked a lot like my mother from the brown skin that was a couple shades lighter than mine, to the hazel eyes. He was handsome and talented and angry. *Always* angry, and sadly, that was my fault. Like I said, I brought out the worst in men, including my own son.

"So I'm supposed to sit back and let some nigga hurt my mama again? That's what you think I'ma do?"

Throwing up my hands, I said, "I just said I won't let that happen again!"

"Yeah, that's what you said before, that you wouldn't let it happen again, that you would leave that nigga alone, and then what happened?"

"Armand, why do you always do that? Why can't we have a decent conversation without you bringing up the past?"

"Because you got a selective memory, so let me jog it for you. You let him come back, he acted good for a week, and then I came home from school to find him choking you. *Choking you*, Mama! I *can't* forget that! I can't forget how I had to pull him off you and beat his ass and make him leave. I can't forget how I had to tell him that if he ever came back, I would kill him. I can't forget that I meant it. And since I can't forget any of that, forgive me for not trusting your judgment when it comes to men. What is it? You lonely? Come back to Miami. Live with me again."

"You're my son. I can't date or marry you, Armand," I said in a soft, defeated voice, because defeat was all I ever felt when he brought up my past transgressions.

"You don't need to date."

"I need companionship!"

"No, you don't!"

I blew out a frustrated breath. "I'm grown, Armand. You're my son, not my guardian, and you can't tell me what I need!"

"I might not be your guardian, but I *am* your boss."

"Are you serious right now? You're gonna pull that card?"

"I'ma do what I need to do to keep you alive. Ain't no more niggas putting their hands on you, and *I mean that*."

I rubbed the back of my neck and sighed loudly. "Not all men hit women, Armand."

"Yeah, but the ones that don't hit women lie and cheat. Niggas ain't shit. *I* ain't even shit. I lie and cheat all the time."

"Armand—"

"What I'm tryna say is, it ain't a single man on this earth good enough for you. Period."

"Boogie—"

His phone chimed, and he held a finger up. After he checked it, he stood and walked around the table, pressing a gentle kiss to my forehead. "I gotta go. Supposed to be meeting up with Scotty and them."

I nodded, deciding I'd take the text from his childhood friend as an out, because I knew how this conversation would end, at an impasse just as it always had. I knew he was coming from a place of love and concern, but in an overwhelming, obsessive way. As I stood and walked him out of my condo, I thought about my life, how I'd tailored it to fit his needs for so many years, ever since that day when he was twelve, and as he put it, he kicked my then-boyfriend's ass. I didn't really date after that, because the couple of times I tried, a teenage Armand terrorized the poor guys into leaving me alone. So I had managed to find some solace in casual sexual arrangements, like the one I had with Elrich, but I was tired of that. I was exhausted from the sacrifices, and honestly, now that he was an adult, it made no sense for me to keep living like that. Something was stirring inside of me that made me want more, and I had to wonder if it had something to do with Leland McClain. I mean, yeah, I liked him, *really* liked him, but being with him would really send Armand over the edge. However, the reality was that it made no sense for me to have to consider my grown son when it came to my love life. Then again, I knew the fact that I *did* have to consider him was my fault; I just didn't know what to do about it. Plus, he *did* save my life, so maybe I owed him the debt of staying single. Or maybe I just didn't deserve love.

Yeah, that was probably it.

*****

It was the second Saturday in July, which followed the last week of our camp—the only week Armand volunteered for—and we'd just had our little summer camp closing ceremonies with several of the NBA guys in attendance. As I sat in my office in the emptying building, I couldn't help but to feel proud and extremely relieved. Our first program of this kind had been a success, Armand was already on his way back to Miami, and I felt like I could breathe again without his overwhelmingly smothering presence. I loved my only child from the depths of my soul, but I was always just as glad to see him leave as I was when he arrived.

Digging in the bottom drawer of my desk, I pulled out a bottle of rum and a plastic cup, had poured myself a celebratory drink and was about to throw it back when the knock came at my door. I knew who it was, knew when he walked into the gym for closing ceremonies that this would be the day I had to break things off with him. He'd texted me a few times while he was in LA, had informed me he'd be back in town today, and I hadn't replied to anything, because I...couldn't. I knew what I needed to do but couldn't find the strength to do it over a text message or a phone call. Now he was pinning me to the wall, forcing me to do it.

I threw my drink back, squeezed my eyes shut at the burning sensation in my throat and warmth everywhere else, and shouted, "Come in!" through the door.

A second later, I was facing a gorgeous giant in slacks, a dress shirt, and tie. I could see his thick muscles bulging through the shirt, his hair was in full, afro effect, and it looked like his beard had grown longer in his absence. Sadly, all I could think of doing was climbing him and letting him satisfy my every need.

As he settled in the chair across from my desk with a serious look on his face, I said, "Glad you came to see me. We need to talk."

He stared at me with those dark eyes, raised his eyebrows, leaned back in the chair, and nodded. "Okay."

I blew out a breath, and blurted, "I can't see you anymore. We can't...we can't have sex anymore."

He puckered his lips and shook his head. "Naw...that's not gonna work for me."

My eyes widened. "What?"

He straightened his relaxed posture. "I said, that's not gonna work for me."

"Um, it's not about what will work for you. It's about what's right. This is...it's wrong."

"What's wrong about two adults enjoying each other?"

"You're too young for me."

He cocked his head to the side. "How young do I feel when I'm inside you?"

"W-what?"

"Fifteen? Twenty? How young, Kim?"

"I-I don't know."

"Here's a better question: how many times have you thought about my age when I'm making you come?"

"Um…"

"When you think about me, is it my age you think about or my di—"

"Leland!"

"I'm Leland instead of McClain now?"

"My son—"

"Is not a concern of mine. You are."

"He *should* be a concern of yours."

"But he's not. I didn't leave Miami because of him. I left because I'm chasing a ring, or at least that's what I thought, but what I realized when I was in LA is that I ended up here because you're here, and I didn't even know when I was asked to be a part of this program that you were moving back here permanently. But here you are, a woman I have wanted since the first time I ever laid eyes on her. I wanted to know if your skin was as soft as it looked and how your lips would taste and how it would feel to be with you. Now that I know, I'm not letting you go."

My heart was beating wildly, and I couldn't look at him. "You—you're gonna have to. This won't work! It can't!"

"Have you even discussed this with Little Kim?"

"McClain—"

"Keep calling me Leland. I got an old name. That should help you deal with this a little better."

"There's nothing to deal with. We're over. We *have* to be."

"Give me a valid reason that has nothing to do with my age or your son, and I'll agree to end this."

"Those *are* valid reasons."

"No, they're not. I already debunked the age thing. And you know what? You're the youngest woman I've been with in years, anyway. Two, I told you, I ain't fucked up about your son. He wanna fight me over you when he finds out? Cool. Whatever. I'm not scared of him.

Now..." He stood and rounded my desk, took my hand, pulling me to my feet, and drew me into his arms. As he leaned in to kiss me, he asked, "If I do this, you're gonna stop me?"

I closed my eyes and nodded. "Yeah...stop," I said weakly, as he kissed me.

He flicked his tongue against my neck. "And this?"

"Yeah. Stop that, too," I whispered.

His hands found my waist, and he rubbed his fingers across the beads that could be felt beneath the fabric of my dress. Leaning in close to my ear, he said, "You got no idea how much these beads turn me on. I was sitting in that gym wondering if you were wearing them."

"They turn me on, too," I admitted.

Sucking on my earlobe, he said, "Damn, you are the sexiest woman I have ever seen in my life."

Closing my eyes, I said, "Thank you, but-but stop. I can't—"

"I wanna eat your pussy."

My eyes popped open. "Huh—what?"

"I realize I haven't done that yet, and how can you make the decision to end this without knowing the full scope of what I have to offer you? I got a long-ass tongue."

"Uh-um...It's about more than sex. It's about keeping the peace and doing what's right, and you should go find you a woman your age so you can have babies and stuff."

"I don't want babies and stuff. I'm too selfish for that, gotta have all the attention." He slid his hand under my dress and into my panties. "I want *you*, and why can't you let the age thing go?"

"Because you are only six years older than my child!"

"Seven, and so? You're only fifteen years older than him."

His finger was inside me, and my knees were buckling. I had to grab him to keep from falling. "Leland—"

He kept playing with my yoni with one hand, cupped my face with the other, looked into my eyes, and said, "I'ma eat this pussy and I'ma eat it good, and if you still don't want me after that, I'll leave you alone. Won't ever contact you again no matter how bad I want you, and I want you *so bad*, baby. Never wanted anyone like this before in my life. So this is my way of begging you to be with me, a'ight?"

Since my yoni was literally a slushy pulsating mess, I stopped arguing, raked the papers to the floor, and let him lay me on my desk. I clamped my eyes shut while he relieved me of my panties, almost bolted to my feet when his tongue met my clit. My entire body tensed up as he licked…and licked…and licked, then slid a finger inside me as he sucked on my clit like it was a damn Blow Pop. Then his tongue replaced his finger as he slipped it inside me, pulled it out, and glided it over my clit over and over again. He tongue-screwed me until my yoni began to convulse and I screamed his name at the top of my lungs, and then he softly slapped his hand against my pulsating vagina. "Am I too young?" he asked.

"Oh!" was my response, as my eyes opened and rolled into the back of my head. I'll be damned if his hand hitting my yoni didn't almost make me climax again. The hell?

He gently smacked my yoni again, making me shudder and moan, and smiled down at me, his beard and mustache glistening with my essence as he said, "You like that, huh?"

I nodded and reached up, wrapping my arms around his neck when he bent over, bringing his face close to mine. "Am I too young, Kim?" he repeated.

"Noooo," I whined.

"So you wanna keep seeing me and doing this?"

"Yessss."

"Only me?"

When I didn't answer him fast enough, he gently bit my bottom lip, making me shudder again. "Only me?" he asked again.

"I-I thought you didn't want a relationship."

"Changed my mind. So answer me."

"*Okay*…yes, only you."

"And you're gonna answer when I call and return my texts?"

"Uh-huh…"

"So you're mine now, right?"

He was inside me now, so I basically whimpered, "Yes."

"And I'm yours?"

"Mm-hmmmmmm…"

"Now that we got that clear…" He slid out and back into my saturated core.

"Uh!"

"See, we were made to do this, baby."

"Le-Le-Leland?" I said against his lips as he kissed me over and over again.

"Yeah, baby?"

"I don't want my son to know about us. Not right now. So we'll need to be careful. We can't—Ooooh! We can't tell anyone about us."

"Whatever you want, baby."

I woke up the next morning in Leland's suite with him lying beside me, wide awake, those dark eyes on me.

"You been up all night staring at me?" I asked, as he reached over and rubbed a finger over my waist beads.

"No, just woke up a few minutes ago, looked at you, and thought damn, she's beautiful."

I reached over and tugged his beard a little. "So are you."

"Thanks. Hey, I gotta head out early to work out, but I ordered breakfast and I'll call you later. Or you can stay until I get back and we can spend the day in bed since it's Sunday."

I stared at him and smiled. "I'll stay, but I was wondering…are you ever going to get a place? How long you planning on staying here?"

He sighed. "I don't know. Been looking, but I can't find anywhere I like. I really want a condo in a secure area."

"Try my building. I know there are a couple of units that haven't been purchased yet. It's a new building, really exclusive and secure."

"Your son got it for you?"

I nodded.

He moved closer to me, kissed me, then lifted from the bed. "Text me the info."

"I will," I said, as I watched him move around the suite naked. After he left, I climbed out of bed, wrapping a sheet around me as I sat at the table to see what was for breakfast—bacon, eggs, toast, and pineapple chunks. I guessed he liked pineapples. Shrugging, I dug in.

# 13

## Kimberly

"Damn, you're actually here?" was the way Zabrina greeted me as I approached the table.

Falling into the chair, I rolled my eyes and set my huge purse on the floor beside me. "Damn...happy National Cheesecake Day to you, too. And I *said* I'd be here, so I'm here."

"Uh-huh, but you been too busy to have lunch, dinner, or anything else with me. You even turned down drinks last Saturday, and I offered to damn pay!"

It'd been two weeks since Leland and I officially became a thing, and I honestly *had* been neglecting my friendship/cousinship with her, but this was new and fun and I hadn't had a real boyfriend in seven or eight years and Leland was just...everything. Passionate, funny, and sexy as hell. Plus he fed me well, which was a big deal to me. I appreciated a man who made sure his woman ate. Never had that before. Hell, I never had a man that cared not to hit me before. Yeah, every single man I ever dated from Armand's sorry ass father to the one Armand had to peel off of me put their hands on me at some point. That's what I meant by me bringing out the worst in men, but Leland had me thinking maybe I was wrong. Maybe it wasn't me. Maybe it was the men.

*Or maybe if you give him enough time, he'll hit you, too, and not just in a sexual way.*

I squeezed my eyes shut to chase that thought away, and when I popped them back open, Zabrina was staring expectantly at me.

"What?" I asked, then took a sip from my sweaty glass of water, averting my eyes from her face.

"I said, has breaking things off with Leland McClain gotten to you like that? I mean, I know it had to be hard as fine as his ass is. And he's rich, too. Girl, I don't know how you did it, but it was for the best. You know that, right? I mean, I get it, so you don't have to avoid—hey, when did you get that bracelet?"

I glanced down at the tennis bracelet Leland had gifted to me a couple of days earlier. I'd woken up to an empty hotel room and the bracelet on my wrist. I'd been trying to give it back to him, but every time I did, we ended up somehow having sex, so I just gave up.

"What?" I asked, because I didn't know what else to say.

"Did Armand give it to you? It's nice, girl!"

"Hey."

I would've known that voice even if I wasn't staring up at him in total and utter shock. And if I didn't recognize it, my vagina definitely did. Did I tell him I was having lunch there? Shit, was he following me? Was he crazy like the other fools I dated in the past?

"Oh. My. God. I-I've wanted to meet you forever! I tried to get to you at that block party, but you were swarmed before I could make it! I'm Zabrina Norris, Kim's first cousin and best friend! Hi!" Zabrina was grinning like a nut and talking all over herself. If I didn't know any better, I'd wonder if she was telling me to break things off with him so she could make a move, because I saw absolutely nothing but lust in her eyes.

He took her limp outstretched hand, bent over, and kissed it. "Nice to meet you, Zabrina."

"Nice to meet you, too! This is Kim—shit, you already know her, and I know you know her."

Leland returned his attention to me and nodded. "Yeah, I know her."

"W-w-what are you doing here, Mr. McClain?" I asked, begging him with my eyes not to out us.

He raised his eyebrows, gave me a quick confused look, and said,

"Oh, right. Uh, my boy Polo wanted to meet up here. I told him I wanted to celebrate me buying a condo and becoming an official St. Louis resident and he suggested we come here, promised this place makes the best wings in town."

I knew he was supposed to be purchasing a condo on the top floor of my building and was happy to hear the deal was sealed. That would make it much easier for us to see each other.

"Polo?! Paul Logan is here, too?!" Zabrina shouted.

I dropped my head, afraid to look up and see folks staring at us. "Z, I don't think he wanted you to announce it," I muttered.

Leland chuckled. "It's all good."

"Why don't y'all join us?" she suggested, as she snatched her purse up from one of the two empty seats at the square table.

I wasted a glare on her thirsty ass, because her eyes were shooting lasers into Leland whose gaze was volleying between me and her.

"Uh, I'm sure he and Polo don't wanna eat out in the open like this. People are already staring, thanks to you," I said.

Her shoulders and face fell. "Oh."

Leland was staring at his phone as he said, "He just texted me to meet him in a private room. How about y'all join us?"

"Uh—" I tried.

"That'd be great!" Zabrina gushed, bolting to her feet with a huge grin on her face.

Leland turned to me, and I gave him a wide-eyed "what the fuck?" look.

He merely smiled, and said, "Follow me, ladies."

The room was one I'd never been in despite the fact that I'd been patronizing Dendy's forever. It was actually a smaller version of the main dining room, complete with tables and booths. The room was empty except for Polo, who was waiting in a booth for us. Yeah, a damn booth. So that meant I would either have to sit across from Leland and try not to look at him or sit next to him and try not to attack him, because at this point, the scent of him alone turned me on.

"Come on, girl," Zabrina chirped, beckoning for me to slide into the booth next to her. I supposed this seating arrangement was the safest. I'd just act like Leland wasn't sitting across from me.

"Polo, man…look who I found out there," Leland said.

"Ms. Hampton! How are things over at King's Dream without us?" Polo asked, extending his hand to me from his seat next to Leland and across from Zabrina.

"Quiet. We're not running any programs right now. Just got the indoor and outdoor courts open to the public while we prepare for our back-to-school events."

"Cool, cool," Polo said, with a nod.

Zabrina nudged me so hard I damn near fell off the seat. In response, I shot her ass a look.

Then she took it upon herself to fling her hand at him. "I'm Zabrina Norris, her cousin."

Polo licked his lips and gave her the same grin he'd been giving me since I met him a few months back. "Nice to meet you. I'm Polo," he said, as he clasped her hand.

"I know! I'm a huge fan! If I could afford some tickets, I'd be at like every game."

"Yeah? I can hook you up with some," Polo said.

"For real?!" Zabrina squealed.

"You'll need one for you *and* your fiancé, right?" I asked. I think she was willing to screw both of them at that point, and I was gonna have to kick her ass if she kept flirting with my secret boyfriend that she didn't know I was still screwing.

She pinched me under the table and I pinched her the-hell right back.

"You're engaged?" Polo asked.

"Do you see a ring on my finger?" she asked, then turned and cocked an eyebrow up at me.

"Wow," I muttered, then let my eyes roam the room as she and Polo talked about…shit, I don't know, because the only thoughts in my head were Leland-Leland-Leland-Leland-Leland-Leland-Leland. And then my eyes shot over to him on their own, and I was forced to take him in from the ponytail atop his head down to his thick lips and that damn beard. His serious eyes were glued to me, and like a magnet, held mine in place. And there we were, transmitting something through our eyes, something I had never, and knew I would never, share with another man, because there was only one Leland McClain.

"...right, Kim?"

I snatched my head around to face Zabrina. "Huh?"

"Um...come with me to the restroom," she said, but I was sure that wasn't what she said the first time.

The door had barely closed behind us when she spun around, looked me in the eye, and asked, "You didn't break it off with him, did you?"

My eyes flitted around the two-stall restroom. "What? Why do you think that?"

"Because the two of you were out there eye-screwing each other, and I have never seen a man look at a woman the way he looks at you. I mean, damn! What you put on him? His ass looks like he's in love or something."

Dang, she stopped drooling over him long enough to notice that?

Still, I said, "No he doesn't, and we weren't looking at each other like nothing."

She gave me a smirk. "Ho', please."

I sighed. "I tried to break it off and then he did some nasty shit to me and I couldn't."

"Uh-huh, I knew it!" She placed a hand on my shoulder and looked me dead in the eye. "Look, ignore anything I said before about him. He ain't playing, and he ain't out for revenge. His ass is crazy about you, and you know what? You deserve to be with him. You sacrificed your happiness to raise Armand, worked two and three jobs to make sure he had everything he needed and wanted. He's grown now, and you need to focus on yourself and what makes you happy."

Huh?

I stared at her for a second, then asked, "You mean that?"

"Yes! Girl, I know Garner loves me, but he ain't never looked at me like Leland McClain looks at you. Shit, I'm as jealous of you as I am happy for you."

As my eyes filled with tears, I said, "I really like him and he's so sweet and nasty at the same time. So far, he's been good to me."

"He bought that bracelet?"

I nodded. "And a necklace and a fur coat."

"Damn, girl. Have y'all even been together a month?"

"Officially? Two weeks, but yeah, it's been about a month since we first hooked up."

"Cuz, you found what me and you have been talking about forever—a real man."

"Yeah, but we're keeping it a secret."

"From Armand?"

"Yes, and that means we have to keep it from everyone else, too. Please don't tell anyone."

"You know I won't. But how long are you planning on keeping this on the hush?"

"I don't know. I need to see where this is going first. No need in telling Armand if this is only a short fling. Plus, I tried to reason with him when he was here, but he's still on that 'I don't need to date' stuff. I mean, it's not like I'm afraid of him or anything like that; I just don't want him starting any more trouble with Leland. He doesn't deserve that."

She nodded. "You gotta let go of the guilt over the past. I think once you do that, you'll have the courage to set some real boundaries with him. He's your son, not your man."

"I know that." I hated when she said stuff like that. It made me sound like a weakling or a nut, and I wasn't either, not any longer.

"And you know he's wrong for always bringing it up," she continued.

"Yeah," I said softly.

"But I really am happy for you, cuz. I truly am."

I gave her a tiny smile. "Thanks, Z."

"Okay, well, I actually gotta pee. Hold up so we can go back out there together."

"Okay."

I shook my head, stared at myself in the mirror over the sink, and then I smiled. As convoluted and crazy as this all was, it was a relief to share it with someone. It made it feel more real.

# Leland

"You fucking her, ain't you?"

I was staring at the door to the private room, waiting for Kim and her cousin to come back. "Who?" I asked, my eyes still on the door.

"You know the-fuck who, nigga! You fucking Daniels' mom? Really?"

"You *wanna* fuck her," I accused, turning to face him.

"Shit, who don't? You know half the league was checking for her from the moment we saw her with him during the draft. The rest of us just got enough sense not to go there. And didn't you say she wasn't your type?"

I shrugged. "I guess I changed my type."

"Daniels good with this?" he asked skeptically.

I shook my head. "He don't know. She don't want him to know. So don't say shit."

"Really, man? When you known me to snitch?"

"Just saying."

"Whatever, nigga. So she don't want Daniels to know, huh? I *bet* she don't. I heard he was wildin' over her in Miami, threatening to kick everybody's ass if they even looked at her. Word is, she went out on a date with some old dude who owns a club down there and Daniels threatened to kill him. They say that's why she moved back here. And we all know the nigga can't stand your ass. The hell are you doing?"

"Shit, man…I think I'm falling in love."

"Got damn."

As the door opened and Kim and her cousin made their way back to the booth, I said, "I know."

# 14

# Leland

She was behind me, her arms around me with her leg kicked over mine. I could feel the steady pattern of her breathing against my back in the darkness. We were in my suite, it was late, I had to get up in a couple of hours for my training, but all I wanted to do was lay up in that bed with her twenty-four-seven.

This was nice and…different. I'd never basically begged a woman to give me a chance before, never kept one around this long, never thought about the future when it came to relationships. Yeah, there was a whole bunch of stuff I never considered before Kim, and the crazy thing was, I couldn't explain the shift if someone put a gun to my head and tried to make me. There was just something inside of her that called to me from day one. Something that told me she needed me, and I damn sure needed her.

"Leland?" I was so deep in thought I hadn't noticed that the rhythm of her breathing had changed to indicate she was awake.

"Yeah?" I answered, placing my hand over her much-smaller one.

"Why do you like older women?"

I sighed. "I don't wanna argue about that anymore, Kim. I thought we were past this age shit. Do I need to quiz you again?"

"No…I didn't mean it like that. I just wanna know why. Like, most of the guys I knew back in the day who dated older women kind of did it for money or stuff like that. That's obviously not the case with you."

I lay there for a minute then turned to face her, pulling her closer to me. She snuggled into my body and kissed my chest. "I don't know. Just always have," I said.

"You've never been with someone your own age?"

"No. Never been attracted to anyone my age. Lost my virginity to my twenty-five-year-old tutor when I was fourteen."

"What?!"

She sounded alarmed, so I said, "It wasn't predatory. I begged her to do it until I finally wore her down."

"She still shouldn't have done it, Leland. I mean, you didn't rape her, did you? You didn't make her do it?"

"No! I'd never do that!"

"Did you care about her? Did you love her?"

"Love? No. But I did care about her. We were together a few more times after that. I enjoyed being with her."

"Where would y'all do it?"

"Her apartment in Houston where my aunt would drop me off."

She was quiet for a minute, then asked, "You think it has anything to do with you losing your mother when you were young?"

"You think I got mommy issues, baby?"

"I-I don't know…"

I slid my hand down her back and clutched one of her ass cheeks. "You think I see you as my mother?"

"Oooo, obviously not. I was just wondering about it."

"I don't know, baby. Maybe it has something to do with my mom's death or the fact that her older sister finished raising me or that my brother married an older woman or that the mail carrier we had was a fine older woman or that I had some sexy teachers? All I know is everyone has preferences and older women are mine. I've never tried to figure out why. I bet you have preferences, too. What kind of food do you like?"

"Hmm, besides anything my granny cooks? I love Asian food."

"Okay, I can vibe with that. You like to drink? What's your favorite cocktail?"

"Mai Tai, hands down."

"I'll remember that. What kind of men do you like?"

I could feel her shrug against me. "Tall men and kind men, I guess."

"Older or younger?"

"I always dated older men until you."

"So that's your preference?"

"I don't know. I was always crazy about my dad, and I only got to see him occasionally growing up because he and my mom split when I was little, so I always thought that was why I dated older guys."

"Y'all closer now?"

"He passed away a few years back, so we never got to have the relationship I wanted us to have, but I know he loved me. He was a sweet man."

"Your son's father was older, too?"

"Yeah, he was twenty when I got pregnant at fifteen. Like I said, you're the first man I've been with that isn't older than me."

"Where is he now?"

"Armand's father? Who the hell knows? Probably locked up somewhere since he can't seem to stay out the pen. I haven't seen him since Armand was like five."

"His father ever reach out to him?"

"No. Not yet, but I'm sure that's coming since Armand is in the NBA now."

"Yeah, probably. So, you raised him by yourself?"

"For the most part. My mom helped me early on. I lived with her until I finished college, so she basically helped raise Armand until he was like eight, and then I moved out because I realized she'd become more of a mother to him than me and I didn't want that. She's never forgiven me for 'taking her baby away from her.' So she refused to watch him for me unless we moved back in. My grandma helped me after that, though."

"Well, I'm glad you had some support. Why didn't you have a man when we got together?"

"Who said I didn't?"

"Shit, I hope you woulda told me before we started fucking, baby."

"I would've."

"That's what I'm saying. So why didn't you have a man?"

She stiffened in my arms. "You want the honest truth?"

"That's why I asked."

She sighed against my chest. "For a lot of reasons that I don't wanna talk about."

"Bad relationships in the past?" That was a thing with all the women I'd messed with—regretful past relationships. Niggas really weren't shit, myself included before Kim.

"The worst kind of past relationships."

"They put their hands on you?"

She hesitated, then whispered, "Yeah, including Armand's father."

"Did Armand see it?"

"Yeah…"

Shit, I didn't know what to say now, but this did explain why dude was so damn crazy when it came to her. After a few minutes of silence, I did say, "So that's why you got sick after all that went down at Shemar's house, why you were crying?"

"Yeah, it hit too close to home, brought back some really bad memories."

"Baby…I'm sorry that happened to you."

"It's not your fault. I just…I don't know why I attracted men who liked to hit me," she said.

"All of them hit you?"

"All the ones I had a real relationship with did. I've never loved or thought I loved a man who didn't hurt me both emotionally and physically."

We were both quiet for a moment or two, and then I asked, "Y-you want me to stop smacking your ass and stuff? Does that bother you?"

"You think it bothers me?"

"I think you like it, but—"

She pushed against my chest until I rolled over on my back. Then she straddled me, making my shit rise as she sat on it. "I like everything you do to me, Leland…especially that."

That was a relief, because I loved smacking her ass…and her pussy. The sound of it did something to me. "Good. So now I know why you need me."

"Did I say I needed you?"

"You didn't have to."

Rolling her eyes, she said, "Okay, I'll bite. Why do I need you?"

"Because you need to know what it's like for a man to treat you right. I do that for you."

"So you think you treat me right, huh?"

"I *know* I treat you *more* than right."

I watched the expression on her face change from what looked like delight to confusion. "Do you need me?" she asked.

"Yeah, baby. I do," I answered.

"Why?"

"Because I need someone to share my world with, someone I can give my heart to. That's you."

She blinked a few times and then smiled down at me. "You're beautiful, you know that?"

"Yeah."

"Wow."

I chuckled. "Hey, you on birth control, baby?"

She frowned down at me and nodded. "Of course I am. I'm on the pill. Why?"

I reached over on the nightstand for a condom. "I'ma send you my latest test results tomorrow so we can go raw. I wanna feel you like that."

Leaning forward to kiss me, she said, "Okay, I'll send you mine, too."

\*\*\*\*\*

"I miss you." Her voice flowed into my ear, and I smiled.

"You coulda came with me," I replied.

"And do what? Hide in a hotel room the whole time?"

"I got a house out here. I told you that."

"Okay, then I'd be hiding in your house. No thank you."

"If you tell your son about us, you wouldn't have to hide."

"It's too soon for that."

"It's been almost two months."

"Exactly. Too soon."

"If you say so. I gotta go do this interview in a minute. I'll call you later."

"Okay. Bye, Leland."

"Bye, baby."

I went to the pictures on my phone and stared at the one I'd taken of her that morning before I left to return to LA. In it, she was asleep, mouth slightly open. Smiling, I closed the picture, stepped out of my truck, and into the studio, glad this was just a two-day trip, because I already missed the shit out of her.

# 15

## Kimberly

I already wasn't in the best of moods because Leland's little turnaround trip to LA had been extended, and while we spent the majority of our time together engaged in sex, I did manage to get the best sleep I'd had in years when I was in his bed. Since he'd been gone, I'd fallen back into a familiar pattern of insomnia, which had my eyes tired and my head throbbing. Add to that miserable condition that Peaches had decided to call in sick and my irritation level was through the roof. My plan had been to stay to myself in my office, but that was impossible now. Peaches' absence meant I'd *have* to interact with people.

*I should take my ass home.*

That was the logical solution, but I'd never been the most logical person, so I decided to torture myself by tackling payroll. My eyes were damn near crossed by 11:00 AM when my cell phone began to vibrate against my desk. I rolled the hell out of them when I saw my mother's name on the screen. I shouldn't have answered it, but my dumb ass did.

"Hello?" I tried to sound chipper but failed epically.

"I'm still alive," was her greeting.

I sighed, reclined in my chair, and said, "Well, I hope so since you're on the phone talking to me."

"You live in the same town with me, and you don't come see me; you don't call. A lot of people wish they still had their mother, and you act like you don't care about yours."

Closing my eyes, I rested my head on the back of my chair. "I care."

"You don't act like it."

"Been busy."

"Boogie stays busier than you, but he makes time to call me."

*Because he actually likes you. I don't.* "You talked to him today?"

"Mm-hmm. He sounded so good. I am so proud of that boy! It's a blessing how he turned out after the shit you put him through getting your ass kicked all over town."

"I guess I get it from my mama," spilled from my lips before I could catch it and reel it back in.

"Oh, you wanna take it there?"

"*You* took it there."

"Yeah, well, I might have gotten my ass kicked a couple of times, but I had sense enough to leave men alone a long time ago. I haven't had a boyfriend in years. And your ass shoulda been taking notes on how *not* to get your ass kicked instead of running head first into any fool who liked to kick ass."

"Gotta go, Ma."

"Still can't stand hearing the truth, huh? Boogie told me you tryna date again. You better not. You know every man you even look at kicks your ass. Some fool be done killed you and that'd kill that boy because as sorry a mother as you are, he still loves you. You heard about that girl in East St. Louis, didn't you? Her boyfriend shot her. You don't—"

*Time to hang up before I curse this woman completely out.* "I said I gotta go!"

I hung up and blew out a breath. So they were still talking about me behind my back? I blamed my mom for establishing that kind of relationship with him when he was little and treating me like I was Armand's sister instead of his mother. That mess had stuck despite the effort I put forth to be a good mother to him after we moved out of her house. He respected me as his mother in some ways but not in others. It irked the shit out of me.

And my mother's lack of respect for me? Well, I was sadly used to that.

A knock came at my office door, and since my mother's call had intensified my sour mood, I groaned, took a deep breath, released it, and yelled, "Come in!"

It opened to reveal a woman I mildly recognized—short, wearing a microscopic red dress, her hair in a flowing weave, her makeup flawless. With a slight frown on my face, I asked, "May I help you?"

Her eyes rounded my office before settling on me. "You Ms. Hampton, right?"

I straightened my posture and nodded. "Yes, and you are?"

"Sheila Townsend, Shemar's mom."

My stomach dropped a little as I remembered the encounter at her house, an encounter that reminded me too much of my past life. "Oh, um…have a seat."

She did, crossing her legs and folding her hands in her lap. She looked nice, pretty without the blood and bruises on her face.

"How are you? Shemar?" I asked.

"We good. A lot better since Domo is locked up."

Good, she hadn't tried to get him out. Leland would be glad to hear that. He'd been worried about Shemar. "That's great. So what can I help you with today?"

She dug in her purse and pulled out a piece of paper. "I was wondering if you could give this to Leland McClain?"

I reached across my desk and took the slip of paper. On it was her name and a phone number. "Um, why?" was all I could think to say.

"So he can check on Shemar. I know they kind of bonded and stuff, and since my mom helped me get my phone back on, I wanted him to have my number." She smiled at me, and that's when I realized what was going on. She was tryna get with my damn man. She'd mistaken his concern and help for him wanting her. She had probably dolled herself up hoping to run into him here. I'd be damned if I gave him that number. Screw that.

So I said, "Um, Ms. Townsend, Mr. McClain doesn't work here. He was just a volunteer, and as you know, the program he was helping out with has ended."

"Yeah, but you know how to reach him, right?" She leaned forward, lowering her voice. "I'm just tryna shoot my shot, you know? We're like the same age and stuff. I think he might like me. Hook a sister up."

*Hellllll, no!*

I stared down at the paper then handed it back across my desk to her. "I'm not in the business of hooking sisters up, Ms. Townsend. If you need the help of the center in an official capacity, I'll gladly assist you, but I can't help you with this."

She snatched the paper from me and huffed her way out of my office while mumbling, "Stuck-up bitch."

*I'll be that before I give my man your number, ho'.*

I closed my eyes and shook my head. *What kind of day is this?*

I got the official answer of "a day from hell" when I received a text from my cousin, Shelby, three seconds after Sheila Townsend stormed out of my office. It read: *U seen this shit, cuz? Sorry motherfucker.*

With it, was a link, a link to a picture on the fucking *Tea Steepers* website, a picture of Leland—*my* damn Leland—with his hand on pop singer Honey Combs' back, obviously leading her somewhere. Short, so light-skinned she was damn near racially ambiguous, big fake-breasted, highly over-rated, no-singing-ass Honey Combs of the group Confections, which she was a member of along with her sisters Sugar and Candy. The caption read:

*Looks like Honey bagged Leland "Fastlane" McClain. The two were spotted entering Leland's LA nightclub, Second Avenue. Get your life, Honey!*

The picture was posted that morning.

"Corny name-having bitch," I muttered. "Sorry cheating-ass nigga," I added.

I closed the Google Chrome app and told myself this was probably my fault for making him keep us a secret. Then I told myself he'd said he was okay with it. Then I fully realized that the text had come from Shelby, who I hadn't told about Leland, which meant Zabrina had told her, which meant her supposed-to-be-keeping-a-secret ass had probably told other people, which meant my damn son was going to find out only to see this man out with another woman, reinforcing his theory that men weren't shit and that I had no business dating. Then he'd tell his BFF, my mom, who'd throw this shit in my face like she did everything else. So after I text-cursed Zabrina out, I grabbed my purse and car keys and left, went home, and collapsed into my bed. By some miracle, I managed to fall right to sleep. When I woke up to a missed call from Leland's ass and a text from him informing me that he was back in town earlier than expected, I rolled my eyes and decided I needed a damn drink.

\*\*\*\*\*

Around ten that evening, I found myself at Plush. I had ignored any calls I received from Zabrina's broken refrigerator ass, so I sat at the bar alone. When a guy asked me to dance, I obliged him and actually enjoyed stepping to *24K Magic* with him. We ended up dancing through two more songs, including a slow one, before he offered to buy me another drink. He sat with me at the bar, and I was laughing at a moderately funny joke he'd just told me when I decided to check my phone. For what, I don't know. Maybe an apology from Zabrina? I actually did have a text, but it wasn't from her. It was from Leland: *Who the fuck is that nigga all up in ur face?*

I frowned, then turned my head. The club wasn't crowded since it was the middle of the week, so I quickly spotted his tall ass sitting at a table near the dancefloor. How in the world had I missed him? My ass must've been drunk.

Me: *What are you doing here?*

DLS: *My woman's been ignoring me so I accepted my friend's invitation to check this place out. Who the fuck is that nigga trying to get his ass kicked? And what the fuck u got on?*

Me: *What friend? Honey Combs?*

DLS: *U saw the picture? Is that why u tryna get that nigga killed?*

Me: *Yeah, I saw it. What the hell was that?*

DLS: *Some fabricated shit. Meet me in VIP and I'll explain.*

"Important message?" the guy asked. I think his name was Vincent, but since I was at least forty-percent drunk, I can't be sure. Hell, I couldn't even remember what fake name I gave him. I had a whole list of them I used when I went to the club.

"Yeah, sorry about this. Give me a second," I replied.

"No worries, pretty lady."

I smiled up at him.

DLS: *What that nigga just say? I will fuck him completely up!*

Me: *None of your business and stop texting me. I'm busy right now.*

I tucked my phone in my purse and resumed my conversation with Vincent. Five minutes later, Leland appeared at the bar, right next to me. I knew that because I smelled him, but I didn't turn to look at him. Instead, I pretended to be interested in whatever Vincent was saying. However, Vincent quickly lost interest in me.

"Leland McClain? I can't believe this!" he gushed.

I involuntarily rolled my eyes.

"Yeah," Leland responded to the guy, his voice caustic. Then he leaned in close to me. "Let me holla at you real quick."

Oblivious to the fact that Leland was not trying to converse with him and was three seconds from beating his ass, Vincent said, "Man, it's great to meet you! Can't wait for you and the Cyclones to hit the court this season! I got season tickets."

"Uh, excuse me," I said, grabbing my purse and leaving the two men behind.

I was almost to the restroom when I felt a hand on my bare arm and tried unsuccessfully to snatch away. Turning to face him with a frown on my face, I hissed, "Let me go!"

Leland leaned in close, and said, "Nope. Bring your ass up to VIP or I'ma tell the whole damn world we fucking. Matter of fact, I'll fly my ass down to Miami and tell your son in person."

"I-I need to pee," was all I could come up with, but it was the truth. That liquor was running right through me.

"Then pee. I'll be waiting for you up there. I'm not playing with you, Kim. Let me see you talking to that nigga again, and I'ma turn this motherfucker out."

So after I peed, I carried my ass to the stairs that led to VIP, where the big burly man who was guarding them gave me a smile and moved aside to allow me access to them. Plush's VIP was a series of roped-off areas, some with varying-sized tables and others with couches. The entire VIP section was empty except for Leland, who I found sitting on a sofa.

"Where is your friend, the one who invited you here?" I asked, as I approached him.

"He left," Leland replied, without looking up at me.

"Who was it?"

"Drayveon Walker."

Drayveon was another member of the Cyclones. But instead of acknowledging that, I said, "Oh, I thought maybe you were here with Honey Combs or one of her sisters. Or shit, maybe you're messing with all three of them."

"Sit down, Kim," was his response.

"I don't want to sit down."

He finally looked up at me with lifted brows. "*Sit down, Kim.*"

Remembering that he was blackmailing me, I plopped down on the couch, scooting away from him, but he slid close to me, crowding me into the arm of the sofa.

"I don't know what makes you think you can play with me like this, but you got me fucked up. You gonna make me catch a charge up in here," he said.

"You're gonna kick your fan's ass? Really, Leland?"

"You think I won't? I will go down there and dot that nigga's eye right now!"

"I think you're a cheating asshole who has the nerve to be upset about me talking to another man when you had your hand all on that no-singing trick's back and shit. I got *you* fucked up? Naw, you got *me* fucked up! I don't care if we're a secret! That was disrespectful as hell! I ain't no Khloe Kardashian!"

"And I ain't no got-damn, Tristan Thompson! That shit he did don't make no sense. Hell, if a nigga wanna fuck around, why get in a relationship?"

"You tell me!" He tried to kiss me, but I pushed him away. "We're in public. Someone could see us!"

"I don't care!"

"I do!"

"Ain't nobody coming up here, Kim! Damn!"

"How do you know that?"

"Because I paid for the whole floor after I spotted you!"

"Oh…"

"Yeah." He backed away from me a little and shook his head. "I'm not messing with Honey's young ass, Kim."

"She's your age, Leland."

"That's what I'm saying."

I rolled my eyes.

"Look, I'm not messing with anyone but you. I don't *want* anyone but you. I saw her when I was heading into my club, we spoke to each other, and I escorted her inside. Then we went our separate ways. That's it."

"Why'd you have to touch her, though?"

He shrugged. "I don't know…it's a habit, I guess."

"Well, you need to break it."

"I know. My bad, baby. But damn, we grown. You supposed to confront me about this shit, curse me out, slap me or something, not ignore me. That shit gave me a headache. Then I come here, and you got a nigga all in your face while you're wearing that little-ass dress. The fuck, Kim?"

"I'm sorry. The men in my past were the types you just have to cut all contact with for them to get the point."

"Well, I ain't them and I ain't done what they did to you. Damn, can you at least put me in the right category? Shit!"

"I said I'm sorry! Give me a break. I had a bad day. Then I saw that picture and it just sent me over the edge."

Concern filled his eyes. "What happened today? You all right?"

"Shemar's mom came to see me. She and Shemar are fine. Her man is still in jail, but she wanted me to give you her number so y'all can *hook up*. When I refused, she basically cursed me out. Then my evil mother called to throw my past into my face like she always does. I haven't been sleeping. And—"

"Wait, why you ain't been sleeping?"

"Chronic insomnia. Been dealing with it for a while now."

"But you always sleep when you spend the night with me."

"That's the only time I sleep, but you weren't here."

He stared at me, then kissed me, then pulled me onto his lap so that I was straddling him and my *little-ass* dress was up over my hips. "Come with me next time."

"Leland—"

He leaned in and kissed my neck. "Don't argue with me, just say yes, baby."

As he gripped my ass with both of his big hands, I muttered, "Okay. Yes."

"I missed you."

"I missed you, too."

"Hey, why you ain't never danced for me like you did for that dude downstairs?"

"I wasn't dancing *for* him, I was dancing *with* him, Leland."

"Same thing. And that damn dress…"

"You really hate this dress, huh?"

"Naw, I love it."

"Good, I pulled it from the back of my ho' closet just for this occasion."

"Ho' closet, huh?"

"Yeah. Not that I'm a ho'; I just like to dress like one sometimes. I firmly believe that every woman should have a ho' closet."

"Well, you gon' have to rename yours the Leland closet, because you can only wear stuff like this for me now."

"Is that right?"

"It's *damn* right."

"Hmm…are you jealous of that guy, the one I was dancing with?"

"Hell, yeah!"

"Because I danced with him?"

"Yeah."

"You want me to dance for you?"

He licked his lips and nodded. "Yeah."

I grinned at him and lifted from his lap. As Migos' *Stir Fry* blasted through the club, I bent over and shook my ass in his face, felt him smack my left butt cheek, then turned around and rolled my hips for him while mouthing what I knew of the lyrics. I moved to turn my back to him again and back it up on him, but he grabbed me and pulled me into his lap, tilted his head to the side, and with heavy eyelids, said, "Come here," before kissing me so passionately I almost fell off his lap.

When we broke apart, we were both out of breath.

Gripping my butt, he said, "Raise up a little."

I did and watched with rapt attention as he unbuckled his belt and unfastened his pants, felt my yoni begin to deliquesce from the mere idea of doing it with him in semi-public, and after he lifted up to pull his pants down, I slid my own panties to the side and sank down on his erection. He pulled the top of my off-the-shoulder dress down and glanced up at me when he found that I was wearing no bra. The look in his eyes was a combination of anger and desire as he lowered his head, taking my nipple into his mouth.

I gripped his shoulders, threw my head back, and moaned loudly as I slid up and down his shaft, and Leland murmured against my breast, "Shit, I think I love you."

# 16

# Leland

"What-up-there-now, Nephew?!"

"What up, Unc?"

Sitting up on the side of the bed, I watched Kim as she ducked into the bathroom. I'd finally moved into my place in her building, two floors above her condo, which I'd still never set foot in, because even though her son hadn't been in town since July, nearly two months ago, she was afraid he might show up and catch me there. What was really crazy was that he didn't even have a key to the place, so it really wasn't like he could just pop in there on us. Nevertheless, us spending time together there was out of the question. I couldn't lie; the whole secrecy thing was getting old and irritating the shit out of me. I was a grown-ass man who'd only ever messed with grown-ass, Mary J Blige, *Just Fine* and Jill Scott, *Golden* women. The types of women who did what they wanted with whom they wanted when they wanted, and that was probably what attracted me to them—their freedom. But Kim? Shit, being with her felt like I was a grown man sneaking around with a chick who was still in high school and had a fucking curfew.

Free, she was not.

I really cared about her and wanted to share what we had with the world, but to keep from losing her, I just went along with this crazy shit for the time being. Because I definitely didn't want to lose her even with the hassle of hiding it from her son. Her son, not her husband. This shit was ridiculous. I mean, we could do nothing outside the four walls of my place.

"Yeah…give me three of those. Uh, I want four of those. Two of those…and fuck it, give me one of those, too."

"You talking to me, Unc?"

"Naw, talking to the lady at this gas station—hold on. How much I got left?"

I frowned. What the hell was Uncle Lee doing? Then I heard a muffled voice say, "You got twenty dollars left, sir."

"A'ight, give me four of them Set for Lifes. Thank you." A pause, then I heard a scratching sound.

"Unc!"

"Shit, I forgot you was on here, Nephew."

"The fuck you doing, Unc?"

"I messed around and won five hundred dollars playing tunk last night so I'm getting me some scratch-offs."

As Kim walked her fine ass back in the room and dug in one of my dresser drawers, I licked my lips, and said, "That's what you do with the money I send you, huh?"

"Shit, gotta do something." I guess he was referring to the fact that he had retired from his factory job a few years earlier.

"I hear you. What's up, Unc?"

"You know Ever's birthday's coming up. Barbie planning a big party, and she got me calling to invite everybody. You the first person I called since you Ever's baby."

"Yeah, I knew it was coming up in a couple of weeks. Already got my eye on her gift. You know I'll be there, Unc. Probably stay at Ev's crib."

"Okay. Barbie say she gonna text you the details after she puts everything together."

"A'ight. I'ma call her, too, see if she needs any money or anything."

"Aw, shit! My ass done won a hundred dollars! Hey, let me get five of them Big Moneys and some Newport 100s—soft pack. I don't fuck around with them boxes."

Shaking my head, I said, "Unc, I'ma let you go." I swear it was hard to clown Neil about his gambling when Uncle Lee's ass was worse than him. He just wasn't an alcoholic. At least not really.

"All right, Nephew!"

I ended the call and looked up to see my woman in one of my Miami Heat t-shirts, leaning against my dresser, smiling at me. So I stood from the bed, walked over to her, and kissed her. "What you smiling at?" I asked.

She wrapped her arms around me. "The finest man in St. Louis."

"Just St. Louis?"

"Okay. Missouri."

"Damn, not the world?"

"Unh-uh...the universe."

I picked her up and she giggled as she wrapped her legs around my waist. "Damn straight. They don't get no finer than me, plus I got a big dick and a long tongue and I'm rich. Shit, I'm winning, baby."

She shook her head. "You are so damn crazy."

"But am I lying, though?"

"Naw, you ain't lying. You're winning, and I'm winning 'cause you're mine."

I nodded. "I'm yours all damn day, baby."

"What was your uncle talking about? You shoulda put him on speaker so I could hear. He cracks me up."

"I wasn't finna have you sniggling and shit at my uncle again."

She laughed. "You use the oldest words sometimes. Sniggling?"

"Old folks raised me. Anyway, he was talking about my aunt's birthday party."

"The one that raised you?"

I nodded. "It's gonna be back home, probably at her house in a couple of weeks."

"You going? Isn't preseason coming up?"

"Yeah, but Barbie—her daughter—knows to schedule it before then."

"So you're about to leave me, huh?"

"Come with me like you said you would the next time I leave

town."

"Leland, you know—"

"Here you go with *that* shit. Look, it's my *family*. They know not to take pictures or run their mouths. Everett will be there, and he don't play that. Never has. Plus, I doubt anyone will know who you are. They ain't really basketball people despite my being in the NBA. My family loves football. Come meet my folks, baby. I want you to meet everyone, especially my auntie."

"I want to, and I'm flattered that you want me to, but…"

I sighed, walked over to the bed, and set her down on it. Then I turned for the bathroom without saying another word.

I was peeing when I felt her hand on my back. "Leland?" Her voice was soft, almost timid.

I finished my business, shook, and flushed, then moved to the sink to wash my hands. "I'm not trying to argue with you, Kim. If you don't wanna go, you ain't gotta go."

She followed me back into the bedroom where I fell into bed and grabbed the remote from the nightstand. "I *do* wanna go. I really do," she said.

With my eyes on the TV, I said, "Then go."

"You know I can't."

I shrugged. "If you say so."

The next thing I knew, she was straddling me. She wasn't wearing panties and her scent wafted into my nose, so of course I got hard as a damn rock, but I still picked her up and sat her beside me, then resumed my channel surfing.

"Are you mad?" she asked.

"Mad? Naw. Fed the fuck up? Yeah, most definitely."

"What do you want me to do?"

I looked at her with raised eyebrows. "I'm not about to go in circles with you, Kim. You know what the hell I want. I want you to come to Houston with me. Shit!"

"I—"

"Can't. You already said that. I heard you. And it's whatever."

I could hear her sigh. "Okay, but I thought you understood my position."

I turned to look at her. "What I understand is that most women *want* to meet my family, beg me to let them meet them, but you?" I shook my head. "Fuck it."

"I *do* want to meet them, Leland. I-are you gonna break up with me over this?"

I eyed her. "Is that what you want?"

"No, but I can tell this whole thing is getting to you and...you deserve a woman who doesn't have all this baggage and stuff that she carries with her."

"Man, Kim...just leave it alone. You say you can't come, cool. I'll go alone, come back here, and we'll keep having sex in secret and eating and watching TV and shit like a couple of teenagers. You were so worried about my age, but I'm grown enough not to let other people run my damn life."

"My son doesn't run my life."

"Yeah, okay."

"He doesn't! It's just that I owe him a lot, and—"

"What? The condo? Your car? You think I can't replace that shit for you? Hell, you could move in here with me and I'll buy you three cars."

"It's not just that he takes care of me. I mean, I put him through a lot with my past relationships, and I don't like upsetting him if I can help it."

I turned from her face back to the TV. "It's cool, Kim. I mean, it's whatever. Do what you gotta do, and I'ma do the same."

"W-what does that mean?"

"Whatever you think it means."

She sat there beside me for a couple of minutes before I felt her lift from the bed. Then she moved around the room, getting dressed.

"I'm gonna just go. I can see I've upset you and you're talking crazy now," she said.

I fixed my eyes on her. "I'm the one talking crazy? Okay."

Her face folded for a second before she fixed it and grabbed her purse from the floor next to her side of the bed.

*Her side of the bed.*

Shit.

This was all fucked up. I should've never messed with her, shouldn't have agreed to this secrecy stuff. But now my heart was in this. Yeah, this was a totally fucked-up situation.

I didn't move a muscle as she left. I was tired as hell and had a damn headache. So I closed my eyes, tried not to think about how much I already missed her, and soon fell asleep.

*****

"Leland, wake up."

My eyes popped open to darkness and quiet. My first thought was that I was dreaming about her. But then she called my name again, so I reached for the bedside lamp and turned it on. She was there, eyes wide with apprehension.

"Damn, I must've slept all day, missed both my workouts. What time is it?" I asked.

"It's after nine. I've been calling you," Kim said, a deep frown on her face.

I groped for my phone on the night table, checked it, and said, "It's dead. What's up?" through a yawn.

"I…can you come with me?"

"Why?"

"Just come with me. Please."

My head was in a fog, I was still half-asleep, and my bladder was about to bust, but I'd follow her anywhere, even though I was frustrated as hell with her. So I climbed out of bed, took her outstretched hand, and followed her through my barely-furnished condo—all I had was a couch and a bedroom set. I'd gotten rid of the stuff I had in my place in Miami, because I was tired of it. Hadn't gotten around to buying much for this new place.

When she got to my front door, she stopped, and said, "Put these on."

How I didn't notice her holding a pair of my shoes is a mystery to me. As I put them on, I asked, "We're leaving? Where we going?"

"You'll see."

"I need to lock up?"

"I have my key. I'll do it," she said.

A few seconds later, we were on the elevator. When she pressed the two, I realized what was going on. "Kim, are we—"

She pressed a finger to my lips. "Just let me do this."

I stared at her for a second, saw her eyes pleading with mine, and I nodded.

When we got to her door, she dug in the pocket of her jeans and handed me a key. "This is yours."

"For your door?" I asked, shocked as hell. She had never even let me step foot in the place and she was giving me a key? For real?

She shrugged. "Try it and see."

I stuck it in the door, turned it, and something swelled inside of me. Dropping my hand, I shook my head and looked at her, this woman who had my heart twisted all the way up. "I ain't never been in love before, but I love you, you know that? I'm not playing. This is not a game. I love the hell out of your ass right now."

She smiled at me. "But wait, there's more. Come inside."

I took her hand again, following her inside her condo. It had the same floor plan as mine, but on a smaller scale. Everything was closer together, and her place was full of furniture, nice furniture but not too nice. The place looked like a home, not a showcase, and it smelled good, too, like flowers or some shit like that. There were those throw blankets folded over the backs of the loveseat, sofa, and recliner in the living room. There was a huge TV, a stereo, the walls were covered in black art, and the tables held family photos, most of which were of her son. Her place was nice, lived in, cozy.

I turned my attention to the other end of the room where there was a dining room table with two place settings, candles, and covered dishes of food.

"What's this?" I asked, as she stepped over to the front door, closing and locking it.

Crossing in front of me and sweeping her arm toward the table, she said, "I realized I've never cooked for you. You probably think I can't cook, but I can throw down in the kitchen, so come eat."

I gave her a grin as I headed to the table. "Baby, I don't know what to say."

"Oh!" she said, as she settled in the seat across from mine. "And I'm going to Houston with you. Let's just...can we still be discreet?"

As she uncovered dishes of chicken spaghetti, salad, and yeast rolls, I nodded. "Yeah, but are you sure about all this? Me being here, having a key, you going to Houston?"

She gave me a tiny smile. "I'm sure I don't wanna lose you, and I'll do whatever it takes to make sure that doesn't happen."

"I wasn't gonna break up with you. This shit was just...you don't have to do any of this if you're not ready. I didn't mean to push."

"I wanna do it for the man who says he loves me."

"It's not just words, Kim. I mean it."

"Then I'll go, and you can keep the key, and tonight, we'll sleep here."

All I could do was smile, and say, "This looks good, and I'm hungry."

"Then let me fix my man a plate."

# 17

## Kimberly

"What you doing?" was how he responded to my hello.

"Um, working? I'm at work, Leland. What else would I be doing?"

"Thinking about me."

"Are you thinking about me?"

"Always. Hey, I want you to check something out."

I was grinning hard as I said, "Okay…"

"Go to YouTube and check out the interview I did with Hot Ones. They finally posted it."

I knew he'd done quite a few interviews recently, most of which I'd already watched, but I didn't recall him mentioning this one. I loved those Hot Ones interviews. "Is there any special reason I need to watch it?" I asked.

"Yeah, because I want you to. 'Bout to head in this gym and get my ass kicked. Talk to you later."

"All right. Bye."

I wasn't lying when I said I was working, but Leland was a distraction, and even after we ended the call, I found myself thinking of him, about how he'd ravished me a week earlier after I gave him that key to my place. I can't lie; that hadn't been an easy decision for me, but I realized I was asking too much of him by expecting him to never want to see the inside of my home, and Armand barely ever visited me anyway. Hell, he was off living his life, which was one of the reasons I left Miami—I was always alone and when I tried to socialize, he blocked it acting a fool with every man who even looked in my direction. So, knowing that although my son liked to try to exercise some control over my life, he wasn't really present in it, never made any surprise visits, and didn't have a key to my place, giving that key to Leland and sharing my home with him was a no-brainer and made more sense than the status quo despite my apprehension. As far as the trip to Houston, I had enough sense to know that when a man wants you to meet his family, especially a man you care about, you need to make that happen. And hell, my *son* was in the NBA, not *me*. We didn't even share the same last name. Most people had no idea who I was unless I told them even with me being on that documentary-style sports show with him after he was drafted, so things would be fine. Well, I *hoped* things would be fine, tried to convince myself they would, because I still wasn't ready for the mess that would come with Armand finding out about us. But the fear of my son finding out about us wasn't enough to change the fact that I was crazy about Leland. Who wouldn't be? Yet, his attachment to me was a mystery. Not in a low self-esteem way, but in a "I've got to be a lot to deal with" way. Nevertheless, he said he loved me and I wanted to believe him.

Since I couldn't get him off my mind, I abandoned my unfinished work and navigated to the YouTube app on my phone, feeling excited about seeing him on the tiny screen as if I hadn't shared a bed with him the night before. The premise of Hot Ones was celebrities being interviewed while eating from a platter of progressively spicy chicken wings. The interviews were usually hilarious as the celebrities struggled to answer questions while trying to maintain their composure with a burning mouth. Leland wasn't that big on spicy food, so I was interested to see how he'd do.

My eyes were glued to Leland in his jeans and plain white, v-neck tee with his favorite gold rope adorning his neck. I could see the tattoos on his bulging biceps, and my heart stuttered at the sight of the big smile he wore.

Beautiful, this man was just absolutely beautiful.

At first, I barely noticed the host or his questions but made myself climb out of the lust pit and really concentrate on everything. The questions were mostly benign, a lot of sports-related stuff that I didn't totally understand, because although my child had always been a talented basketball player and I understood the sport, I never really watched games unless Boogie was playing, and I knew little to nothing of the business side of things. So all the talk about buyouts and player stats flew completely over my head.

They talked about Big South and music in general; then the host said, "Name your favorite rapper of all time besides your brother."

By then, they were up to the third hottest wing, and Leland was sucking in air and puffing out his cheeks. I could also see his knee bouncing up and down and his hand gripping the edge of the table. He was trying to meet the challenge and not drink any milk, but those wings were kicking his ass.

"Uh—whew! Damn, uh…Little Kim," he said, then winked at the camera.

My mouth dropped open. Was he referring to—

"Lil' Kim?" the host repeated. "A female rapper, huh?"

Leland nodded, cleared his throat, blew out air, and said, "Yeah, man. I love me some Little Kim. I'm kind of obsessed with her. Be thinking about her all the time." He licked his lips, winked again, and coughed.

With my hand muffling my mouth, I said, "This man is crazy."

"So you're a big fan of hers?"

"Man, I Stan for her like a motherfucker."

My eyes were wide as I watched him continue the interview. He made it through all the wings then gulped the milk down, and screamed, "Shit! I made it!"

After I was done laughing at his silly butt, I texted him: *You are a whole fool, Leland McClain!*

DLS: *U watched it? Did Little Kim hear my shout out to her?*

Me: *I'm about tired of you and Little Kim sneaking around behind my back. I thought you loved me, not her.*

DLS: *Shiiiit, I love both of y'all. Can't wait to see y'all later. My place or urs?*

Me: *Yours because you seem to think I'm gonna cook when you're at my place and I ain't cooking tonight.*

DLS: *That's a damn shame. Don't even wanna cook for me with all this penis I been giving u.*

I rolled my eyes. He was so damn silly. Just as I was typing out my reply, there was a knock at the door, which meant Peaches' ass was predictably away from her desk.

*I really need to fire this chick.*

"Come in!" I yelled, looking up from my phone to see Zabrina opening the door and stepping into my office with a crazy look on her face.

I slammed my phone down on my desk and shook my head. "Oh, *hell* no. Turn your ass right back around."

"It's been two weeks! Come on, now. I have apologized a thousand times via text, left messages on your voicemail, Facebook messaged you, sent IG DMs. You gotta forgive me! It was an accident!"

I scoffed, "You accidentally told a secret you promised to keep? Really, Z?"

"It slipped out! Shelby was talking shit about you never having a man and I told her you keep a man and she said they must all be ugly or married since you're never seen with anyone and I said, shiiiid, Leland McClain ain't ugly. It just came out. My bad!"

I sighed. "I don't know why I told you in the first place."

"Because I'm your BFF, that's why!"

"I'm beginning to wonder why. Damn snitching ass..."

"It's *Shelby!* Hell, she's *known* for lying. Ain't nobody gonna believe her."

Well, that was true. Shelby was a huge liar, but that wasn't the point. "It doesn't matter. You weren't supposed to tell anyone even if you were using the information to ratchetly defend me. Now Shelby's ass is steady sending me links to stories about Leland even though I lied and told her he wasn't my man. Half the stuff she sends is just plain crazy, and the half that ain't crazy is out and out lies where he's supposed to have been somewhere with some woman at a time when I know for a fact he had my legs in the air in his bed or mine!"

"Daaaaamn, y'all getting it in like that?"

"Girl…"

"Shit!"

"It's so good, Z, that I almost wish you could experience it, too. Almost, but not really, because I don't mind kicking ass over him."

"I know that's right! He just look like he can give you some ass-kick-worthy sex!"

"You have no idea—wait, where was I? Oh! Anyway, I told the fool to stop sending stuff, but you know she's stupid. See what you started?"

"*I'm sorry*, but at least you know she won't tell Armand because of that time he cursed her out when he heard her talking shit about you, and even if she did tell him, I'm sure he wouldn't believe it."

"I know, but you hurt my feelings. You're my best friend and my cousin and I trusted you and you don't see me telling your man about you damn near screwing Polo Logan on top of a plate of buffalo wings."

"Wasn't nobody trying to screw him."

I gave her a smirk.

Rolling her eyes, she said, "Whatever."

"I don't want this to get out yet, Z. Is that so hard for you to understand?"

"Actually, yeah…because if that was my man, I'd pay for one of those four-second commercials on YouTube announcing it."

"Well, you don't have a crazy-ass son. And before you say it, I know this is not normal. I just need time."

"Time for what?"

"Just time!" I shouted, more frustrated with the entire situation than her betrayal.

"Shit, okay! Do you forgive me, though?"

"You know I forgive you. I actually missed your crazy ass."

She hopped up and scurried around my desk, wrapping her arms around my neck, hugging me tightly while rocking us back and forth. "I missed your crazy ass, too."

\*\*\*\*\*

My eyes searched the darkness in his bedroom as I lay on my back with his head on my stomach, his long arms encircling me. I lifted my hand and rubbed it across his hair which he'd had braided in cornrows.

"Why you ain't sleep?" His voice was husky and saturated with drowsiness.

"Why aren't *you* asleep?" I countered.

"You thinking about the trip to Houston this weekend?"

"No. You?"

"I'm excited about it. What is it? You wanna back out?"

"I just said I wasn't even thinking about it, Leland. I'm not gonna back out. I'll just deal with the consequences if Armand finds out about us."

He lifted his head. "What you mean consequences?"

"Why do you think you love me?"

"Why you curving my question?"

"Why're you curving mine?"

I felt him sigh against my skin. "I don't *think* shit, Kim. What? You think I'm too young to know I'm in love with you?"

"I didn't say that. I just wanna know what it is that you love about me."

"Hmm, your smile, your heart, your dedication to your son, even though it's making things hard for me. Your beauty...your booty."

"Leland! Be serious!"

"I am! I just love everything about you. Most of all, I love you for the job you have."

"My job?"

"Yeah...you're in a position where you don't have to work at all, but you choose to work that job, in that neighborhood. You have a heart for service just like I do. We got more in common than you think, baby."

"I guess we do."

"And it don't hurt that you got some good pussy and you're sexy as hell."

"Wow."

"Just telling the truth."

"Mm-hmm...well, thank you for loving me, Leland."

"Don't have a choice. Now, what did you mean by consequences?"

I hesitated, let my eyes search the darkness again, and said, "Nothing. I was just saying something."

"You scared of him? Of what he can take from you? I told you, I got you, baby."

"It's not that. It's—like I said before, I put him through a lot with past relationships and he worries about me. I don't like upsetting him. That's all."

"I wouldn't put my hands on you, Kim."

"I know that, but he doesn't. He just doesn't trust my judgement and I can't blame him. I don't trust it, either."

"But it's not really his business. You know that, right?"

"Yeah, I know that. I just..."

"It's all right. You need time and I'ma give it to you, but you need to know I ain't going nowhere and that this ain't temporary."

"This coming from a man who told me he didn't want a relationship..."

"I also told you I changed my mind. You got a problem with that?"

"No, I don't. Can't think of anyone else I'd ever want to be with."

"Me either, baby. Me either."

# 18

# Leland

I watched as her eyes surveyed the interior of the jet. She looked nervous, almost scared, as she sat across from me. I actually couldn't believe she didn't back out of going to Houston with me, was expecting her to change her mind up to the moment we boarded, but I was glad she didn't. I was also glad we were traveling in a private jet. I could only imagine how much more nervous she would've been had we taken a commercial flight together.

"Hey, did you know today was Make a Hat Day?" I asked, trying to pull her out of whatever thoughts had her eyebrows all tangled up.

Her eyes met mine as she shook her head. "Uh, no...I didn't."

I raised my eyebrows. "What? You ain't keeping up with your holidays no more?"

She shrugged and folded her hands in her lap. "I haven't thought about holidays much since you and me became a thing."

"For real? Why?"

"I used to have to find a way to appreciate every day. You give me that now."

Shit, I couldn't do nothing but stare at her, and I guess I freaked her out, because she asked, "Uh, did I say something wrong?"

I blinked a few times, placed my hand on my chest, and said, "Naw, baby. I just...I never had anyone to say nothing like that to me before."

"Well, I mean it. You do. I'm...I'm glad you're in my life even if you do like listening to fake jazz."

"Smooth jazz ain't fake jazz, you damn hater."

"If you listened to regular smooth jazz, but all you wanna listen to are jazz versions of R&B songs."

"Whatever. Your ass be humming when I play it, though, and Little Kim told me I have good taste in music."

"The way you and Harvey keep her satisfied, she'll probably say anything she thinks you wanna hear."

"Who the hell is Harvey?"

Her eyes scanned the small cabin, probably looking for the flight attendant. "Your penis."

"Why in the hell you give my penis that nerdy-ass name?"

"That's an insult to every man named Harvey! I think it's a nice name."

"Naw, that name is an insult to my dick."

"Then what would you name it?"

"I don't know, something that says big and black like Hakeem or Rashad or Malik. Not no damn Harvey. Harvey sounds like he's only an inch long and can't get hard. Shit, that name makes my dick sound like it has asthma or something."

"Leland!"

"What? It's the truth!"

"Okay, okay…I got a better one."

"It better say *long and strong* or I'm rejecting that motherfucker, too."

She smiled. "Tyrone Jones."

"Hell, yeah! That name says, 'Mandingo dick.'"

"Mr. McClain, we'll be landing soon," Marnie, the flight attendant, said.

I nodded. "Thanks."

As Marnie left, I looked over at Kim whose eyes were wide as she covered her mouth with her hand. Her "You are so stupid," was muffled.

"You like it."

"Yeah, I really do," she admitted.

Leaving my seat, I took the one next to her, and as she fastened her seatbelt, I leaned in and kissed her cheek. "You still okay with this trip?"

She nodded and gave me a smile. "As long as I'm with you, I'm more than okay, Mr. McClain."

# Kimberly

I was so nervous before I even got on the plane that I was nauseous, and that ramped up exponentially once we landed at a private airstrip and climbed into a limousine that took us to a small town on the outskirts of Houston—Leland's hometown. So much could go wrong on this trip. What if his family didn't like me? What if I didn't like them? What if…what if I went through all the trouble of meeting his family, maybe even getting to know them, and we didn't work out? It'd happened before. I put in a lot of time and energy with my last boyfriend and his kids only for him to end up beating my ass and choking me out. Or what if I went through all this and Armand found out and ran Leland away? Yeah, he said he could deal with Armand, but he didn't know him like I did. My only child was full of rage, prone to being violent, and could be very persuasive when he wanted to. I didn't want him to hurt Leland but knew he would in the name of protecting me and my honor. Leland didn't deserve that. Not at all.

"You don't like it?" he asked, pulling me back into the room with him. We were at his brother, Big South's, house, had just arrived two hours ahead of his aunt's noonday party. Evidently, my introspection had drowned out his voice.

"What?"

"I was asking if you're still okay with staying here? I mean, I could get us a room if you'd prefer that." His thick eyebrows were knitted together as he spoke.

"No, this is fine. It's a beautiful house."

He moved closer to me, sliding his hands up and down my bare arms. "Then what is it?"

"I'm just...I'm nervous, Leland."

He reclined his neck and smiled down at me. "About meeting my family? Don't be. They all crazy as hell, so you'll fit right in."

"I hope so—wait, are you calling me crazy?"

He nodded, and with raised brows, said, "Yeah."

"I'm not half as crazy as you, 'round here talking to vaginas and stuff."

"Vagina, singular. Yours is the only one that speaks to me, and anyway, stop worrying. Everything will be cool." Checking his phone, he added, "You hungry? Tired? Wanna take a nap?"

"No. I think I'm good."

"Okay, you want a tour of the house? A walk around the property? Some sex?"

"Wow, really? Are you serious?"

"When am I ever not serious about that?"

I faked a yawn. "You know what? I *am* sleepy after all."

Grinning down at me, he snaked his long arm around my waist and pulled me close to him. "Fake ass." He kissed my neck, sliding his mouth up to mine. "Come on, baby. Let's do it before there's a house full of people here."

Then he kissed me, letting his tongue caress mine. So when his mouth left mine, I said, "Mmmm, okay."


*****


"Leland, stop! You know I'm too old and stuff to dance now!"

I couldn't wipe the grin off my face as Leland grabbed his Aunt

Ever's hand and pulled her to her feet. The party was in full swing with Aunt Ever's front yard crowded with long tables and chairs and teeming with family members, the scent of barbecue permeating the air. I was sitting at a table with Big South—*Big-motherfucking-South*—and his wife and both their daughters, trying not to stare at them. I was crazy about Leland, no sense in denying that, but his brother? Damn, was he fine and just…magnetic. Geez, it was hard to take my eyes off him, and his wife? She was so beautiful in an odd way, and he was obviously crazy about her as had been reported on all the blogs. I knew they'd been through some scandals since they'd been together, but none of that seemed to have put a damper on the heat that obviously flowed between them.

"Hey, Tick! You see them pineapples I grilled for you? I know you was looking for them earlier," Uncle Lee Chester yelled from across the yard. I couldn't get over Big South's family nickname but managed not to laugh.

"Naw, where they at?" Big South asked, with a serious look on his face.

"Over here by the grill!" Uncle Lee shouted, as he took a swig from a can of beer and rubbed his round stomach.

"A'ight, I'ma come get Jo some."

"Aye!" Leland shouted from where he was dancing with his aunt to some old blues song. "Get Kim some, too!"

What was with this family and pineapples?

Seeing the confused look on my face, Jo said, "Girl, just eat them. I'll explain later."

Twenty minutes later, Leland was sitting at the table beside me, his arm draped across my shoulders as I inhaled another plate of ribs, because damn! Uncle Lee was a true grill master! I hadn't tasted anything that good in a long time, probably because I'd been on a diet of chicken and vegetables forever, trying to get back to a size ten when a size sixteen wouldn't let my wide ass go. One thing about Leland, though, if I didn't think I looked good before him, I thought I was super-fine with him from the way he attacked me every chance he got. He made sure I knew I was desirable to him, and I couldn't lie and say that didn't make me feel good.

"Have you met the twins, Kim?" Jo asked me. "Wait, we brought Neil with us, so you met him when we first got here, right?"

I looked up from my plate and nodded. "Yeah, but I haven't seen him since then."

"He's probably somewhere pouting," Big South said, and I had no idea what that meant.

Jo elbowed him, and he shrugged. "Have you met Nolan? I haven't seen him yet," she said.

I wiped my hands and mouth with a napkin and gave her a smile I hoped wasn't riddled with food. "Yes, Leland introduced me to him and Svetlana."

Jo's mouth dropped open. "His new girlfriend's name is actually Svetlana?" she asked, her eyes shifting from me to Leland.

He shrugged. "Hell if I know."

I frowned as I turned my attention to him. "Why'd you tell me that was her name, then?"

"Because he's a fool," Big South interjected.

"Whatever, nigga. Don't be bad-talking me to my woman," Leland countered.

"Ain't nobody bad-talking your ass."

"It's an inside joke, Kim. Neil has a problem with Nolan's dating practices and likes messing with him by calling all of his girlfriends the same name—Svetlana," Leland explained.

"Shit, it fits all of 'em," Big South muttered.

"Y'all need to leave Nolan alone," Jo said.

"Naw, Nole need to leave them Nordic chicks alone," Leland said. "Don't make no sense."

I lifted a brow and nudged him. "Maybe that's his preference. Like you told me, everyone has preferences."

Leland looked from me to Big South and they both shook their heads, saying, "Naw, that ain't it," in unison. "Speak of the devil," Big South added under his breath.

Nolan was approaching the table. I knew it was him and not Neil because of what he was wearing—khakis and a white Oxford shirt, the same thing he was wearing when I met him earlier. His twin, by contrast, wasn't nearly as neat in baggy black jeans and a retro *Higher Learning* t-shirt. Neil and Nolan were identical, but easily distinguishable by their styles and demeanors. Just that quickly, I could tell Nolan was the more confident of the two.

"Hey, everybody," Nolan greeted, as he grabbed a chair from a neighboring table and placed it next to Leland, plopping down in it.

After we all greeted him, Big South asked, "Where's Svetlana?"

"Damn, really? You too, Ev?" Nolan replied.

"My bad, man. What's her name?"

"Danya."

"Danya? That's the same chick from the benefit last year? She don't look the same," Leland said.

"No, it's a different woman with the same name," Nolan clarified.

"You found two Yugoslavian motherfuckers named Danya?" Big South asked, confusion in his voice and on his face. His wife just shook her head while she bounced her little girl in her lap.

"She's not Yugo—you know what? Never mind. Hey, Jo…did Bridgette come with you guys?" Nolan asked.

Jo looked at him with wide eyes, then looked at Big South and back at Nolan again. "Bridgette? No, she's working on a film right now and couldn't make it."

"Oh, right. She's an actress, isn't she?" Nolan asked, seeming genuinely interested in this Bridgette person's career. "I've got to remember that. Well, I guess I better go check on Danya. She's taking a nap." He hopped up from the chair and left.

At that moment, as Leland and Big South exchanged a look, Uncle Lee Chester appeared at the table. "What-up-there-now, young folks?!" he shouted, and I almost choked on the coleslaw I'd just stuffed into my mouth. The man was hilarious, and I really don't think he was trying to be funny, but with him standing there in a straw hat, a faded Amerson Family Reunion t-shirt, denim shorts that were so tight they damn near gave him a testicular camel toe, white tube socks and black Florsheims combined with that signature greeting of his, it was hard to keep a straight face in his presence.

"It's all you, Unc. You clowned on that grill today!" Leland said.

"Yeah, Unc! Them ribs was on fire!" Big South agreed.

"They sure were!" That was Jo.

"The best I've had in a long time," I added.

"Thank you! Thank you!" He fell into the folding chair next to mine, snatched the towel from around his neck, wiped his sweaty face, sucked his teeth, stuck a toothpick in his mouth, and smiled. "Leland! Where you find Kimmy here at?" His voice was so loud next to me that I actually jumped.

Kimmy?

"She's the director of a community center I volunteered at," Leland replied.

"Oh, yeah? She a pretty one. Chocolate like my Lou. I ain't know you liked 'em like I like 'em, Nephew! Ha-ha-haaaaaaa!"

Leland reached across me and slapped hands with his uncle. "Shiiiid, ain't nothing like some chocolate, Unc!"

"I-know-that's-right!" Uncle Lee Chester shouted, releasing a long wheezing laugh, then tilted his head to the side. "Oh, hell. Got a call. Probably Lou's crazy ass." After pressing the button on his earpiece, he said, "What-up-there-now?!"

I turned and eyed Leland, who shrugged. Across the table, I could see Big South whispering something in Jo's ear while she tried unsuccessfully to stifle a giggle.

"Got damn, woman! Shit! I just got off the grill! I ain't leaving yet!"

My eyes widened. If that was his wife, they must've had a crazy relationship, because judging from the reactions of everyone at the table, this wasn't unusual.

"Lou, look now...I'ma be home after we through celebrating! You coulda brought your ass over here instead of sitting up in that house watching got-damn *Murder, She Wrote!* Hell!" he shouted, then tapped the button on his Bluetooth earpiece, returning his attention to me. The toothpick bounced up and down as he asked, "My nephew treating you right? You know he spoiled as hell. That's Ever and Tick's fault. They always gave him everything he wanted."

I laughed. "He *is* spoiled, but he's good to me."

"Oh, shit! We gotta dance to this one, baby," Leland said, hopping up and reaching for my hand. "We'll be back, y'all."

"All right, Nephew! Who the DJ? I wanna hear some Rufus Thomas. I'm tryna walk the dog! Ha-haaaa!!!!" Uncle Lee Chester called after us as I followed Leland a few feet from the table to where some of his other relatives were already swaying to a song I had never heard before but knew was old because all of the music that had been pouring from those high-quality speakers had been old.

As he pulled me into his arms, I said, "What you know about this song?"

"A lot. The Whispers were my mom's favorite group. She used to play this nasty-ass song, *In the Mood*, all the time."

I laughed as I rested my head on his chest and closed my eyes. This man…he was just *everything*, and being in his arms was like being home. It was like I'd always wanted and needed him in my life but had been so wrapped up in the misery of my past that I didn't know it. In that moment, as we moved in perfect rhythm with one another to the music, I fully realized that God created Leland McClain for me and me for him. It was the best feeling, a feeling of completeness I didn't know was possible. I hadn't known him long, but what I felt for him, what he gave to me, seemed to transcend time.

He released me enough to cup my face in his hands and lean down to gently kiss me before resuming the dance. I was so full of emotion by the time the song ended, I was near tears. But I managed to fight them off and was wearing a smile when we returned to the table.

"Damn, Leland…I thought you was gonna molest her out here in front of everyone for a minute," Big South quipped.

His adorable little stepdaughter lifted her sleepy head from his shoulder, and muttered, "Damn," softly.

I stifled a giggle, while Ella, Big South's older daughter, let hers rip. Jo rolled her eyes. Big South looked like he wanted to disappear, and Leland fell out laughing.

"Dang, she stay repeating you, man!" he said.

"Only when I curse, though. Man…" Big South shook his head.

"I told you to watch your mouth around her," Jo reminded him.

"I know. I know."

"She is too cute, though," I said. "Both of you all's girls are beautiful."

"Thanks," Jo and Big South said in unison.

"Yeah, them girls pretty as hell. So Kimmy, where you from?" Uncle Lee Chester queried.

"Lee! You harassing Leland's friend?" Aunt Ever said before I could answer. She was tall and wide, a sturdy but attractive woman I'd only met briefly almost two hours earlier as the yard began filling with Leland's family.

"I ain't doing shit but talking to the girl. You too damn sensitive about this boy!" Uncle Lee Chester responded.

"Oh, hush." The frown she wore for her brother eased into a smile as her eyes slid over to me. With an outstretched hand, she added, "Kim, honey. Come sit with me."

I swallowed and looked at Leland who gave me a little nod. "Go ahead. Ella here owes me a dance."

Ella, who'd been quiet most of the day, grinned at her uncle.

I smiled as Leland leaned in to kiss me, then he hopped up and rounded the table, grabbing Ella's hand and leading her to the designated dancefloor area.

Leland's aunt was basically like a mother to him, and from talking to him, I'd gathered they were close. So I expected an interrogation at some point, just not in the middle of her party. Nevertheless, I took her hand and let her lead me to a round resin table where she dropped into a large white matching chair with a grunt. On the table was a paper plate that held rib bones and barbecue sauce, a half-empty bottle of beer, and a pile of dirty napkins that stirred in the light wind.

"Barbie," Aunt Ever said to a younger version of herself who had been introduced to me as her daughter. "Can you give me and Kim here a few minutes alone?"

Barbie stood from her seat, chirped, "Yes, ma'am! I'ma go get some more cake," and bounced her voluptuous frame away. All the women on Leland's mother's side of the family were full-figured from his aunts to his cousins. No wonder he wanted my big ass.

"Have a seat, baby," Aunt Ever offered.

I was sure I looked as nervous as I felt as I took Barbie's vacated chair.

"I'm glad you and my Leland could make it. When Barbie told me she was planning this party, the first thing I told her was to make sure to plan it so that he could come. That boy…" She shook her head and sighed. "I love my kids and all my nieces and nephews, but Leland? He's got a special place in my heart."

I smiled. "I believe you have a special place in his, too."

She nodded. "We have a special bond." As she leaned back in her chair, I watched her eyes scan the area around us. "He was so broken right after my sister died, so sad. Such a sad child." Her eyes were back on me. "Tick—Everett wanted to take him and raise him, but he was young, had just married that foreign girl, so I stepped up, moved into their mother's house and raised him so he wouldn't have to move away from here. All my kids was grown, so it was just me and him and Kat—his sister. Kat was sixteen, really a grown woman. She handled their mother's death better than Leland did. That baby was an orphan at eleven, both parents gone. He loved his mother so much and Lord knows she loved him. Losing her, it broke something inside of him that it took a long time to get fixed. When I got him, he cried all the time, was so sad for so long. Everett paid for his counseling, took him with him on tour, put him in a lot of activities. Leland had seen the world by the time he was eighteen. I did my best to love him and raise him right, but I think Everett made him the man he is today. A good man."

I nodded. "He *is* good, very sweet to me. Spoiled, but sweet, kind. I don't think he'd ever do anything to intentionally hurt me."

"I know he wouldn't. I hope you wouldn't do anything to hurt him, either."

"No, ma'am. Never. I-uh-I care deeply for him. Never felt like this for any other man."

"He's young. Got to be younger than you, because I know that boy. All he wants is an older woman."

My heart skipped five beats. "Um…yes, ma'am. I had a problem with that at first, but although I'm older, Leland is much more mature than I am in a lot of ways. He lives with a sense of freedom I wish I possessed."

"Hmm, probably because life made him grow up real early, made him take control of things before he should've had to."

I nodded in agreement.

"Your son…he doesn't like my Leland, does he?"

*She knows about Armand?*

*Of course she does. Leland had to have told her.* "My son doesn't like a lot of people. But I think he'll like Leland if he gets to know him."

"I'm sure he will. Well, I like you, and I can tell Leland is crazy about you. Never seen him like this with a woman before. But, can you do me a favor, sugar?"

"Yes, ma'am. Anything."

"I don't want him hurt. He's already lived through enough pain to last him two lifetimes."

"I just want to be with him and try to return the happiness he's given me since I've known him."

She nodded and we kind of just sat there in a mutual, peaceful silence.

"He still having those headaches?" she asked.

I frowned. "Heada—"

Loud voices, what sounded like an argument, interrupted me. I turned to see Leland and his brothers—all of them—running…somewhere. Aunt Ever got to her feet and was rushing in the same direction as literally everyone else. So of course, being that I'm black, I followed the crowd.

When I met Kat, Leland's big sister, shortly after we arrived, all I could think was that she had to be the tallest, prettiest woman I'd ever laid eyes on. She closely resembled Leland, who was gorgeous by any standards. And her style was impeccable, makeup was flawless. But now, with a crowd of family members surrounding her, she looked disheveled. She'd been fighting, and from the looks of her husband, *her very handsome husband*, the battle had been a fierce one.

Big South had ahold of her arm, attempting to pull her toward his house, but she was trying to get to her husband, obviously to do more damage.

Leland was holding him back as he heaved breaths and shook his head. "She's crazy! She's fucking crazy!" her husband—I think Leland called him Wayne—shouted.

"I'm crazy?! *I'm* crazy because I'm tired of you screwing anything with half a pussy?!"

There was a collective gasp, and I think she must've really shocked Big South, because he let her go. With lightning speed, she was on her husband again, pummeling him mercilessly. Leland tried to pull her husband out of her reach. Nolan pulled on Kat until Big South finally lifted her off her feet. She writhed and kicked at her husband, while yelling, "That motherfucker gave me a VD! I'ma kill him! I'ma kill him!"

Big South carried her to his house. Jo was on his heels with her little girl, who somehow managed not to wake up from her long nap, on her hip. Ella was right behind them.

I turned back to Kat's husband in time to see Leland let him go, mumble, "Man…" and then punch the hell out of his brother-in-law, knocking him out cold.

\*\*\*\*\*

"You a'ight in there? You been in there a minute," Leland asked through the bathroom door.

I was so glad we had our own bathroom in his brother's house, because I had been in and out of it nearly every hour on the hour since the party ended. Had to decline drinks in the living room with Big South just so I could stay close to the toilet, and that broke my heart because Lord knows I loved me some Big South! I was a fan, a huge one, and had been trying unsuccessfully not to appear star-struck since he arrived.

"I'm fine, just…like I told you, I haven't had this much pork in a while, years. Those ribs tore my stomach up."

"I know they did since you ate a whole damn slab by yourself."

I rolled my eyes. "No, I didn't!" I lied, because I probably did eat a whole slab. Shit, I lost count of how many ribs I ate.

"And you ate about three of them grilled pig feet. You country as hell."

"No, your uncle is some kind of grill sorcerer. I've never liked pig feet, period, but those grilled ones were…oooh, my stomach! They were fire!"

"Yeah, they were. Uh, you sure you don't need anything? Some milk of magnesia, Pepto Bismol, ice water, Glade, a whole pack of incense, a box of matches, a new ass?"

"Fuck you, Leland."

"Hell, I had plans of fucking *you*, but now? I don't think so…"

"Whatever. I bet if I come out there and strip, you won't turn me down."

"You damn right. Hey…"

"What, baby? I'm tryna get finished and you bugging me is not helping the process."

"I'ma leave you alone, but uh…you ain't tryna shit your way out of brunch in the morning, are you?"

I rolled my eyes again. "No, Leland. I ate too much. That's all this is. I am not trying to get out of going to this business brunch with you. You said it's at the guy's house, right? And it's not like we'll be taking selfies for Instagram. I'm fine with going."

"A'ight. I'ma go back to bed. I'm tired as fuck."

"Okay. Hey, are you okay after all that with your sister and her husband?"

"Kat's okay, so I'm okay."

His sister was spending the night at his brother's house, too. I had no idea where her husband and his black eye had gone, just knew that he'd left after he regained consciousness. "Good. You think he'll sue you for hitting him or press charges or anything?"

"Naw, not unless he wants me to collect on the money I loaned his ass to start that car detailing business of his."

"Oh, okay. So you didn't know they were having problems?"

"No one did. I mean, I knew they weren't all that happy, but I didn't know dude was cheating on her. They been together since high school. This is just all messed up."

"Yeah, it is. Hey, go on to bed. I'll be out as soon as I can."

"A'ight."

About ten minutes later, I was climbing back in bed with him. It was after midnight, I was exhausted, and I hoped and prayed my disgruntled stomach was now empty.

Leland flipped over, throwing an arm over my waist and pulling me to him. He snuggled close, kissed my neck, and murmured, "I hope you're done."

"You can't want that any more than I do."

"Hmm, I'm glad you came with me. It's been a good day despite that stuff with Kat."

I smiled in the darkness, turning to face him and press my lips against his full ones. "It has, and I'm glad I came, too. Your family is so nice. Everyone made me feel really welcome."

"Especially Everett, huh?"

It was so strange hearing him refer to his brother by his government name that for a second, I had to wonder who he was talking about. Finally, I replied with, "Yeah, it was great meeting him. He's super cool."

"You got a crush on him, don't you?"

"A crush? How could I possibly have a crush on him when I got a rich man with a big dick and a long tongue sharing my bed every night?" So, yeah, I actually did have a crush on him, an innocent one, but I wasn't going to tell my man, who happened to be his brother, that.

"Damn straight. Do you know how lucky you are?"

I smacked my hand against his hard chest. "You are such an arrogant asshole."

"But you love it."

"Actually, I love your uncle. He is too funny."

"He loves you, too, *Kimmy*. Gon' fuck around and get his old ass kicked."

"You need to quit! He was just being friendly."

"Naw, I saw that look in his eye. He was probably ready to break out his Viagra for you."

I laughed so hard at that, my stomach cramped up.

"That shit ain't funny. Hey, what was you and Jo talking about when I walked up on y'all after all that stuff went down with Kat and Wayne?"

"Me and Jo? Oh! She told me why you've been feeding me pineapples."

"For real? Good, then I expect you to add them to your grocery list permanently. Ev said it's important for you to keep your levels up."

"Levels? Pineapple levels?"

"Yeah."

Before I could reply again, my phone buzzed, damn near making me jump straight to my feet. Who the hell was calling me so late? No one ever called me at that hour—oh, shit...was it Armand?

Panic shot through me as I swiftly untangled myself from his legs and arms, flipped over, and grabbed my phone. Seeing that it was Elrich and not Armand sent me into a different type of panic. Had something happened to or at the center?

"It's work," I said, as I accepted the call. "Hello? Elrich? Is everything okay?"

"Uh, no. There was a break-in at the center. Someone broke one of the front windows, but the alarm went off. They didn't get much before they ran off. The broken window was the only physical damage to the building, and I managed to board it up."

"They didn't get much? Well, what *did* they get?"

"Just the laptop at the front desk. They didn't mess with the desktop up there. So they were probably on foot and just took what they could carry. I got the call from the alarm company since you're out of town this weekend, and I met the police up there, filed the report and everything. I hate to disturb you but wanted to keep you in the loop."

My hand was on my chest as relief flooded me. At least they didn't tear the place up or steal more than that one computer. "It's fine. I'm glad you called. I'd hate to walk into that mess unaware on Monday morning. Thank you."

"No problem. So…are you enjoying your trip to…where was it?"

I hadn't told him or anyone else, including Zabrina since she could no longer be trusted to hold water, where I was spending the weekend, so he was fishing, which was odd for him. Yeah, we used to have sex with each other, but he never seemed interested in my life all that much. I'd always liked that about him, because I preferred to talk about myself and my life as little as possible.

"Uh, yeah. It's been great. Elrich, I should probably—"

"I miss you."

Huh? "What?"

"I miss you, Kim. Things with my ex are just not what I thought they'd be, and I realized everything I wanted, the kind of relationship I've been trying to build with her, I already had with you."

Relationship? We never had a relationship. We were literally just fucking, so what in the entire world was going on here? "Um, what are you trying to say?" I knew what he was trying to say but hoped the question would make him change his mind about saying it. However, what my question, or maybe the crazy way I was sounding, actually did was make Leland not only sit up, but turn on the bedside lamp, climb out of bed, and walk around it to stand his entirely too fine ass in boxers right in front of me. He was frowning as he peered down at me.

"I'm saying, I want us to start seeing each other again, but this time, I want it to be more than sexual."

My eyes climbed my man, then fell to the floor. If I had been about twenty shades lighter, I would've been beet red at this point as I tried to find words of response that wouldn't tip Leland's crazy jealous ass off to the reality of this conversation.

"Um, that's not possible right now, Elrich."

"Oh, really? Why?"

I looked up at Leland, who raised his thick eyebrows, and then I dropped my damn eyes again. Then I held the phone, because...shit!

"There's someone else?" he deduced.

Thank God he said it! "Yes."

"Oh."

"Yeah...Elrich, I gotta go."

"Okay. Um, bye."

"Bye."

I ended the call, and without looking Leland in the face, said, "Um, that was Elrich, the center's social worker. He was just letting me know there was a break-in at King's Dream, but he handled it for me."

I looked up in time to see him nod. "Good," he said, before walking back around to his side of the bed, flicking the lamp back off, and climbing in beside me. After we had both settled back in each other's arms, he said, "The social worker is a dude? You never told me that."

"I'm sure I did. But anyway, yeah...it's a man. Elrich O'Neal. He was there before I came on."

"He sounded old."

My heart leaped in my chest. "You could hear him?"

"I could hear his voice. Couldn't make out what he was saying, though."

"Oh...yeah, he's an older guy."

"You fucking him?"

"What?! Why you ask that?"

He released me and reached over to turn the lamp back on. Looking me directly in the eye, he asked, "Shit, you *are* fucking him, aren't you?"

"No!"

"You *used* to fuck him?"

"Uh—" My phone started buzzing again, and I wasn't sure whether to be relieved it had interrupted this conversation or to feel anxious about it possibly being Elrich again. Or Armand.

It was Elrich.

Shit.

To be clear, that would've been my reaction if it was Armand, too.

I reached for the phone, but was too slow, because in the midst of my almost-panic, Leland's quick, long-tall-ass had rounded the bed and snatched the phone up from the night table.

His eyes narrowed as he looked at the screen. Then he accepted the call, put the phone on speaker, and as I stopped breathing, answered it with, "Aye, Elroy?"

"Hello?" came Elrich's uncertain voice. "I think I have the wrong number?"

"Naw. You tryna reach Kim Hampton, right?"

"Y-yes?"

"This her man. Look, homie…I'm finna be knee-deep in her pussy in a minute so I'ma need you to stop calling, a'ight?"

"Uh…"

He ended the call and handed me the phone. All I could do was stare down at it and hope that Elrich didn't call back, because Leland had just proven he was a complete-damn-fool. Then I decided to stop hoping and just turned the phone off.

The room went black again as Leland turned the lamp off and climbed back in beside me.

I turned around, eyed his silhouette, and said, "I can't believe you just did that."

"Believe it. That nigga was scouting pussy. That's the only reason he called this late. Shit, if he handled everything with the break-in, there was no reason for him to call at all."

"Leland—"

"And don't bother lying about the fact that you been fucking him, because I *know* you have. He's old, and his ass is too familiar, calling like that."

"So I just go around screwing any old man? That's what you think of me, Leland?"

"No, but you screwing that one."

"*Screwed.* Past tense, and it was over before me and you got started."

"Yeah, I figured that."

"So why'd you act like you thought I was still seeing him?"

"I was testing you."

"Testing me? Negro, what?!"

"I—"

"You know what? I should go. I mean, you obviously don't trust me, and you just embarrassed the hell outta me by answering my phone and saying what you said, and—"

He pulled me to him, holding me tightly. "I'm sorry. Shit, I'm kinda crazy when it comes to you, baby. Dude had to know he wasn't getting in no more."

"I had already told him that."

"And he still called back."

That, he did. I blew out a frustrated breath. "Leland—"

"Look, I wasn't really testing you. Shit, I don't really know what the fuck I was doing. I just…I love you, Kim."

"I know you do, but you have no need to be jealous. No man can hold a candle to you in any category, Leland. Ever."

"Shit, I know."

"Conceited ass."

"Again, you love it."

"You know what? I do."

"I know you do."

"How are the headaches?"

"Head—Damn, Aunt Ever told you?"

"Yeah. Why didn't *you* tell me?"

"Same reason you didn't tell me about your insomnia. I don't have them when I'm with you. They're supposed to be tension headaches. I guess you take my tension away."

"I don't see how."

"Me either. It's a miracle with how you be working my damn nerves."

"Shut up!"

He laughed and kissed my forehead.

Silence settled over us, and just as I could tell by his breathing pattern that he was drifting off to sleep, I said, "Um, aren't you supposed to be knee-deep in my pussy right now?"

"You down? I mean, can you handle it with your stomach problem?"

"I can always handle it, Leland."

"Well, shit, get up here and ride this thang then."

# 19

## Kimberly

I stood in the bathroom mirror and checked my makeup for the tenth time, jumped when I saw Leland appear behind me, then turned around and spread my arms wide, presenting myself to him. "You approve?"

With intensity in his eyes, he nodded. "I always approve, baby."

"Well, that's good to know. You ready?"

He nodded again. "Yup."

He was wearing black jogging pants, a white t-shirt, and black *South* sneakers. I was wearing a white sundress and gold strappy sandals. So I asked, "Is that what you're wearing?"

"Yeah. What time is it?"

"Uh, let me get my phone so I can see."

Following me from the bathroom into the bedroom, he said, "You need a watch."

"I know. Wait, you're not wearing yours?" Picking up my phone, I said, "It's nine-thirty," without waiting for his answer. When I turned around and looked up, he was smiling at me while handing me a small bag, like the kind of bag jewelry comes in. I was becoming very familiar with those bags.

My mouth dropped open. "Leland, what is this?"

He shrugged. "A watch. Check it out."

I pulled the box out, opened it, and gasped. It was brilliant with diamonds and obviously expensive. Shaking my head, I said, "You gotta stop. You are spending too much money on jewelry and stuff for me. And the jet we took here? You're gonna go broke!"

"Kim, I've been in the NBA for eight years. If my ass goes broke from buying a few pieces of jewelry, I need to. And I didn't pay for the jet."

"You didn't?"

"No. Let me put that on you so we can go. The car is outside."

I sighed. "Okay."

The business brunch meeting was at the gorgeous beachfront Galveston home of business mogul Derek Hill, more than an hour's drive from Big South's home outside of Houston. It was a three-story structure with wrap-around covered porches on every floor. We were driven there in a limo that, along with the jet we flew to Texas in, belonged to Sable Inc., Hill's company. Leland said he and Hill had known each other for a while, ran in the same social circle, and had been talking about doing business together for years. This meeting was about a new film production company Hill was starting, and he evidently really wanted Leland on board because he'd spared no expense making this meeting happen.

I knew Leland co-owned a nightclub in LA and had his hand in other business dealings, but this meeting seemed big, *huge*, and something about knowing I was getting ready to see my man conduct big-time business turned me completely on. I was excited and a little nervous about meeting these rich people, but there was no other place I'd rather be at that moment than with him.

We were greeted by Mr. Hill's very friendly and tiny wife. I instantly liked her and loved her style. She wore a bright yellow romper on her short but filled-out frame and bedazzled turquoise sandals. Her toes were painted a peach color and her hair was in long, blond, Senegalese twists. She was the perfect combination of ratchet and sophisticated.

"Hi! So glad you two made it safely!" she gushed. "Oh, I love your goddess braids, and you are just gorgeous!"

"Thank you!" I replied. "You look beautiful. That shade of yellow is so pretty."

"Aw, thanks. I bet it would look even better against your skin. Hey, Leland!" she said, peering behind me.

"'Sup, Greer. This is my girl, Kim. Kim, this is Greer Hill, the lady of the house."

She grinned. "We're not that formal around here and he knows it. Leland is a friend *and* one of our best customers. He's been chartering our jets from time to time for a while now."

"Really?" I asked, looking at him.

He nodded. "Yeah, I like the privacy sometimes."

"Well, y'all come on in," she invited us. "It's hot out there!"

We followed her into her home, through a spotless foyer with shiny mahogany flooring into a beautifully-decorated living room which boasted huge windows that opened to a breathtaking view of the gulf. I almost tripped over my own feet from gawking at it. She led us up not one, not two, but three spiral staircases to the rooftop patio where we were to have brunch. Standing beside an elegantly-set table with a smile on his face was Derek Hill, all dreadlocked, tall—but shorter than my Leland—and fine. His wife stepped into his arms and kissed his cheek as she announced our arrival. They looked so good together, *really* good.

Ungluing my eyes from the photogenic couple as Mr. Hill and Leland shook hands, I took in the panoramic view of the ocean and the exclusive neighborhood surrounding us. It was beautiful in an unbelievable way. I'd never owned a home, had never desired to because I was always so busy working and trying to give my son a decent life. Armand had the means, but only owned a condo in Miami in addition to the one he bought for me in St. Louis. All either of us knew were apartments. But now, seeing the world through Leland's eyes, seeing how Leland, his brother, and the Hills lived, I realized what I'd been missing. Leland had invited me to his home, his beachfront home in LA, more than once. I'd declined more than once, because I was scared of upsetting Armand while Armand was off continuing to live his life. Maybe I needed to start living mine.

"Thanks for having us, Mr. Hill," Leland said, before introducing me to this powerful man. And once the introductions were done, we all sat around the table, and the brunch meeting began.

# Leland

I placed my fork on the edge of my plate and lifted the linen napkin to wipe my hands, my eyes on the view of the ocean as I considered Derek Hill's proposal. It all sounded good—great, to be honest. But one thing was bothering me.

I glanced over at Kim, who was taking a sip of her water with her eyes wide and glued to me, then redirected my attention to our host. "Derek, I'm not gonna lie. What you're proposing sounds really good, like something I'd love to be a part of. Partnering with you to launch a new studio, a mecca for black screenwriters, directors, and actors? The possibility of finding the next Ava DuVernay or Ryan Coogler or Dee Rees and giving them a chance to share their vision with the world? That's something I would definitely love to put my name and money behind, and honestly, I'm honored you want me to be a part of this vision."

"But?" Derek Hill asked, as he reclined in his chair.

"But, I'm sure you know my brothers, Everett and Nolan, are launching a film production company."

He nodded. "McClain Films. I'm well aware of that."

"Then you've gotta know I'm not trying to be my brothers'

competition."

Leaning forward, he said, "But that's just it. We wouldn't be their competition. From what I've heard, your brothers are looking to make mainstream movies along the lines of *The Best Man* and *Love Jones*. They're planning to revive the black love cinematic renaissance of the nineties."

I nodded.

"What I'm proposing is a company that specializes in small, art house-type productions like *Moonlight* and Lee Daniels' *Shadowboxer*. You ever seen that one?"

I shook my head. "No, can't say that I have."

"I have," Kim said, speaking for the first time since we took our seats. Her eyes swung between me and Derek as she added, "It's very different, definitely not mainstream at all. It's-it's provocative and dark and intriguing and-and shocking. It makes you think."

Derek smiled, and I had to admit that I was impressed with my woman myself. "Yes!" he said. "Those are the kinds of movies I want to make, stories that other studios would shy away from. Stories that are gritty, real…provocative and dark and intriguing and *shocking*. What I'm proposing is that the art will come first, and the money and accolades will follow. I believe that."

I glanced over at Kim again to see the glimmer in her eyes. This thing, this proposition, was exciting to her, and her excitement combined with Derek's obvious passion for this venture, was beginning to rub off on me. "I can't lie," I said. "I'm liking what I'm hearing. How many partners are you planning to bring on?"

"Three, including myself."

With lifted eyebrows, I said, "Three? So, who else besides me?"

"Actually, a writer. A street lit author you might have heard of. His moniker is Street, but his government name is Lorenzo Higgs. He wanted to be here to meet you today, but his wife is due to have their fifth son any day now."

"I've never heard of him. Not much of a reader." I heard a glass thud against the table and turned back to Kim in time for her to give me a slow smile. "Let me guess," I said. "You've heard of him?"

She nodded, looking like an excited teenager. "Yes, I've read some of his books. He's phenomenal!" she gushed.

"That, he is," Derek agreed. "He's written several books, has his own publishing house, and just recently completed his first screenplay, a paranormal love story."

"Paranormal! Wow, I didn't know he wrote anything besides street lit!" Kim shrieked.

"This is a new undertaking for him, and I believe it would be a perfect fit for this company. I'd like for it to be our first feature," Derek informed us.

"This sounds…hell, it sounds like I need to be signing on the dotted line after my lawyer looks over everything. But before you have your folks send the contracts to her, can I see the numbers again?" I had the money to invest, more than enough, really. To be honest, the only real apprehension I had was attached to the fact that this would be the first business venture of this size I'd be entering into without consulting Everett first, but I knew it was time to cut that cord. It was time for me to stand up and be my own man. Everett had taught me well how to conduct business and grow my wealth over the years. It was time for me to apply that knowledge independently.

"Sure. As a matter of fact, if everyone is finished eating, we can head down to the living room for drinks and I can show you the figures on my computer in living color."

"Yeah, that sounds good."

Shortly after that, we headed downstairs where we talked more business, drank some of his expensive bourbon—the same bourbon my brother had turned me on to—and then the Hills took turns bragging about their little girls. Kennedy and Sable, I think were their names. They were in Italy with their grandparents, according to Greer. We had a good time, and before we left, I gave Derek my word that if my lawyer liked what she saw, I was on board. I felt good about that, like I was investing in the future, a future that I hoped was full of me loving the incredible Kim Hampton.

\*\*\*\*\*

"Wow! Seeing you in action in there was just...wow!" Kim said, as the driver pulled the limo out of the Hills' driveway.

I shot her a lopsided grin. "In action?"

"Being a business man and using that good business grammar. Leland, you have no idea what it did to me seeing you poring over those figures with Mr. Hill. Then, when you shook his hand and said you looked forward to making money with him?" She scooted closer to me on the seat and softly pressed her lips to my ear. "That turned me all the way on."

I licked my lips as I turned to look her in the eye. "For real?"

She nodded.

"Well, shit...I felt the same way when you were talking about that movie Hill mentioned. And you know about the author he was talking about, too? I was like, damn, what doesn't my woman know?"

"That turned you on?" she asked.

"Like a motherfucker."

Her eyes narrowed as she leaned in and grabbed my bottom lip with her teeth, bit down on it, then swiped her tongue across it to ease the pain.

I held up a finger. "Hold that thought. Driver, take us to the nearest hotel."

She frowned slightly. "A hotel?"

"Yeah, me and Tyrone 'bout to tear you and Little Kim up!"

# 20

# Leland

I had a lot on my mind that morning, from the situation with my sister and her husband to this new business venture I'd decided to enter into. My sister was grown. Hell, she was older than me, but I was still worried about her, had basically begged her to fly back to St. Louis with us, but she'd refused, deciding to stay in Houston at Ev's place while her husband flew back to their place in LA. I kind of hoped she didn't take Wayne's ass back but didn't want to push her in any direction. I honestly just wanted her to be happy, whatever that looked like for her.

The business deal, I believed was solid, but it still felt foreign to be standing on my own with it. Then there was the fact that we were flying back home that morning. Kim had been so relaxed in Houston, so open to my family and even the Hills. I wasn't looking forward to going back to being closed up in bedrooms with her again, but like I said, I'd do what I had to do to keep her.

As the limo pulled to a stop, she grabbed my hand and smiled at me.

Leaning in to kiss her cheek, I said, "I'll be right back, and then we'll be on our way to the airport."

"Can I go with you?" she asked softly.

I looked at her for a second, and then asked, "You sure you want to?"

She nodded. "Yeah, unless you...do you need to go alone?"

I shook my head. "No, you can go. I was gonna tell her about you, anyway."

I held her hand as I led the way, taking the stone path I'd walked so many times before, but usually alone. It felt good not to do this alone for once. When I stopped, I nodded at the huge, marble headstone that stood before us proclaiming this the final resting place of Randall and Juanita McClain, my parents.

Instead of talking to my mother like I had planned to, like I usually did, I stood there and stared at their names. And when I opened my mouth to speak, my words were directed at Kim.

"I never knew my father, because I was a baby when he died, but my mother? She was…she was an angel. She loved me, spoiled me, and even when she yelled, 'Leland Randall!' and I knew I was in trouble for something, I was never afraid of her. She disciplined me with love. I remember I hated to be apart from her for any reason, including to go to school."

She didn't reply, just squeezed my hand, I guess to let me know she was listening.

"I made it home first that day, so I was the one who found her. She was on the floor, and even at eleven, I knew she was gone. But I called nine-one-one anyway." I blew out a breath. "Can you imagine that? Losing your mama, your whole world, at eleven and being the one to find her…dead?"

"No, I can't," she whispered.

"I remember feeling so helpless…and alone. After my mom died, I could be in a room full of people and I'd still feel alone. I remember feeling like shit like that would always happen to me, like bad stuff was gonna follow me around for the rest of my life. And on top of losing my mom, the kids at school would fuck with me, tell me I thought I was better than them because of who my brother was. I was always fighting and arguing. I believed I'd never be happy again."

"Do you still believe that?"

"Naw, I can see the good in my life now. I got good friends like Polo and I got my brothers and sister, Aunt Ever, Uncle Lee, even Aunt Ever's boyfriend that she puts out the house every other day.

I'da introduced you to him, but he's in the dog house right now."

She chuckled.

"And I got a good career. I live a good life. Then there's you. You're a good thing, too," I continued.

She stood there for a moment, then dropped my hand and wrapped her arms around me. "I love you," she said into my chest.

"You don't have to say that just because—"

"No, it's the truth. I love you, Leland. I do, with all my heart. I just don't have a good track record when it comes to love, so I was reluctant to say it, but I do. I love you, and I…I need you."

Something popped in my chest, like my damn heart snapped or something at hearing her say those words. "Kim…"

"And I know I'm not easy to love. I'm crazy. I do stupid stuff. I overreact. I'm difficult to be with, but I'm glad you haven't given up on me. I'm glad you love me, and I want you to know you don't ever have to feel alone again, because you have me. And you're not helpless, you're strong and smart and talented and so powerful. You make me feel special. I love you so much, Leland."

I squeezed my arms around her and closed my eyes. "I love you, too, baby, more than I know how to show you."

We were quiet, standing there holding each other in the middle of Hartfield Cemetery in my hometown. Then something came over me, and before I could stop myself, I said, "I want you to have my baby."

She stiffened in my arms. "What?"

"I…want you to have my baby."

"Are you serious?"

"Yeah, I think I am."

"You *think* you are?"

"I know I am."

"But didn't you say you didn't want kids?"

"Yeah, but that was before I fell in love with you. Now I want that more than anything."

"Leland, my only child is twenty years old."

"I know that."

"Then you know it would be crazy for me to have children twenty-plus years apart."

I didn't know how to reply to that. I just knew what I wanted and that was for her to have my baby.

"And I'm thirty-five."

"And?"

"That's too old for me to be getting pregnant, Leland. See, that's what I was trying to tell you before we got in so deep with each other. You need a woman who can give you kids!"

"That woman is you!"

"No, it's not!"

"Yes the-fuck it is! Kim, you are not old, and I wish the-hell I knew why you think you are!"

"Because I have a grown son!"

"That you had when you were a kid! Look, it's women way older than you having babies."

"I know that...I, um...Leland, this thing we have, it's dizzying and fierce and makes me light-headed sometimes. It feels like I'm on a rollercoaster ride that's about to fly off its tracks any second. It's scary enough for me without adding a baby to it. I'm just not ready for that," she said. "Not right now."

I released her then grabbed her hand, sighing as I said, "You're right. It's too soon for that. Forget I said it. Let's just go."

She looked like she wanted to cry when she said, "I didn't mean to upset you. I just. I do love you, but—"

I released her hand and held her face in my hands. "You love me. That's more than enough for me. I'm not upset, baby. Not at all. Come on, we gotta get to the airport." I leaned in and kissed her, then smiled down at her.

She wrapped her arms around my neck, kissed me, and then took my hand, letting me lead her back to the limo.

# 21

# Kimberly

More and more, I was beginning to hate my job. Not that anything about it had changed. No, it'd always been hectic, stressful, and overwhelming, to put it lightly. I suppose what had changed was me and my priorities. Before, my main goal had been to stay busy and to keep my mind occupied, and yes, to help others. I still had a desire to help others, but I had a new passion that more than kept my mind occupied—Leland McClain. Since that trip to Texas a few weeks earlier, we'd grown closer and closer, had spent nearly every hour I wasn't at work and he wasn't at practice or working out together, and when he left earlier that morning for a preseason game in Memphis, I was crushed. He'd offered for me to tag along, and while that was tempting, I had to work, and I still wasn't trying to be out like that with him. He'd been right about his family not posting anything about us and neither had the Hills, but I wasn't going to push it.

A knock came at my office door, and before I could acknowledge it, it eased open, and as expected, Elrich stepped into my office with a pinched brow and apprehension in his gray eyes. He would be considered attractive by anyone's standards—neat, fit, handsome, and compassionate. He was a keeper. I realized that, just not *my* keeper. I had thought he understood that, that we had an understanding from day one of our dalliances, but I'd evidently thought wrong, because since his encounter with Leland on the phone, he'd barely said two words to me despite the fact that we'd had several meetings since then. I asked questions to assess his progress with whatever issue involving whomever it involved, and he kind of just grunted his answers. That needed to end. We were adults, professionals, and while Leland had crossed the line, so had Elrich, to be honest. He needed to get over this ASAP. So I had summoned him to my office.

"You wanted to see me?" he asked, in a less-than-friendly but not quite antagonistic tone.

"Yes, have a seat."

"I'd rather stand."

"And I'd rather you had a seat."

He rolled his lips between his teeth before dropping into a chair in front of my desk, and then he just stared at me.

"You wanna tell me what's going on?" I asked.

"With what?" he asked.

"Your attitude as of late."

He shrugged, rested his left leg on his right knee, and relaxed his posture. "I don't have an attitude."

"Yes, you do. Either you have an attitude or somehow lost half the words in your vocabulary."

He chuckled bitterly. "You have your new boyfriend talk crazy to me, and I'm the one being interrogated? You are something else."

I leaned forward with a frown tattooed on my face. "I didn't have him do anything. He's an adult. He does what he wants, and I apologize if he hurt your feelings."

"Hurt my feelings?" he scoffed. "No, he didn't hurt my feelings. *You* hurt them by turning me down for a thug. What is he? A drug dealer?"

"What?! Why would you think that?"

"Because he sounded like one!"

He had raised his voice and I'd never known him to do that before, so after I calmed myself down, I said, "Elrich, did you think what we had was more than what it really was?"

He sighed. "No, I just...I think I made a mistake with you. I should've demanded more."

"Demanded? That wasn't going to work with me; I can tell you that right now." *The only man who can get away with that is Leland McClain.*

"I know. It's just that I care more about you than I realized when we were…when we had our arrangement. It didn't dawn on me until after we stopped seeing each other."

"Well…I'm sorry, Elrich. I didn't know."

"Would it have made a difference if I had known then? If I had told you how I felt?"

"I don't know," I lied. The truth was, I now knew what love was. It was what I felt for Leland, what I'd never felt for Elrich. I don't think I could've fallen in love with him even if I'd tried. He just wasn't the one.

"Is this thing with the new guy serious?" he asked.

I nodded my response.

Blowing out a breath, he said, "I guess I have myself to blame for letting you go."

"No, I'm a firm believer that things happen as they should, as they're meant to. You're a great guy, Elrich, and I know there's someone out there for you."

"Thank you for that."

"And in the meantime, can you stop giving me attitude?"

He gave me a slow smile. "Yeah, sorry about that."

"And I'm truly sorry if I hurt you in any way or led you on or—"

"You didn't, so there's no need for you to apologize."

We were both quiet for a minute or two before he stood, and said, "Well, boss…I better get back to work."

"Okay, thanks for meeting with me."

"No problem."

*****

"So you two have been together since college? Wow!" I said to Kendra, Polo's girlfriend. She was petite, rail thin, and appeared even younger than her age in the little dress she wore. I was the oldest person at the table, and sitting there looking at her, I felt it. But she was sweet, a gracious hostess, and the food was good. Nothing fancy, just some shrimp tacos and dip and chips, but delicious. When Leland told me we were invited to have dinner with her and Polo after he got back in town, my first reaction was to panic, but he assured me Polo was a friend of his who would keep us a secret for as long as he asked and that Kendra would do the same. And despite having to miss my stiletto step class, the evening had been enjoyable.

"Actually, me and Polo met in high school, been together since eleventh grade."

"That's amazing!" I said, my eyes wide as they shifted from Kendra to Polo.

She nodded. "Yeah. I mean, it hasn't been all perfect or anything. We've had our ups and downs, but we love each other, so we stick it out." She wasn't lying about things between them not being perfect. From what I'd seen on social media, Polo stayed getting caught with other women.

"Yeah, I love this girl, just can't get her to marry me. I done asked a million times," Polo said.

"Really?" I asked, as Leland moved his chair closer to mine and draped his arm across my shoulders.

Kendra shrugged. "I don't see the point. We're good like this."

Polo shook his head. "Naw, she's convinced we'll get a divorce. She says as long as we stay like this, we might fight or break up, but we always get back together. She feels like divorces are final."

"That's an interesting way of looking at it," I said.

"It's what I've observed in my family. Folks stay together for years, break up, make up, then they decide to get married, get divorced, and that's it. I'd rather have Polo in my life like it is than not at all," Kendra admitted.

"I don't know why you want this fool," Leland quipped. "He ain't shit."

"I know the king of Ain't Shit Land ain't talking," Polo rebutted.

They went back and forth trading insults for a few minutes, and then they both laughed.

"You two are a mess," I said, with a grin on my face.

They slapped hands across the huge, glass-topped table. "My nigga for life," Polo said.

"On everything," Leland agreed.

"So," Kendra began, "you two must be serious. I've been begging Leland to have dinner with us forever, so when Polo said he finally accepted, I almost fainted. Then I found out he was bringing a date and almost had a stroke. As long as I've known him, he's never introduced me to any of his girlfriends."

"Really?" I said, glancing at Leland.

"Never had a girlfriend before Kim, Kendra," he said.

"You don't have to lie for my benefit," I directed to Leland.

"I ain't lying. I had acquaintances, friends. You're my first real girlfriend."

"Do your friends and acquaintances know that?"

He shrugged. "I ain't never lead them to believe otherwise."

"Well, you two look good together. It's good to see my friend with a woman with viable eggs," Polo said.

Kendra smacked his arm as he threw his head back and laughed.

"Oh, you got jokes, huh? You lucky I'm in a good mood tonight," Leland said, then leaned in and kissed my cheek.

"Y'all are so cute! Hey, since these two are so close, maybe we can hang out when they're on the road, or will you be traveling with Leland?" Kendra asked.

I shook my head. "I have a job, so it would be difficult to travel with him."

"Well, I don't work, but I'm not with the road life. Tried it, but hated it."

"I bet. But yeah, we can hang out sometimes when I'm off. That'd be nice." It really would be nice. I liked Kendra's spirit.

"Great! I'll get your number before you two leave."

"Okay."

Leland leaned in to kiss me again, this time on the lips. "I love you, you know that?" he whispered.

"I love you, too," I whispered in response. When I looked up, both Polo and Kendra were grinning at us.

# Leland

"That was fun!" Kim chirped, as I pulled out of Polo's driveway.

"See what a nice time we can have outside a condo?"

"I went to Texas with you, Leland. We've been out together before tonight."

"But we need to do it more often."

She didn't respond. So I said, "Don't you think it's time to tell Armand about us so we can stop hiding this? I mean, it's only a matter of time before he finds out anyway."

"I'm not ready yet."

"Baby—"

"I'm not ready. Just…I need more time."

Sighing, I said, "A'ight, Kim. A'ight."

# 22

"You get the tickets?"

I leaned back in my chair and bit my bottom lip. "Yeah, I got them."

"So you gonna make my games?"

"All of them? Probably not, Boogie. I have…I have work, you know?"

"What? You think I'ma fire you for taking off to see me play?"

"No, of course not. I just hate missing work. This place seems to fall apart in my absence."

"You talking about the break-in? Don't blame yourself for that, Ma. You deserved to take that trip with your friends. Shoot, I told you, I got you. You ain't gotta work at all. I actually don't like you working at that place. It obviously ain't safe."

"Don't start that again. I *want* to work here."

"Yeah, I know." He sighed into the phone. "So you're really not coming to my games? For real, Mama? What you got to do besides that job that's so important?"

*There's this man that I'm crazy in love with and I like spending every waking hour with him and I want to go to his games and cheer him on even if I have to wear a wig and shades to do it because he's just that important to me.* "Nothing, I…I'm gonna try to make as many as I can. I'll definitely be at the one here in St. Louis."

"Good. That's next week. Hey, let's go out to eat afterwards."

"Okay, that'd be great! You know I've been missing you."

"You could at least come visit me sometimes, Ma. You know?"

"I know, and I will. Love you, Boogie."

"Love you, too, Mama."

After I ended the call, I sat back in my chair and blew out a breath, I loved my son, but I'd spent years up until that point centering my world and my every action around him. He was used to that, so it made sense that he expected the status quo—me following him around, watching him play even after I moved back to St. Louis—to stand. But I didn't want that anymore. Things had changed, unbeknownst to him. He was still important to me, but he wasn't my world anymore. I was focused on my own happiness for once, and an integral part of that was Leland. The responsible thing to do would be to tell Armand the truth, that I was in a new relationship with a wonderful man whom I adored and that I wanted to spend time building on that, but fear obscured my view of what was right, what needed to happen.

I sat there for a few more minutes, mulling over everything in my life and wondering if being with Leland was the right decision to make, experiencing those old familiar feelings of doubt again. I mean, anything I felt I needed to keep a secret couldn't be right, could it?'

*It's the secrecy that's wrong, not the love.*

That thought made me shake my head at myself. My life had been so ridiculously messed up that I had a skewed view of what was good and appropriate. Of course being in love with Leland wasn't wrong. Being afraid of my son's reaction to it was. But shit, I couldn't help it. I just…couldn't, and to be honest, not only did I know I was frustrating Leland, I was frustrating the hell out of myself.

As my phone chimed with a text, I closed my eyes and sighed. *Soon. I'll tell Armand soon.*

Letting my eyes fall to my phone, I read the text from Leland: *U have no idea how much I love u.*

As I typed out, *I love you more*, I decided I'd tell Armand about me and Leland when he was in town the next week, over dinner.

Or at least I'd try.

*****

The night of the Cyclones vs. Heat game, I found myself faced with a dilemma. Armand had sent me tickets for seats located on the visitor's side—third row from the floor, right behind the team's bench, which, of course, wasn't really a bench. Leland had given me and Zabrina season tickets right behind the Cyclones' team seats. Leland's tickets were better, but it would look really strange to my son for me to sit there instead of using the tickets he'd sent me. Plus, he sent three, including one for Zabrina's man. It just made more sense to use those. I could only hope Leland would understand that and not be insulted that I wasn't sitting where he expected me to, because my coward ass didn't tell him I'd be using Armand's seats. Hell, he didn't even know he'd sent tickets to me.

Yeah, I was fucking things up and I knew it.

Anyway, we arrived early, grabbed some food from concessions, and settled in our seats in time to watch the players warm up. My eyes darted from one end of the court to the other, taking in the awesome athleticism and skill of both my son with his low-cut fade and my man with his thick hair pulled up in a messy ponytail. Like always, I couldn't believe I created a person who was as talented as my Armand and wondered where in the world he got it from. I would say his father, but I honestly wasn't sure. We weren't together long enough for me to learn much of anything about him. Malcolm Daniels was older, twenty-five or twenty-six to my fifteen, a neighborhood drug dealer who showered me with gifts in exchange for me not asking him any questions about…anything, but who had no time or need for kids. So he quickly dismissed me when he found out I was carrying his child but came back around from time to time during the first few years of Armand's life, even gave him his last name. We had a very volatile on-again-off-again relationship until Armand was about five when I finally came to my senses and got tired of him kicking my ass when the mood hit him. Then I moved from him to Shawn, a local radio disc jockey old enough to be my father who drank like a fish and kicked my ass on the side. After him was Dre—the man Armand had to peel off me.

"Damn, Armand looks good out there!" Garner, Zabrina's man, declared.

I peered over at him sitting on the other side of Zabrina and smiled. "He always does. He's just got it, you know? Always has."

"Yeah, he's been a star since he was a little boy," Zabrina said.

"True," I agreed.

"And Leland? Damn. This is gonna be some game," she added under her breath. I guess I was supposed to believe Garner didn't know about me and Leland. Yeah, right.

My response was to nod. Leland was definitely talented, too. So yeah, this was going to be an awesome game.

While on the floor, Armand did a quick search of the area where we were seated and then grinned, giving me a salute and making me feel like he was back in high school when I wouldn't dare miss a game and happily sat amongst the other parents with my chest puffed out with pride. I was proud of my boy, always would be, and seeing that smile on his face gave me confirmation that I'd made the right seating decision. Then my eyes slid to the opposite end of the court where I could see Leland doing the same thing, peering into the area where I would have sat if I'd used the tickets he'd gifted to me. My heart sank as he stared for so long a team member had to tap him on the shoulder to get his attention.

I sighed, returning my attention to the Heat's warm-up until both teams left the floor.

"I'ma go get some more beer. Y'all want anything?" Garner offered.

Zabrina and I gave him our requests, and after he left, my cousin turned and looked me dead in the eye, then pulled me into a hug. "Girl, I am so proud of you!"

With a slight frown, I asked, "For what? Armand? Girl, you know I didn't give him those skills."

"No, for bagging Leland McClain. Seeing him out there in action? Damn! Just how fine can one man be?"

"Do you know how many times you've told me that Leland is fine, Z?"

"Shit, do you know how fine he is?"

"Uh, yeah. I see him naked all the time."

"Got damn."

"Child…"

"It's just wrong for him to look like he looks. Hey, you know what? Y'all need to come have dinner with me and Garner sometimes!"

"First of all, Garner knows about us?"

In response, she gave me a sheepish look and a shrug.

"Second, I'm not bringing him to your house so you can thirst for him in my face. I love you, Z, but you already know I will kick your ass over my man."

"Damn, what you think I'ma do? Rape him?"

"Uh, yeah!"

We stared at each other for a second and then both burst into laughter. We were an odd pair who shared a sick sense of humor, but I wouldn't have it any other way.

"Well, you could at least bring him to one of my shows. I got that residency at Plush that I auditioned for."

"You did?! That's great, Z!"

"Yeah, so you gonna bring him?"

"I'll think about it."

As Zabrina went about the business of snapping an obligatory "I'm at an NBA game and I got a good seat" selfie, I pulled my own phone out with the intentions of quickly browsing Instagram and found a text from Leland. Dang, was he texting me from the locker room or something? Wasn't he supposed to be paying attention to the coach or whatever?

It read: *Where u at?*

I swallowed and typed out my reply: *In the arena, sitting with Z and her man.*

DLS: *Where? I didn't see u.*

Me: *On the visitor's side in the seats Armand got us.*

DLS: *Why u ain't tell me u were gonna sit over there? I was looking for u.*

Me: *I forgot.*

I was ashamed at how quickly I typed that lie out.

There was a pause before he sent: *U still coming over after u have dinner with ur son, right?*

Me: *Yeah. I'll call you when I'm on my way.*

DLS: *Ok. Love u.*

Me: *Love you too. Good luck.*

DLS: *I'm texting my luck right now. See u later, baby.*

Well, that text had me grinning like a fool, so much so that I didn't hear Z talking to me, so she leaned in close and read the text.

"OMG, he is so sweet! Damn, I hate you, Kim!"

Rolling my eyes, I said, "He's all right, I guess."

The game was nuts! It hadn't been that long since I'd attended an NBA game because I attended virtually all of Armand's the previous year, but it was still easy to forget how electrifying it was to sit in an arena and watch these giants at their athletic peak as they squared off against each other. Half the time, I didn't know where to look. Both Leland and Armand were equally impressive, but while Armand excelled at getting the ball through the hoop, Leland's speed was truly something to behold. For a man that size to move that fast? It's just something everyone should see at least once in their lifetime. Watching it on TV does not compare.

From the moment the starting line-ups were announced and the players engaged in their ridiculous handshake rituals, to the second the buzzer sounded indicating the end of the game, I found myself standing or screaming or smiling. I was both hoarse and exhausted by the time we were ready to leave, having cheered almost nonstop for both sides, garnering some odd looks, but I didn't care. If it was possible, I wanted both teams to win, but that night, the victory went to the home team. The Cyclones won by four points. Yeah, it was one hell of a game!

After I said goodbye to Zabrina and her teddy bear of a fiancé—he finally gave her a ring so she was now claiming him—I rushed home to freshen up and wait for Armand to pick me up as planned. We had decided to check out a new ramen shop that stayed open late, and I couldn't wait to spend time with him although I knew he wouldn't be in the best of moods after losing the game. But I was used to that, and bad attitude or not, he was still my only child.

This Thursday-night, seasoning-opening game ended at close to 10:00 PM. Having to fight the traffic around the arena, it took me nearly thirty minutes to make it home, so I knew it would be a minute before Armand arrived with all the post-game interviews and stuff he was obligated to do. So I settled down on my sofa, sent a congratulatory text to Leland, and then went to his Instagram page where he had posted a sweaty picture of himself wearing a big smile on his face, still in uniform. The caption read: *Thanks to my good luck charm, we got that W, baby! #FastlaneMcClain #Number12 #CycloneFever #IStan4LittleKim*

Again, I found myself grinning like a fool. Leland had absolutely no sense.

And the most ridiculous thing was that Lil' Kim had actually commented on the post saying she wanted to meet him.

An hour passed, then another, then another. I had texted and tried to call Armand several times to no avail and was beginning to get worried. Had he gotten into some trouble because of the loss? Gotten into a fight or something that landed him in jail or worse, the hospital? There was truly no telling with him having the anger issues that had plagued him since he was young. A little after 1:00 AM, Leland texted me, asking when I was coming over. Before I responded to him, I tried to text Armand again. While waiting for him to answer, I checked his Instagram page to find a video he'd just posted. I mean, it was posted like a minute earlier. I watched him in a club, a strip club, with some girl dancing on him. I didn't care about that. Hell, he was a grown man. What pissed me off was that he had me sitting up in my place waiting for nothing. I was just about to text that to him when a call from him popped up on the screen of my phone.

"Hello?" I answered through a sigh. "Where are you? I been waiting for hours!"

"My bad, Mama. I forgot I was supposed to pick you up, ran into Scotty after the game and he kidnapped my ass." That was followed by laughter from a whole group of guys.

"Well, you could've called me and let me know you changed your mind."

"I forgot! I just said that. Dang! But I'm on my way now. You still hungry?"

"Yeah…but it's too late to go out to eat now. Just bring me some Taco Bell or something."

"Okay, I got you. Be there in like twenty minutes."

"Okay."

No sooner than I'd hung up with Armand, there was a knock at my door. I smiled, thinking he was already here the whole time we were on the phone and was just messing with me. I'd heard music in the background, but more like car music than club music.

Swinging the door open, I said, "Hey! I thought you said twenty min—" I cut myself off when I realized it was Leland and not Armand who'd knocked.

"You thought who said what?" he asked, before leaning in to kiss me.

My eyes rolled around the area outside my door. He'd said twenty minutes, but still…

"Hey! What are you doing here?" I asked, giving him the best smile I could manage.

"You didn't answer my text."

"You didn't give me a chance to."

"If you say so. Can I come in?"

"Uh, Armand is on his way over. So…"

"He's coming back? Spending the night?"

"Uh, he's just now coming. He said he forgot we were supposed to be going to dinner, but he's gonna bring me something to eat now."

Leland frowned down at me. "You ain't ate yet? You been waiting for him all this time?"

I nodded. "Yeah, like I said, he forgot."

"And you *still* waiting for him?"

"Well, yeah. I'd like to see him, and I just talked to him. He's on his way."

"Where he been?"

"Why does that matter?" Now, I was getting irritated. Time was running out. Leland needed to go home before some mess popped off.

"I just wanna know what would make someone forget their mother."

"He didn't forget *me*, he just forgot he was supposed to come pick me up."

"That's the same thing, Kim."

"Well, he remembered and he's on his way now."

"You already told me that a couple of times."

"I know."

We both stood there and looked at each other.

"Well?" I said.

"Well, what? You dismissing me so your son can come bring you some food at damn near two in the morning? What kind of shit is that? He ain't got no respect for you to do you like that."

"He's my son, Leland."

"So? That means he should have the utmost respect for you! What kind of son does this kind of shit to his mother?"

"Look, you don't know anything about him, and I'm not dismissing you, I just…can we talk in the morning? He'll be here any minute."

He shook his head. "Look at you, all nervous about your son finding me here. You know what, Kim? I'm over this shit…like, for real."

As he turned to leave, my heart fell to the floor. "Wait!"

"What? You gonna call your son and tell him never mind, not to come so late?"

"N-no. I just wanna ask you…what do you mean you're over it."

"What do you think I mean, Kim?" he asked, and then he left and I backed into my living room, shutting the door and resting my head against it.

Despite several calls and texts from me, Armand never showed up that night.

# 23

I missed Leland.

He'd been on the road doing his job for the past two weeks, two weeks during which he'd ignored my phone calls, texts, emails, and DMs. He'd left the day after Armand stood me up without so much as a goodbye. So had Armand, but add to that, that he also gave no explanation for not showing up that night. I guess now I knew how Leland felt when I ignored his calls in the past—like shit. The only difference was that I deserved to be ignored. I honestly deserved the loneliness I felt without him, but that didn't make it any easier to cope with.

I couldn't sleep, barely ate, and was about a second from losing my entire mind. I loved Leland, but more than that, he loved me, and I needed that. I needed to feel loved by him.

But he wouldn't talk to me.

Sighing, I let my eyes roam my desk—paperwork, a half-eaten sandwich, two bottles of water, and my dormant cell phone. I wished I was anywhere besides the four walls of my office. No, I wished I was somewhere, anywhere laid up under my man, or ex-man since he had broken contact with me. But more than that, I wished I'd handled things with Leland better, not put so much weight on keeping things a secret, and most of all, I wished I wasn't so afraid to tell Armand about us and that I had the courage to deal with his inevitably bad reaction to the news.

But I just couldn't, and now I was alone.

All alone.

When a knock came at my office door, I had no idea how long I'd been sitting there staring at my desk but sat up straight and adjusted my blouse before yelling, "Come in!"

Peaches, who I still hadn't fired, peeked her head in the door and gave me a wide-eyed look. "Um, I'm getting ready to head out, Ms. Kim. Remember, I told you I have a doctor's appointment and need to leave early?"

I stared at her for a moment because, no, I didn't remember that, but in my current state of mind, I might have tuned the information out, so I finally nodded. "Okay, See you tomorrow."

"Thanks. Have a good evening."

I nodded again and jumped a little when my phone began to buzz. My heart was speeding out of control as I grabbed it and checked the screen. Seeing that it wasn't Leland but some unknown number, I closed my eyes and slumped back in my chair as I answered it. "Hello?"

"Hey, Kim?"

I frowned, took the phone from my ear, and checked the number again, then activated the speakerphone, and said, "Yes. Who am I speaking with?"

"Hey! This is Kendra, Polo's girlfriend!"

"Oh, hi, Kendra." I tried to sound enthusiastic but wasn't very convincing.

"Hi! So, I was wondering if you're free for lunch tomorrow. I'd love to meet you somewhere. I really enjoyed having you and Leland over the other week, and if you're like me, you're probably going crazy missing him like I'm missing my guy."

I swallowed and blinked back tears. "Yeah, I am."

"So, lunch? My treat. There's a Thai place I've been wanting to try."

I didn't feel like having lunch with her or even climbing out of bed in the morning, for that matter, but nevertheless, I said, "Sure. That'd be nice."

# Leland

I hit the button to ignore Kim's call and went back to my baked fish and my conversation with Polo. We were in Indiana for a game the next day, had been on the road for two weeks, and although we had an excellent record, I was tired as hell and missed the fuck out of Kim. But as much as I missed that woman, I couldn't deal with the incognito shit that went along with being with her. I was tired of hiding and ducking and dodging. I wasn't scared of her son, not at all. Shit, wasn't nothing he could do to hurt me short of killing me, and I was sure things wouldn't go that far. So no, I wasn't afraid of his silly, childish ass, but if and whenever this shit got back to him, I was going to look like a damn wuss. I wasn't trying to go out like that, plus, this shit was stupid. I was grown, she was grown, and hell, so was he. This wasn't a two or three-year-old kid we were talking about. It wasn't like us being together really affected him. He might not like it, but he'd get over it. He'd have to if she put her foot down, but she wasn't going to do that. She was always going to worry about how he felt about it. It seemed to me that she was more concerned about his feelings when it came to our relationship than she was mine, and to me, that was extremely fucked up.

I tried to tell myself that maybe it was me, maybe I was the wrong one in all this. After all, the closest thing to a father I'd ever been was my connection to the kids I'd mentored over the years, but that had nothing on Kim's bond with her son. She was a young, single mother, had sacrificed and struggled a lot to get him to a place of success. Maybe all that struggle and motherly love trumped the love I'd been trying to give to her. Maybe no matter what, she would always choose him over everyone else, including me. And maybe that was right, but that didn't mean I had to settle for it. See, maybe what was right for her was wrong for me.

Maybe we just weren't meant to be.

I missed and loved that woman like a motherfucker, but maybe loving her meant letting her go so that she could deal with whatever she needed to handle with her life and her son on her own terms and in her own time. Maybe to love her, I had to sacrifice being with her, and I loved her enough to do that although it hurt the hell out of me.

"Man, are you listening?" Polo asked, pulling me back into that restaurant with him.

I nodded without looking up from my plate. "Yeah, shorty you met in Denver last week is tripping. I heard you."

"You ain't got no advice for a nigga?"

I looked up at my friend who specialized in fucking his relationship with a good woman up and said something I should've said to him years earlier. "Yeah, stop fucking all these other chicks before you lose your woman."

He actually looked shocked. "Damn, really?"

I nodded. "Yeah, really."

Picking up his fork and pushing his food around on his plate, he said, "Humph, you act like you ain't out here getting all the ass you can, too."

"I'm not. Not since I got with Kim."

"But ain't y'all broke up? You been ignoring her calls for weeks now."

I shrugged. "She still got my heart, though. Ain't nobody else gonna come close to her until I get over her."

"So you're telling me you ain't messed with nobody else since you two got together?"

"That's exactly what I'm saying. I love her. Don't want nobody else."

"Shit, man…I love Kendra, but I still got needs."

I shook my head. "Whatever, man. All I know is, your ass would die if she did this shit to you."

"That would never happen," he said smugly.

"A'ight, if you say so."

"I know so. Shit, she tell me her every move when I talk to her, and I talk to her every day when we on the road. You know she had lunch with Kim the other day."

I dropped my eyes to my plate again. "Yeah?"

"Yeah, said she seemed kinda sad. I told her y'all been into it and shit. She said Kim didn't mention it but that she said she missed you."

Grabbing my napkin, I wiped my hands and stood from the table. "I'ma head on up to my room. I'll holla at you later, man."

"A'ight, man."

I'd barely made it into my room when she sent another text message to add to the collection of the ones she'd sent over the past couple of weeks.

Little Kim: *I miss you and I love you. Please call me.*

I fell into the bed, placed the phone on my chest, closed my eyes, and in no time, had fallen asleep.

*****

"You sure you don't wanna come with us, man? They say that club is always lit. It's new and one of the hottest spots here in Detroit. We won! We need to celebrate, man, and shit...I'm tryna see what I can get into, you know what I mean?" Polo said, as he elbowed me and did that little snicker he did when he thought he was being clever. Polo was my boy, had been for a long time, but he was stupid as hell.

So I said, "Naw, man, I'm good, and your ass needs to listen to me and not be tryna get into shit but your room—alone."

As we approached the door to my room, he waved his hand up and down. "There you go with that shit again, and I ain't even planning nothing like that. I'm just tryna get some drinks and vibe a little, that's all."

"For your sake, I hope so. Catch you later, man."

"A'ight, man. See you in the AM."

The first thing I noticed when I opened my door was the music, the second thing was the scent—a familiar mixture of pears and cocoa butter. Kim's body wash and lotion. Then I saw her—tall, dark-brown skin, long, thick legs and thighs, nice little waist, wide hips, full breasts. There she stood in the middle of my suite wearing nothing but turquoise waist beads, her soft skin illuminated by what had to be a thousand candles.

Got. Damn.

It had been close to three weeks since I'd seen her and…shit!

I couldn't move or talk or even blink. All I could do was stare and feel confused and excited and aroused and angry and happy all at the same time. I was a fucking lunatic in her presence, but I was glad to see her. And my body? Shit, it was ecstatic.

She tilted her head to the side and smiled, widening her stance and placing her hands on her hips. She'd changed her hair, had it re-braided into a swirling cornrow pattern with braids that hung past her shoulders. If she didn't look like a damn queen…

"Hi," she said softly.

"Hi. What are you doing here?" I heard myself say as I let my eyes tour her body from head to toe and back. Then I swallowed, licked my lips, and fixed my eyes on her face.

"I missed you and you wouldn't talk to me."

"I didn't think there was anything we needed to talk about."

"Well, there is. We need to talk and I really wanted to see you, so here I am."

"How'd you know where to find me?"

"Kendra told me."

"How'd you get in here?"

"Polo helped with that."

I shook my head. So he was in on this, huh?

"So you see me. Now what?" I asked. I was trying to play hard, but my damn dick was hard as steel, and my mouth was watering just from the sight of her. Shit, she was fine!

She lost the smile, giving me a serious look. "Now, I apologize and beg for your forgiveness. Now, I tell you I love you and wait for you to tell me you love me, too."

"And what if I don't tell you that?"

She dropped her gaze to the floor and shook her head. "Then…I don't know what I'll do if you've stopped loving me." Looking up at me again, she added, "Have you stopped loving me?"

"It doesn't work like that."

"So you still love me, then?"

"Yeah, I do."

"Then let me apologize."

I watched as she stepped closer to me and fell to her knees. In what seemed like seconds, my jogging pants were down to my ankles, her warm mouth was around me, and all my damn common sense had disappeared.

# 24

# Leland

"Dre was my third real boyfriend besides Armand's father and another guy I dated," she said, as I lay next to her in the room still illuminated by the candles. She stared at the ceiling as she continued to speak, "He was older, had a good job with a liquor distributor, and he was really nice to me and Armand at first. We dated almost a year before he moved into my place. About a month after that, he hit me for the first time during an argument but promised not to ever lay a hand on me again. By then, I knew the cycle, had already dealt with it twice before and watched my mom endure the same treatment when I was a kid, but I still forgave him because I thought I loved and needed him.

"It was a few months later that he hit me again. A few months after that, he evolved from punching me to choking me. I fought back. I always fought back."

She rolled over and looked me in the eye. "I think one of the reasons I let it go on for so long is that he was helping me pay bills, and hell, I was tired of struggling. Social work doesn't pay much, and neither did my second job at a department store." She sighed and shook her head. "Anyway, anything would set him off. Like, if the light bill was higher than he thought it should be or I started my period a day earlier than usual or we ran out of toothpaste. Anything would make him pounce on me, but the crazy thing is, he never hit me when Armand was home. We might've argued after he went to bed, but he never put his hands on me when my son was home, until...

"I don't even remember what he was mad about that day, but I do remember us arguing and I guess I said something that really pissed him off, because things quickly escalated from us cursing each other out to him pinning me to a wall while squeezing my neck. I had started blacking out when Armand burst through the front door, home early from basketball practice, and literally pulled Dre off me and beat his ass. He...he *saved my life*, Leland. And later that night, he told me he'd heard Dre talking crazy to me some nights, had even seen him hit me once when I thought he wasn't home. He talked about remembering his father and my other boyfriend hitting me, and from that point on, our roles became blurred. He was still my son, but he also became my protector. I was his mother, but always felt like I owed a debt to him for what I put him through because of my bad decisions. I promised myself I'd put him first from that point on, and that's what I did, what I still do. And then I became dependent on him. For a long time, I really believed he was all I had. When he left for college is when the insomnia started. I couldn't sleep in my apartment alone. I guess I felt like I needed him there.

"Then there's the issue of his anger. Because of the abuse he witnessed, he's full of anger, rage, and has control issues, especially when it comes to me. I made him what he is today. It's my fault he's how he is."

"I understand that, I really do...but I can't do this secret shit anymore, baby. I don't care how angry he is. I don't care how he reacts. Whatever debt you think you owe him, you paid it and then some. You lived for him. Now you gotta move on, let him live his life the best way he can while you do the same thing. If you saw your mom get hit, that's what you knew, and that's why the same thing happened to you. It's a cycle, yeah, but what your son chooses to do, how he chooses to act as an adult ain't on you. It's on him. You can't change the past, but you can damn sure live a better life now. But look, if you're not ready to let all this go, to put the past behind you and put your son in his place, ain't nothing I can do about it. I guess maybe I moved too fast with you, so I'm sorry for that. I love you, but I can't do what you want me to do anymore, Kim."

"But—all I want you to do is love me."

"While hiding it? I can't. Not anymore. That shit is stressful, and to be honest, it's crazy as hell. I think what I like best about dating older women is the fact that they do what they want and couldn't give a fuck what anyone thinks about it. Me and you? We don't have that. I can't be with you when I don't have control over *how* I can be with you. That just ain't gonna work for me. I don't like feeling helpless and shit, and that's how this thing with you makes me feel, helpless like a motherfucker."

"But I…I don't want us to hide or keep this a secret anymore. I wanna be with you freely. I don't wanna lose you. My life has been a mess these few weeks without you. I've been so miserable."

I stared at her for a moment, then said, "You saying you're gonna tell your son about us?"

"I'm saying I love my son, but I've made some mistakes as a mother. I'm saying he does not respect me because I have never demanded it of him, and yes, I've sacrificed a lot for him and you're right, it's time for me to let him live his life and for me to live mine…with you."

"But?"

"I'm not ready to tell him. I'm not going to pretend I am. I just…let's just be together the way you want us to and whatever happens, happens."

"So when he finds out, what? We're over?"

"No, when he finds out, I'll deal with it. I'll let him know this is what I want."

I rolled over on my back and took my shift staring at the ceiling. "You not telling him, just letting him find out? That still ain't right, baby. It's-it's—"

"The coward's way out," she interrupted me. "I know it is, but it's as far as I can go right now. Please tell me you're okay with this. Please don't give up on me. I promise things will be different. I'll go wherever you want me to go, do whatever you want me to do. I just…I need you, Leland. I really, really need you."

I rolled back over, reached for her, pulled her to me, and after I had kissed her, I squeezed her in my arms, and said, "Okay, baby. Okay."

# Kimberly

"Okay, everyone, it looks like that's all I had on my list for today. Darren and Trisha, I want to congratulate you on organizing Trunk or Treat. The kids really enjoyed it and the costume contest."

They both smiled and thanked me.

"Oh, and those of you working with the kids in the after-school program, be sure to give those forms out for the Thanksgiving food baskets."

I watched as they grabbed stacks of the forms from the center of the table in the small conference room, and just as I was preparing to formally dismiss my staff from our weekly meeting, a soft knock came at the door.

With a slight frown, I said, "Come in!"

Leland peeked in the door with a sheepish look on his face. "Your secretary said I could find you here."

I stared at him for a second, shifted my eyes back to the people sitting around the table, and seeing that their eyes were collectively on my man, told Leland, "Just a second," and then officially adjourned the meeting.

Leland stepped into the room as my staff, including a bewildered-looking Elrich, filed out.

As soon as the window-less space cleared and the door closed, Leland moved closer to me and gave me a soft kiss on my lips. "Hey," he said, smiling down at me.

"Hey, what are you doing here?"

"I came to take you to lunch."

There it was. He was testing what I'd told him in Detroit. It'd been a couple of weeks since then, and he'd been so busy on the road and practicing that he hadn't made me make good on my "no more secrecy" promise. Now he was seeing if I'd follow through.

"Okay," I said, turning to grab my notebook and other paperwork. "Let me take this stuff back to my office real quick."

"A'ight, can I walk with you?"

I held my papers to my chest and nodded. "Yes, of course you can."

We were halfway down the hall to my office when his cell rang. "This is Derek Hill. I'ma head outside and take this. I'll wait for you out there."

"Okay. Be out there in a second."

I'd managed to set my papers down, grab my purse, and was about to leave my office when the door opened and in walked Elrich. He quickly closed the door behind him, and asked, "What's going on?"

"What do you mean?" I asked, confused, ready to go to lunch, and wishing I could take the rest of the day off so I could climb Leland like the tree he was.

"Why is Leland McClain here? Something going on with one of our kids again? Shemar Townsend?"

I blinked a few times before realizing what he was talking about. It'd been a while since the whole Shemar Townsend thing popped off, not that I could fully forget about it. "Oh," I said. "No, nothing's wrong. Leland and I are just having lunch together."

"Leland? Not Mr. McClain?" he inquired, with both his eyebrows and the octave of his voice raised.

"Yes? Is something wrong with me addressing him by his first name?"

Elrich stood there staring at me and blocking the door, mute.

"Elrich? Is something wrong?"

He finally snapped out of whatever stupor he was in and shook his head. "Uh, no. See you later," he said, and then he left.

I stood there in my office for a couple of minutes, trying to make sense of that exchange, and then I also left, joining Leland in his SUV.

"So, tell me again how you found this place?" I asked, eying my sketchy surroundings—dim lighting, and not the "creating ambiance" kind, but rather the "low bulb wattage because we ain't got no money" kind, tables with chairs that did not match the table or each other, worn laminated menus, and the yucky brownish booth we sat in definitely looked like it'd seen better days. As far as Chinese restaurants go, The Lucky Sun was not impressing me at all.

"I Googled hot pot and this was the first place that popped up," he answered nonchalantly.

"So, you've never eaten here?" I asked, inspecting the artwork of geishas and fountains that hung on the walls.

"Nope, but I had a taste for hot pot, so here we are."

I fixed my eyes on him to find his on me. "So, what exactly is hot pot? Some kind of spicy soup or something?"

He grinned as he shook his head. "You're close, but no. You see this thing right here?" he asked, pointing to what appeared to be a hot plate or stove surface element embedded in the center of our booth's table.

I nodded.

"It's like a hot plate. The controls are here at the end of the table."

My eyes shifted to what he was pointing to. "Okay…"

"So, they're gonna put this big stainless-steel bowl of soup base on the hot plate, and it'll boil. I'ma ask them to make one side mild and the other spicy, because it's actually not that spicy. They use this divider thing in the bowl and the soup base will have seasoning in it for each side. Once it starts boiling, we'll cook our food in it."

"What food?" I asked, with a slight frown.

"Well, it comes with a starter platter of stuff like enoki mushrooms, baby bok choy, shrimp, fish balls, sausages, tofu, probably a few more things. They provide us with little net things and ladles and chopsticks that we'll use to put the food in the base, let it cook, and then fish it out and eat it with rice or udon noodles. I prefer the noodles, but we'll have to cook them, too."

I leaned back in my seat across from him. "So, let me get this straight, we are paying these folks to cook our own food in their restaurant?"

He shrugged. "Well, yeah. I guess that's one way of looking at it."

"Leland Randall McClain, that is the whitest thing I have ever heard in my life."

He chuckled and rubbed his hand down his beard. I loved when he did that. "Naw, baby. It's actually fun. The food cooks real quick, too. I love hot pot. Been addicted to it since Ev introduced me to it years ago. I promise you it's good. I mean, you said you like Asian, right?"

"Mm-hmm, we'll see how good it is."

"Aye, we can add more stuff like pork, beef, extra shrimp. You wanna do that?"

"Yeah, may as well go for it, right?"

He gave me another smile as the server came and took our order which amounted to a ridiculous amount of food that I didn't think either of us would ever finish once it was placed all over the table.

The soup base started boiling almost as soon as they set it on the hot plate thing and turned it on, which shocked me. And as I slid my eyes up to our uncooked spread, I almost jumped out of my seat. "What the hell are those?" I asked.

"What?" Leland asked, holding a clump of bok choy over the boiling bowl.

"Those," I said, pointing to what I was referring to.

"Oh, those are the mushrooms I mentioned."

"Why do they look like stalks of grass? I don't know about this, Leland."

Grinning, he said, "It's gonna be good, baby. You'll see."

"Yeah, and can you turn those around. I feel like they're looking at me."

"You talking about the shrimp?" he asked, sounding completely confused. "This your first time seeing shrimp with the heads still on them or something?"

I shook my head, my eyes on the plate of shrimp. "No. I've seen that before. I just don't *like* seeing it."

"You scared of them?"

"N-no. They just…it's like I said; it feels like they're looking at me. It's just something about seeing them intact. I can't stand to look at a whole lobster, either. Creeps me the hell out."

He gave me a smirk, and I could tell he was trying not to laugh at me, "So, I guess I'ma have to peel them by myself, huh?"

"Hell, yeah! I ain't touching them sum-bitches!"

He burst into laughter.

"Stop laughing at me because I have a crustacean phobia. It's not funny!"

"A crust—wow, baby. Okay, I'm—woo, shit! That was funny. The look on your face? Damn! But I'ma stop laughing, though."

"You are such an asshole."

"But I'm *your* asshole."

"Whatever."

He slid out of the booth and scooted onto the bench I occupied, moving close to me and nuzzling my neck. "I'm sorry, baby. I was just playing."

I rolled my eyes. "Like I said, *whatever*."

He kissed my cheek and left my side, sliding back into his own seat and chuckling the entire time.

"So, did you enjoy lunch?" Leland asked, as we left The Lucky Sun with full bellies.

"What do you think? I'm about to pop! Everything was so good! Thanks for taking me there and letting me experience something new."

"See, I told you it was good. Even the shrimp, huh?"

"Fuck you," I muttered, smacking him on his arm.

He wrapped said arm around me and pulled me close to him as we approached his truck. "You so damn violent with your sexy ass."

I smiled. "You need to stop being mean to me."

"I ain't mean to you. Hey, I been meaning to ask you something."

"What?" I asked, as he opened the passenger door for me.

"You wanna come to my game in Mexico with me?"

I waited until he'd climbed behind the wheel before I said, "Mexico? What would I do?"

"Shit, go to the game, and after that, there's a break in my schedule so we can just hang out there and chill for a few days."

I thought for a second, and said, "Yeah, I think I'd like to go. I've never been out of the country."

"For real, baby?"

"Yeah."

"Well that's definitely about to change now that you're with me. And hey, make sure you pack some of them ho' clothes you got in that ho' closet."

"I thought I wasn't supposed to wear those clothes out in public anymore."

"The exception to that rule is when you're with me. You can wear them then, because I'll be present to fuck anybody up who looks at you."

"Wow."

"And some extra waist beads."

"Any more requests, Mr. McClain? Should I pack panties or just forgo them altogether?"

"Shit, since you taking requests...can we take a private jet and you just go naked, no luggage or anything?"

"Really, Le—" A knock on my window interrupted me, and when I turned to see who it was, my heart jumped into my throat.

I fumbled with the window control button for a few seconds and then just decided to open the door, snatching it open and jumping out onto the parking lot. I must've confused the hell out of Leland, because in seconds flat, he was standing beside me.

"I thought that was you! I had just parked my car when you walked out of there," Scotty, my son's best friend damn near since birth, said as he pulled me into a hug.

As I returned his hug, I could hear movement—Leland's crazy ass.

"Good to see you, Scotty!" I gushed, as I backed away from him a bit. "Hey, do you know Leland McClain?"

Scotty's eyes shifted to Leland and narrowed. He was Armand's ride or die friend, so that, of course, made Leland an enemy. They were so close; the only reason Scotty was in St. Louis instead of following Armand around the country was that his parents had made him stay in college. "I know *of* him," he replied.

"Well, let me introduce you two. Scotty Smith, this is Leland McClain. Leland, Scotty is one of Armand's closest friends."

Proffering Scotty his hand, Leland said, "Nice to meet you, man."

Scotty looked at his hand for a moment, and then smiled at me. "I gotta grab this food and head back to campus, Ms. Hampton. I'll tell Boogie I saw you."

*That's what I'm afraid of,* I thought, but managed to give him a weak smile as I said, "Okay."

As he drove me back to work, Leland asked, "You all right?"

I glanced at him and nodded. "Yeah, why?"

"Because I been talking to you for the last five minutes and you ain't said nothing."

"You have? I'm sorry. Guess I've just been in my head."

"You worried about what dude said about telling your son he saw you?"

I shook my head. "No, I'm not." Of course I was lying, but I wasn't about to go down that road with Leland. I loved my son, but I also loved Leland, and shit, I was trying to keep him now that I was fortunate enough to have him again, because he was truly good to me and I really believed he was good *for* me, too.

"You sure?"

Now he was beginning to irritate me by making me lie repeatedly, so I sighed, and said, "I'm good, Leland. Just don't feel like going back to work."

"Shit, then don't. Take off the rest of the day and come home with me."

I turned and looked at him, took in his handsome face, the thick hair that was in a huge Afro at that moment, and saw into him to that big heart of his that made me feel so special and loved, then I reached over and grasped his hand. "Okay."

# 25

# Kimberly

"What's up with you and Leland McClain?"

I adjusted the phone on my ear as Leland bent down and kissed my cheek before leaving for practice, gave him a smile and a little wave, and then answered my son's question. "What are you talking about?" I replied, although I was sure Scotty had already reported back to him, probably told him about Leland's arm being around me as we walked to his vehicle.

"I'm talking about you and him kicking it."

"Kicking it?"

"You was over at The Lucky Sun with him, right? Scotty said y'all looked real friendly."

"Yeah, we had lunch together. He's a nice guy. You'd know that if you took the time to get to know him."

"Naw, he's a thirsty nigga who's tryna get with you, Mama. That's what he is. He been sniffing in behind you since I made the team last year."

"You think every breathing man is sniffing in behind me. Son, your mama looks good, but not *that* good."

"Naw, I know what I know. Why you think I can't stand him? I caught him looking at your booty one time."

*Really?!* If my child only knew just how hard I was grinning at that moment. "Why didn't you tell me this before now? You had me wondering what was going on between you two."

"I didn't tell you because you're too nice to people. I didn't want you to get sucked into being all motherly with him because his folks are dead and then let him flip it on you and end up getting you in bed."

"Boogie, you need to stop. So, how've you been? Getting ready for your game tomorrow?"

"Uh-huh, and that's another thing. I heard you been going to a lot of Cyclones home games. What's up with that?"

"You heard?"

"Yeah, I got folks everywhere. I be knowing what's going on."

"So, it's a crime for me to support the home team?"

"Yeah, when you ain't been to none of my games."

"I did go to your game when you played here, Boogie. I can't follow you around the country. I have a job, you know?"

"You ain't never got to work and you'll still get paid and you know it."

"But I don't want to do that, son."

I could hear him sigh into the phone, then I heard a female voice say something and knew he was about to hang up. So I said, "Go ahead and take care of whatever whoever that is is talking about."

"Why you gotta say it like that?"

"Because you have a different 'friend' hanging around you every time I talk to you."

"Man...I gotta go. Love you, and stay away from Leland McClain, for real. Don't make me have to mess him up."

"Love you, too, son. Bye."

# Leland

This thing with Kim was going so well, I didn't know what to think. We were together as much as we could be with me working all the time. We had lunch together most days when I was in town and even went to the movies together a couple of times. We were deep in that regular, normal couple shit and I was loving it just as much as I was loving her. And my ass didn't even think I could fall in love, never really wanted to, but I also didn't think I'd ever be with Kim Hampton.

I spent Thanksgiving playing ball in New York while she stayed behind in St. Louis to celebrate with her grandmother, whom I hadn't met yet, and some of her other family members, including the mother she didn't get along with. From what she told me, she'd have been better off in New York with me. She talked to her son a couple of times a month, but he was just as busy as I was, too busy to try and micromanage her life. So as he'd always been, he really was a non-factor when it came to me and Kim unless she made him a factor, and she hadn't done that since we reconciled in Detroit.

I was honestly shocked that we hadn't hit the gossip blogs yet, but then again, I wasn't exactly LeBron or Steph. Shit, I wasn't even on Mike Conley's level of famous in the league. I was more like Tristan Thompson before he got with Khloe. And plus, my brother's fame pretty much overshadowed mine, not that I minded. I didn't want the kind of fame that required bodyguards and shit like that, anyway. I mean, there were stories about me with women, never Kim, but the thing is, the women were famous, super-famous like Honey Combs. They were all more famous than me, so the stories were really about them with me as the blogs' favorite co-star for some reason, despite the fact that all these chicks were my age and it was common knowledge that I didn't mess with women my age. That just goes to show you how inaccurate their information was. Kim was probably happy they were missing the true story, and me? I didn't care. I was just glad she stopped tripping about us being together in front of people. Otherwise, she wouldn't have been in this club in Mexico City on Christmas night, grinding on me to some Latin-electronic song. She was lit as hell and hadn't had a drop of liquor. She didn't seem to care about the fact that we were in that club with several of my teammates and their dates. While I nodded to the music, not really dancing all that hard, she spun around and backed up to me, rolling her ass on me and making me want to attack her right there on that dancefloor in front of everyone. Then she turned to face me, dropping into a squat and rubbing her face on my groin. My eyes shot around us, and yeah, half my damn team was staring at us with their mouths hanging open. So I reached for her, pulling her to her feet. She smiled up at me with low eyelids, slipping her arms around my neck and kissing me as she jumped on me, wrapping her legs around my waist and grinding against my now rock-hard dick. My baby was on fire! Here in this club, she was freer that I'd ever seen her be.

She had on some of her ho' gear—some little white shorts and a low-cut sparkly gold wife-beater shirt thing. Only I knew she had on blue waist beads, too. Man, I loved sliding my hands over them through her shirt. This woman, *my woman*, was beautiful, the finest thing in the club, hot as hell, and it just made me happy to see her have so much fun. It didn't hurt that Kendra had made the trip, too, and was out on the floor egging Kim on. We lost the game the night before, but you couldn't tell from the way we were all turnt all the way up in that club in Mexico City.

"I'ma suck you into a damn stroke when we get back to the room. Tyrone ain't ready for me," she said into my ear, then licked my earlobe.

"Damn, I love you," was my reply.

*****

"Leland," she moaned, her voice heavy with exhaustion. It'd been a long night, we'd danced until the club shut its doors, and the sun would be up again soon, but all that damn dancing and her teasing had me ready before we got in the suite good. So I had to get a taste of her before I went to sleep.

"Oooooo, Leland," she whimpered.

She had a mean grip on my head as she slid her pussy all over my damn mouth, riding my face as my tongue tried to keep up with her pace. She liked the way my mustache and beard scratched her down there, and I liked the way she moaned and wiggled and whined.

"Oh…oh…ohhhhhhhh!" she screamed, as she jerked and vibrated and then fell onto the bed on her back.

I climbed out of the bed and smiled down at her as I unfastened my pants with one hand and rubbed her pussy with the other. Then I buried my face between her legs again and felt her twitch from the flick of my tongue against her clit. "You taste like candy, baby. Best tasting pussy on Earth."

She whimpered her response as I let my tongue play with her clit, licking it then pulling it into my mouth and sucking on it until her whining became screaming, her body began to convulse again, and I could feel her walls squeeze around my fingers. Then I spread my body over hers and settled between her legs as I slid my tongue in her mouth, letting her taste herself. She kissed me like she hadn't kissed me in years, like she missed kissing me, and I kissed her with the same passion.

As our tongues collided, I slid inside the hottest, wettest, tightest pussy I had ever had the pleasure of experiencing, closing my eyes and mumbling, "This pussy right here! I will never get used to how good you feel."

In response, she raised up and clamped her mouth to my neck, sucking on it so hard that it actually hurt, but shit, I couldn't think about anything at that moment but what was between her legs and how it made me feel. I closed my eyes, rested on my elbows, and kept with a slow pace as I eased in and out of the woman I loved more than I loved my own damn self, would fuck up the world for her, would fight a damn lion for her.

"I love you so much, baby," I groaned, as she threw her head back and dug her nails into the flesh of my back. Her walls contracting around me told me that another orgasm had hit her.

Still, she managed to scream, "Ohhhhh, shit! I love you, toooooooooo!"

It wasn't long after that, that I got mine, shouting her name as I emptied inside her. Once I caught my breath, I fell on my back and pulled her on top of me. Sometimes we slept like that.

"I don't know why you like me laying on you like this. My big ass gotta be heavy."

"You ain't big; you're perfect."

"I'm knocking on a size eighteen's door, Leland. If I didn't work out and try to eat halfway right, I'd be big as a house!"

"I don't care. I love all of you. I love these thick thighs and this ass?" I grabbed a handful and squeezed. "You know I love this ass."

She laughed. "Yeah, you definitely love my ass."

I had to laugh at that, too. "And do I even need to mention my obsessive devotion to Little Kim?"

"Please don't."

"You're a hater."

"I sure am. I'm sick of you and Little Kim."

I chuckled as I rubbed my hand down her soft back. "Hey, I wanna ask you something."

"If it's about what I promised to do at the club, I'ma still do it. Just let me catch my breath. You wore me out, baby."

"Naw, you good, baby. That's not what I was gonna ask."

"Okay…"

"Uh, I need to tell you something first."

"You sound serious."

"This *is* serious."

"I'm kinda scared to hear what you've got to say now," she said, as she lifted her head and looked me in the eye.

"Don't be. Just some stuff I want you to know."

She kissed my chest and then laid her head on it again. "All right, tell me."

I lifted my eyes from her face to the ceiling. "I been in the NBA since I was nineteen, was a second-round pick, so I ain't never made Kobe money, but my brother, Everett, taught me how to manage it, set me up with some good accountants and lawyers, told me about investing it, mentored me about starting businesses and stuff, so now, I'm worth around sixty million, not counting my current contract with the Cyclones. They're paying me ninety million over the next five years, with bonuses if we win the championship. I own a house in LA, the condo in St. Louis, the nightclub in LA, got an endorsement deal with Frost Menswear and another one with Spartan Vitamin Water. I finally signed the deal with Derek Hill, so I am an official co-owner of HMH Films."

"HMH?" she asked.

"Hill, McClain, Higgs."

"Wow, baby! I'm so proud of you! That's wonderful!"

I smiled at her, then returned my attention to the ceiling. "Thank you. Um, where was I? Oh, I own like five cars, the SUV I drive in St. Louis, and four more parked at my house in LA. I—"

"Why does it feel like you're trying to convince me that you're a good catch when I already caught you?" Kim asked, interrupting me.

"Because I want you to know everything about me before you marry me. I want you to know I can take care of you, that it would be my pleasure to take care of you for the rest of our lives."

She slid off of me and sat up in the bed. "Are you proposing, Leland? You-you wanna get married?"

"Yeah, baby. I mean, I don't have a ring to put on your finger tonight, but I can fix that in the morning. Will you marry me?"

"I'm wondering if you're just doing this because you're drunk or if I'm hallucinating and none of this is really happening because *I'm* drunk."

"Neither one of us is drunk. We ain't drank shit, Kim."

"I meant, drunk off of sex."

"Kim, stop playing. I know what I'm saying, and you heard me correctly, baby."

"But we haven't even been together that long. It's only been like what? Six months? Not quite six months?"

"That's long enough for me to know I want to spend the rest of my life with you."

"You're being impulsive. First, you want a baby, and now you wanna marry me?"

"I thought we settled the baby thing."

"We did, but marriage? You haven't thought this through."

"Yes, I have. I've thought about this a lot."

"But...what if it doesn't last? What if it all falls apart?"

"It *will* last and it *won't* fall apart. And you know what? What difference does it make anyway? We've got *right now*. We have today, so let's live for that."

She fell silent and I can't lie, her reaction was fucking with my heart. Nothing was ever easy with Kim. She couldn't make decisions without torturing herself. And even when she did make a decision, it was usually in favor of what she thought other people—specifically, her son—would approve of, not what she really wanted. I knew it was best that I steered us in a different direction before she kicked my heart all the way into my ass by totally rejecting me, or at the very least, pissed me off by bringing our ages up again, so I said, "Just think about it. You ain't gotta answer tonight, okay? I just wanted you to know I want you to be my wife."

She looked over at me and nodded. "All right."

# 26

"What the fuck is going on?!"

I pulled the phone from my ear and closed my eyes. I knew my son cursed, had heard him do it several times before, but never, ever directed *at* me. He was pissed, had probably seen the same pictures I'd seen floating all over Instagram of me with my body wrapped around Leland in that club in Mexico. It hadn't taken long for the images to go viral. We were still in Mexico when they first started popping up on Twitter, and now, just under a week later, the gossip blogs were all over them and the story of Leland McClain and Armand Daniels' mom being an item—that's actually how they referred to me, like I had no other identity.

My first thought when I saw them was, *finally*. Finally, someone, probably someone from Leland's team or one of their dates, had exposed us. It was about time. Or at least I *thought* it was. I thought I was ready for Armand to know, but hearing the anger in his voice and knowing it was directed at me, I wasn't so sure. I knew I probably should've just been up front with him from the beginning, but I also knew the outcome would've been the same. Either way, he would be upset, but with it being revealed to the world at the same time he found out, there was a layer of embarrassment added to his rage.

Placing the phone back to my ear, I asked, "What?" as I rested an elbow on my desk and peered down at the papers littering it.

"You know what! You all over social media with Leland McClain in damn Mexico! At first, I thought maybe folks had it wrong. Some of the pictures were so grainy, I really couldn't tell if it was you for real. Then I saw that video of you grinding on him, and I knew it was you! What the fuck was that?!"

"First of all, you need to calm down and stop all this screaming, Armand."

"No, first of all, are you and him...are you and him together?"

"Yes." I said it. I couldn't believe I really said it.

Silence from my son.

"Hello?" I said.

"End it. End it today or I'ma kill him. I'm not playing, Mama."

"I can't."

"What you mean, you *can't*? I bet you *can*!"

"I can't because I love him and I *want* to be with him."

That's when the call ended, when he hung up on me, and I quickly dialed Leland's number. When he didn't answer, I started to panic, thinking that Armand was in town without me knowing and was making good on a threat I knew he was more than capable of carrying out. I had gathered my things and was headed...somewhere when Leland finally called me back.

I answered the phone with, "Hey, I just talked to Armand and he knows about us and—"

"He said he's gonna kill me. I know. Just got a call from him."

"He called you?! Is he here? Did he say he's here?"

I knew he had a game in New York that night, because although I didn't attend his games, I kept up with his schedule and watched him play on TV as often as I could. So he should've already traveled there in preparation for the game, but I wouldn't have put it past him to miss the game just to come here and wreak havoc.

"Naw, he's in New York. I saw something he posted on IG from there. He's pissed, though, was talking all kinds of shit to me. You gave him my number?"

"No! Of course not! Why would I do that?!"

"I wouldn't care if you did."

"But I didn't! I wouldn't!"

"Okay, okay. Baby, you need to calm the hell down. Where are you?"

"At work. Where else, Leland?" I was so on edge and I wanted to cry, but at the same time, felt an overwhelming sense of relief that the cat was finally out of the bag.

"I'll be there in a minute."

"Don't you have practice or a work-out or something? I don't want to interrupt your day. I just…" The tears came and I couldn't stop them. Hell, I didn't really want to stop them. I *needed* to let them fall.

Leland said something I couldn't make out over my own sobbing, and about ten minutes later, after I managed to halt the waterworks, there was a knock at my door. Since Peaches was off for some reason I couldn't even remember, I yelled, "Come in," without bothering to check myself in a mirror. I knew my eyes were swollen, but the only somebody I was expecting was Leland and he didn't care how I looked. Over the past months, he'd seen me at my best and my worst, and he still loved me.

But it wasn't Leland. It was Elrich. So I sighed and dropped my chin into my chest. "Um, Elrich? Can we discuss whatever it is you need to discuss later? I'm feeling a bit under the weather."

"I bet you are. Probably got the chicken pox from that child you've been screwing."

I closed my eyes and shook my head. "That's none of your business."

"It's everybody's business when you do it in this building. What the hell is wrong with you?!"

My head snapped up. "What are you talking about?"

"This!" he said, flinging something onto my desk. It was a still from a surveillance video, a still of me and Leland kissing in the front lobby of King's Dream the evening all that mess went down with Shemar and his mother—our first time together.

My eyes rose to meet his angry ones. "Where'd you get this?"

"I've been checking the surveillance footage from the lobby, trying to see if I can see the person who broke in, and I ran across this footage."

"Why would you be looking at footage this old, Elrich?"

"That's not the point. The point is, I saw it all, even when he picked you up and carried you in here, I guess. So *he's* why you wouldn't get back with me? Is he the one who said that shit to me on the phone?"

"Elrich, there wasn't any getting back with you when I was never with you in the first place, and you are acting real crazy stalkerish right now for us to have had a purely sexual relationship."

"I'm in love with you!"

I think he startled himself as much as he startled me, because after he shouted the words, he just stood there with his eyes on me, then his face became flushed and his gray eyes shifted to the floor.

"I-I'm sorry. I didn't know. Um…Elrich, I don't know what to say."

"Obviously, you're not going to say what I want you to say, that you love me, too," he nearly whispered, his eyes still on the floor.

"If I said that, it wouldn't be the truth."

"You love him?"

I closed my eyes and sighed. "Elrich—"

"God, I messed this up trying to reconcile with Adana. I had you and just gave you away."

"I take it you're that Eldridge dude, huh?"

*When did Leland get here and how did I not hear him come in?*

Opening my eyes, I saw a bewildered-looking Elrich standing beside a gigantic Leland who looked like he was three seconds from tearing the older and smaller man's head off, probably fueled by his earlier conversation with my son.

Elrich didn't respond, or maybe he was afraid to.

"Look, man…she ain't a damn puppy. You ain't never have her in the first place. If you did, she wouldn't be mine now, and since she's mine, you need to keep your damn distance before I *make* you keep your distance."

A second after Leland's threat filled the room, Elrich slipped out my office door in silence. Then my eyes met Leland's as I blinked back a new supply of tears.

"Get your shit and let's go before I have to kick some ass around here."

"But—"

"But nothing. This place won't fall apart without you, and if it does? Fuck it. Let's go, Kim."

So I grabbed my stuff and left.

# Leland

She was quiet, her eyes glued to the TV screen as the Heat battled the Knicks. Did I want to watch her son play after he called and threatened my life? *Hell*, no. But…he was her son, and she loved him, and I loved her for that. So I sat my ass on my sofa with her snuggled close to me and watched the game, just happy to have a free night with her. Happy to be with her, period, because even with all her crazy ways, the back and forth we went through in the beginning, and the existence of her crazy-ass son, I truly loved this woman.

*Commentator One: Armand Daniels is really struggling tonight.*

*Commentator Two: Well, Bill…I'm sure that has to do with the rumors that are spreading about his mother and his former teammate, Leland McClain. I'm sure that's affecting his concentration.*

*Commentator One: Dave, that might be it, but if he doesn't pull himself together, the Heat will be adding yet another loss to their already disappointing record.*

*Commentator Two: As the one player who usually puts up the most points, let's hope he's in better form during the second half of the game.*

I glanced at Kim to see her staring down at her phone. Then she looked at me and quickly turned her attention back to the TV.

"You got a call? Zabrina?" I asked.

"No, my mother. I talked to Zabrina earlier, when you left to pick up dinner."

"You gonna answer it?"

Shaking her head, she leaned forward and placed her phone on my new coffee table. "No. She won't have anything good to say to me."

"About us?"

"About anything. But yeah, I'm sure she's calling to convince me I'm ruining my life by being with you, not to mention she's close to Armand, so I'm sure she'll want to add something about how I'm hurting him, too."

"Do you think us being together is hurting him?"

She hesitated for a good minute, then looked over at me. "No. Armand doesn't get hurt. He just gets angry. It's all he knows—anger. And the only way he knows how to deal with it is through violence."

"Yeah, well, I ain't worried about him being violent towards me. I just wanna make sure you're good. I know this is hard for you, dealing with the fallout, and I'm sorry."

"You don't have any reason to apologize, Leland. I made this mess a long time ago. This is all on me."

"Don't do that, baby. Don't talk like that."

"But it's true. And I'm so sorry you have to be a part of this. I don't regret being with you or falling in love with you, but I do regret that you have to deal with this mess. I regret that my son is probably going to catch the first flight here as soon as the game is over and try to hurt you."

I turned and looked her in the eye. "I'm not some kid, Kim. As a matter of fact, I'm bigger than your son. I don't wanna kick his ass, but if he comes at me wrong, I definitely ain't gonna fold. But hopefully, he'll come, and me and him will just talk. Maybe he'll be done calmed down by the time he gets here and we can handle things like adults. Whatever goes down, we're gonna handle it together. Okay?"

She reached for me, wrapping her arms around me. "I love you so much."

As I held her in my arms and closed my eyes, I said, "I love you, too, baby."

# 27

## Kimberly

The day after the shit hit the fan progressed like any other day. Contrary to what I expected, Armand did not pop up in St. Louis the night before or early the next morning, so as per usual, I went to work, was thankful that Elrich kept his distance, talked to Leland on the phone, and went to the Cyclones home game later that evening. We would've ridden home together had we not arrived in separate vehicles. I wanted to be up under him so bad, I almost suggested leaving my car on the lot but decided against it. We made it to our building at virtually the same time and quickly decided to spend the night at his place. We usually stayed at my place because Leland said it felt homier than his, but with Armand sure to pop up at any moment, I wasn't comfortable staying there. No, he didn't have a key, but I didn't put it past him to kick my door in. I was sure he had no idea where Leland lived, or at least I hoped he didn't.

Leland wrapped his arm around me as we walked into the building. "I'm tired as shit, but I can't wait to get this victory pussy."

"Victory what?" I asked, trying not to laugh. Leland was a straight-up nut, but I loved that about him.

Leland nodded a greeting to the night security guard stationed in the lobby of the building then leaned in close to my ear, and said, "You heard me, and don't even try to pretend you don't wanna do it. Your ass stay ready, and here lately, you been on fire for real."

After we'd stepped into the elevator, I kissed him, then wiped my lipstick from his mouth with my thumb. "How can I help myself when I got a man with a big dick and a long tongue?"

"Shiiiid, that's what I'm saying."

I rolled my eyes and watched the numbers light up on the panel.

Once we reached his floor, I paused just outside the elevator doors. "Hey, I'ma run down to my place and grab my iPad and my phone charger."

"A'ight. Hurry up, because Tyrone is ready to get to work."

Shaking my head, I pressed the button on the elevator. "I bet he is."

Once I made it to my place, I unlocked the door and headed straight to my bedroom, guided by the light from the ensuite bathroom, the only light I'd left on. As I entered the bedroom, I jumped at the sight of a man sitting on the bench at the foot of my bed.

Armand.

I slapped my hand to my chest and closed my eyes as my heart galloped uncontrollably. "Boogie! You scared me! How did you get in here?!"

He blinked, angled his head to the left, and said, "With a key."

"A key? What key?"

"*My* key, Ma."

"You have a key to my place?"

"Yeah. I bought it. Why wouldn't I have a key?" he said, matter-of-factly.

"Why didn't you tell me you had a key?"

"Where's McClain?" he asked, ignoring my question.

"Not here."

"I can see that."

I just stood there and stared at him. I didn't know what else to say. I definitely wasn't going to tell him where Leland was.

"You know what? It don't matter where he is," Armand said, then stood and crossed my bedroom, opening my closet door.

"What are you doing?" I asked.

Ignoring me, he rummaged in my closet, finally turning around holding a suitcase. "Pack your stuff. You're leaving with me."

"What?"

"You're leaving with me. Tonight. You're moving back to Florida where I can watch you. I'll have someone put your furniture in storage and close this place up later." He held the suitcase out to me. "Here. I never should've let you leave Florida in the first place."

I looked at the suitcase then raised my eyes to my son's face. "*Let* me? I'm not moving anywhere, Armand."

"Yes, you are. *Here.*" He shoved the suitcase at me again.

Shaking my head, I said, "No, Armand, I'm not. I'm not going *anywhere.*"

"Either you leave with me or I kill Leland McClain. It's up to you. You say you love him? Then you better pack and come on." He sounded so cool, calm, and lethal.

"You're gonna kill him and go to prison? Really?"

"You wanna find out?"

I opened my mouth to try and reason with him but shut it when I heard my front door open and close. A second or two later, Leland's voice drifted from the front of my condo to my bedroom, "Aye, what's taking you so long? The only excuse I'm accepting is that you're in your bed, butt-ass-naked, on your knees, ass in the air, pussy facing the door so I can climb up in that motherfucker and squat behind you, and me and Tyrone gon' hit it froggy style."

Squeezing my eyes shut so I wouldn't have to see the rage in Armand's, I said, "Um, Leland...my—"

"Nuh-uh, I ain't tryna hear it. You better be ready, because after I froggy-style you, I'ma flip your sexy ass over and eat the shit out of your taco, stick my tongue all the way in your pussy. Then I'ma have you put your feet on my chest and butterfly them thick thighs open so I can fuck you some more until you scream."

Opening my eyes, I could see my son's nostrils flare, saw the vein pulsing in his neck, watched as he clenched his fists. Panicked, I moved toward the bedroom door, hoping to stop what I knew was about to be a horrible situation, and had managed to call Leland's name again just as he made it to the door, a confused expression on his face. Not another word left my mouth before I felt my son yank me back into the room with such force that I landed on the floor.

# Leland

That nigga was fast, but I'm the one they call Fastlane, so I ducked before his fist connected with my face. When he came at me again, I ducked again.

"Daniels, calm the fuck down! I ain't tryna fight you!" I yelled.

"Motherfucker, you ain't fucking shit here! And who is Tyrone?! You gang-banging my mama?!" he shrieked, voice on soprano level. His eyes were wild as hell. I mean, yeah, what I said would upset any son, but shit, I thought we were alone.

"Man, I wouldn't have said that shit if I'd known you were here. That was for her, not you."

He came at me again, and I dodged him again.

"Daniels, shit! I'm not gonna fight you! I'll talk; we can talk, but we ain't fighting!"

"You're right. Ain't gon' be no fighting. I'ma just kill your ass!"

"First of all, I ain't no damn punk. I *can* fight. I'd just prefer not to because I respect your mother."

"Respect?! You call that shit you just said respect?!"

I sighed. "That was…she's my woman. We play around like that. How you talk to your woman?" We did play like that, but I definitely intended to do all the stuff I described. On my mama, I did.

"Your *woman*? What the fuck made you think you could get with my mama? You must be out your damn mind to think I'ma let this ride!"

"It's not about what you're gonna let happen, man. She's your mother, but she's also a grown woman, and we love each other. I wasn't thinking about you when I got with her. I was thinking that I liked her."

He shook his head. "You—I see what you're trying to do. You're trying to take my mama from me on some petty shit. Well, I'm 'bout to end that right now. She's leaving with me. Tonight. You gonna have to find you another victim."

"Naw, she staying with me, where she belongs."

"Where she belongs? Where she belongs?! Motherfucker, that's my mama you're talking about! My *mama!* She ain't shit to you!"

"She's *everything* to me! She's my wife!" I said, slapping my chest with my hand.

His face went pale so quick, I almost felt sorry for his crazy ass. "You're lying. You better be lying," he said, as he stepped backward a bit.

"Ask her If I'm lying. We're married; right, baby?"

# 28

# Leland

*One week earlier…*

I felt her shaking me but was so deep in sleep that I couldn't open my eyes, and instead, groaned and turned my back to her. It felt like I'd only been asleep for ten minutes, and I was feeling the after-effects of playing a hard game and then backing it up with hours of clubbing and sex. My whole body ached, my head pounded, and my eyelids were glued together. But I knew the headache had more to do with her reaction to my proposal than any physical exertion.

"Leland, wake up," she said, voice loud, clear. It sounded like she'd gotten her rest. I was jealous.

"Let me sleep, baby. I'm tireder than a motherfucker," I mumbled.

"But our flight leaves in a couple of hours."

That made my eyelids come unglued. "Flight? We're here for two more days."

"No, we're leaving for Vegas in two hours. You gotta get up."

I flipped over and stared at her, fully dressed, make-up on her face. She looked serious. No, she looked determined as hell, like a woman on a mission. "You changed our flights?"

She shook her head. "I got us new tickets."

"Why? I mean, I love Vegas, but why?"

"Because we're getting married today. I think we could do it here in Mexico, but I wanna do it in the states to be sure it's legit. Not that it wouldn't be legit if we did it here, but—"

I sat up in the bed, dragging my hand down my face and stretching my eyes to be sure I was really awake and hearing what I was hearing. "You wanna get married in Vegas?"

She nodded. "Yeah."

"But I thought—last night you said—"

"I know what I said, and it had more to do with my fears than anything, my fears and the fact that I still don't trust myself to make the right decisions sometimes. Dre, the ex who tried to choke me to death? We were engaged once. I agreed to marry him after he had kicked my ass a couple of times because I was just that damn stupid."

"Baby—"

She squeezed her eyes shut and shook her head. "No, let me finish."

I gave her a nod. "Okay, baby."

She sighed and adjusted her body where she was sitting on the bed, folding her hands in her lap. "I've made some really dumb decisions, done things I deeply regret, but even though I might have given you a hard time and put a lot of restrictions on us being together, I know choosing to be with you was not a dumb decision. I don't regret a single moment I've spent with you. The first good decision I made in my life was deciding to have Armand even though I was young and afraid and in a horrible relationship with his father. The second good decision I made was deciding to give us a chance. I love you, and although I'm scared and nervous, I'm not unsure. I know marrying you is the right thing to do.

"I called you impulsive last night, but after lying in this bed and thinking about it, I realized it's not impulsiveness; it's that sense of freedom you have that's just foreign to me. If you want something, you go for it. If you want to do something, you do it. You trust yourself to do what's right for you, and because I know you love me like no other man ever has, I trust you to do what's right for me. So, yes, I want to marry you."

I left the bed, walked around to her side, and reached for her hand, pulling her to her feet. Then I stared down at her and closed my eyes real tight, because my ass was about to cry. But I didn't. Instead, I grabbed the back of her head, and kissed her for so long, I was sure both of us almost lost consciousness. Then I held her beautiful face in my hands, and said, "I wish there was some way I could tell you how much I love you. I wish I could show you how deep in my soul you live. I wish I could make you see how much better my world is with you in it. I know I can't do all that in a way that you'll really get it, but I'ma try. I'ma spend the rest of my life trying."

She smiled up at me. "I'm gonna hold you to that."

I kissed her again, just a peck this time, but even that made my heart thump in my chest. When I said I loved her, I meant that in the realest way. What I felt for her would last until I took my last breath. I knew that as sure as I knew my name.

"I'm good with Vegas, real good with us getting married today, but I still ain't got a ring. When I brought it up last night, I didn't mean we had to do it now. I was thinking we could have a wedding and your son could walk you down the aisle and stuff like that."

She wrapped her arms around me and leaned against me. "I don't need that, and let's face it, it might take years for my son to accept us being together. I don't want to wait that long. I want to be your wife. I want to start our life together, our forever, today."

I squeezed her to me and kissed the top of her head. "I'm so glad I found you."

"I'm glad you found me, too."

We flew to Vegas that afternoon, and around eight that evening, a James Brown impersonator pronounced us a funky husband and wife, and then I took my baby to our expensive-ass Las Vegas suite and consummated the shit out of our marriage.

# 29

# Leland

*Now...*

She didn't answer me, and for a moment, I started to wonder if she
was back on that secret shit again, but that didn't make sense after
the show she put on in Mexico. Hell, him knowing we were married
would probably make the whole situation better.

Maybe.

Then I noticed him. He'd turned his back to me so that he faced
Kim as he waited for her response, too, but his hands were on his
head, fingers laced together as if he was trying to understand what he
was looking at, as if something was wrong, or he'd done something
he shouldn't have.

"Kim?" I said.

Nothing. Complete silence.

Daniels didn't move, just stood there like that with his hands on
his head. And then something hit me. The whole time we were
arguing, she hadn't said a word. Not one single word, and knowing
her like I knew her, that was strange. No way she'd let us go at it that
long without at least trying to intervene or get a word in. She loved
both of us. That, I knew. She didn't want us to fight.

"Daniels," I said, trying to get his attention as my heart tripled in
rate. Something was wrong. Something was very wrong.

He still just stood there. Didn't reply, didn't move, didn't do a
damn thing, and that pissed me off, because now I *knew* something

was wrong with her and his ass wasn't doing anything about it. So I shoved past him to find her on the floor of her bedroom, lying in front of her dresser, unconscious with blood on the beige carpet next to her head. It looked like she'd hit her head on something, probably the dresser. As I fell to the floor beside her, a flash of Daniels snatching her out of the doorway and shoving her somewhere popped into my head. I didn't know if I should move her or if it would hurt her for me to move her. I was a damn basketball player, not a fucking doctor. All I knew was something needed to happen and that she needed help and that Daniels did this shit to her and that if I lost her, I was going to kill his ass, stepson or not.

"Call nine-one-one!" I shouted at his frozen ass.

"I-I didn't mean to hurt her. I never mean to hurt her. It just…it happens. Is she okay?"

I looked up at him, and screamed, "I don't know! Call nine-one-one! Now, man! She's pregnant!"

That snapped his ass out of that stupor. He stepped back a little, looked down at his mother, and mumbled, "Pregnant?"

I turned to Kim, placed my hand on her cheek, and whispered, "You're gonna be okay. You *gotta* be okay. Everything's gonna be okay."

Seeing that he still hadn't moved a muscle or pulled out a phone, I hopped up, dug my phone out of my pocket, and dialed nine-one-one myself. While I was on the phone with them, I watched him stumble backward through the doorway and then run out of the apartment.

# Kimberly

I awakened keenly aware that I was in the hospital. Specifically, the emergency room. I knew the smell of them, was familiar with the look of them, but was most acquainted with how they made me feel—ashamed, ashamed of how I got there. Embarrassed that Malcolm had hit me so hard, I couldn't stop my nose from bleeding, or that Shawn had given me a concussion, or that Dre choking me had caused my tongue to swell up...or that Armand had broken my arm. I hated it, hated the pain and the shame and the pitied looks from some nurses, the disappointed looks from others because of my repeat visits and refusal to name my assailant. But since most visits were as a result of my own child's uncontrollable rage, how could I? What mother would tell on her son, especially when what he'd become was her fault? I'd hit my head, but I remembered. I remembered the all-too-familiar rage I saw coursing through him before he snatched me out of that doorway. I remembered my head connecting with the dresser, and now I was here. In the emergency room.

Again.

I felt one huge, warm hand squeeze mine and another resting on my stomach, redirected my sight to my left, and my eyes met his—dark, full of concern and more love than I'd ever thought it was possible for eyes to hold.

Leland.

"How do you feel?" he asked.

I lay there trying to decide how I felt. Sad, ashamed, hurt, but at the same time, adored in his presence. Since that was all so contradictory and confusing, I asked, "How long have I been here?"

"A couple of hours. You got a concussion."

"Again?" I said dryly, giving him a smile he didn't return.

"Kim—"

"The baby?"

"The baby's fine."

I blew out a breath as I let my hand rest on my stomach. "Is Armand here, too?"

He shook his head. "No, he took off before the ambulance made it to your place."

I nodded. "Yeah, he can't handle stuff like this, even when he's the reason behind it."

"Uh…Kim, I know you probably don't want to talk about this, but he…your son said some stuff that made it sound like this isn't the first time he's hurt you."

I sighed, blinked back tears, and told myself that if I just went ahead and told him, I wouldn't have to worry about it. It would be done, finally out in the open. A secret I'd held since Armand was a boy would no longer be a burden I bore alone.

"Armand was twelve or thirteen when he pulled Dre off me and beat him up. By then, he was taller and bigger than me, and after that, his anger issues became more evident. Remember, I said our roles were all muddled? He was my protector, couldn't stand the idea of anyone hurting me. And I came to depend on that. The problem was, all that he had witnessed made it hard for him to cope with things. His anger? He just couldn't control it, and more often than not, I received the worst of it. He never *meant* to hurt me; it was more like I ended up being hurt because there was no one else there. He'd shove me, but he was so strong, I'd fall into or against something and get hurt, like what happened tonight. Or he'd twist my arm while trying to get me out of his way and break it. Stuff like that.

"Seems like I was always going to the ER for something. I went so much, the nurses begged me to report my partner. *My partner.*" I shook my head. "I never told them it was my son. I couldn't tell them that. He had a bright future in basketball. Everyone said so. If I told on him, it could ruin him."

Leland squeezed my hand tighter in his. "Did you ever…why didn't you get him some help? Or did you? Did he get counseling or something?"

"I tried. I mean, I brought it up, but that made him even angrier, so I left it alone, learned how to stay out of his way when he had his episodes, and by the time he went to college, things were better. Today is the first time anything like this has happened in years, because I learned how not to trigger him, but this? Us? That's a huge trigger for him. He doesn't like to feel like a situation is out of his control."

"He said you were leaving with him."

"That's what he wants, but I told him no."

"I told him we're married and about the baby."

I shrugged as I reached up to rub the back of my throbbing head. "He needed to know. I just wish I'd been the one to tell him. I wish I'd told him about…everything. Maybe that would've softened the blow."

"I don't think anything could've softened the blow for him if he likes to have control over you and your life, and from what I can see, he does. So, is this why you were afraid for him to know about us, why you wanted us to be a secret? You were afraid he'd hurt you?"

I shook my head. "I was more afraid of the consequences of someone finding out if he hurt me. Something like this could end his career, and that would kill him."

Leland stared at me, had this look on his face like he wanted to respond to that but wasn't sure if he should.

"I know that sounds crazy, but first and foremost, I'm his mother. I know it's wrong for him to hurt me, but I still want to protect him. And you know he didn't mean to hurt me tonight, right? That's how it usually goes. He loses control and I get hurt. It's rarely intentional."

"I understand all that. I really do. But he won't be hurting you again. I guarantee that, Kim, and he damn sure won't be hurting my baby."

I nodded, knowing there was no sense in arguing with him and believing he would walk through hell to protect me and our child. "Did you call the police?"

"No, but I should've. Hell, the nurses have been looking at me sideways like I did this to you."

I frowned. "What?! Did you tell them that's not true?"

"Yeah, I lied, told them I came home and found you like this, but they'll still want to talk to you."

"I'll tell them I was feeling light-headed and fell. I'm pregnant, so it's plausible."

"You really need to be truthful, baby. I think maybe part of the problem with your son is he hasn't had to deal with the consequences of his actions because you feel so guilty about everything. But baby, you don't deserve to be hurt by him or anyone else."

I closed my eyes and nodded. "I know."

"Hey, I'm here no matter what. I just want what's best for you, okay?"

I finally let my tears fall as I said, "Okay."

*****

Leland had a meeting about some restaurant he was considering buying the next morning, but I had to make him leave me. He wanted to stay, to watch me, make sure I was okay, and it took repeated reassurances that there was nothing he could do for me to convince him to leave. After all, I was well-versed in concussions and knew what to do—rest and take a Tylenol if I needed to, but I probably wouldn't, because I hated taking medicine when I was pregnant.

Pregnant.

I couldn't believe I agreed to have his baby, but I wanted to, and from the moment he asked, could think of nothing else but finally having a child whose father had some common sense. I kind of obsessed about it until I told him I would do it right before Thanksgiving when he was getting ready to leave for New York. He damn near crushed me to death after hearing the news, and I stopped taking the pill the next day. His young-ass sperm evidently hit the target a week later. I didn't realize I was pregnant until right before we left for Mexico which was when I told Leland, and now, I was a little more than five weeks along, another reason he didn't want to leave me. But I reminded him that this wasn't my first journey down that path, either, and reassured him that Armand wouldn't be coming around anytime soon. Like I said, he couldn't deal with stuff like this.

Finally, he left, giving me explicit instructions not to go to work. Hell, I couldn't even if I wanted to with the way I was feeling.

Around eight that morning, shortly after he'd left, I called King's Dream, plugged in Peaches' extension, and after her usual lackluster, "King's Dream Community Center, Peaches speaking," I said, "Good morning, Peaches. This is Ms. Kim."

"Oh, good morning," she said stiffly. Peaches was...Peaches, so I didn't let the tone of her voice bother me.

"Hey, I won't be in today. I had a little accident last night and—"

"Elrich needs to talk to you. Hold on."

I frowned and muttered to myself, "Okay..."

The next voice I heard was Elrich's. "Ms. Hampton?"

Since when did he start addressing me like that? "Um, Elrich? Is something going on?"

"You could say that. Mr. Daniels asked me to let you know you've been terminated. Effective immediately. Peaches will pack your office up, and you can come by anytime to pick your personal items up. Do you have anything in the break room we need to collect for you?"

"Um, excuse me? What did you just say?"

"You've been terminated."

"My son *fired* me?"

"Yes. Effective immediately." He sounded like he was really enjoying this.

*I should've never booty-called his ass. Ever.*

"I heard that part, Elrich! What I don't get is why? You know what? I'll just call him." I hung up before Elrich could reply.

I wasn't sure if Armand would answer his phone. He could've still been dodging facing knocking me out or just plain busy, but after a couple of rings, I heard his, "Hello?"

"You fired me?" was how I greeted him.

"Yep. Promoted Elrich to director."

"On what grounds? Because I married Leland McClain?!"

"No, because you screwed him in the building. That's gross misconduct. And don't try to deny it. Elrich showed me the footage of y'all kissing and him carrying you to your office. Doesn't take a genius to know what happened next."

I closed my eyes and rested my head on the headboard of Leland's bed. Elrich was really a rejected piece of work. "Armand, don't do this."

"*You* did it. Oh, and I had the locks changed at your place. Didn't figure you needed it anymore since you're married now."

"What?! But my things are in there!"

"Your *husband* can buy you some more things. But if you change your mind and leave him, come to Miami, I'll take care of you."

"I can't believe you're doing this!"

"I can't believe you married him!"

"I married him because we love each other and he is the only man besides my daddy who never put his hands on me!"

"So you're throwing stuff in my face now?!"

"No, I'm just stating facts! You gave me a concussion and instead of checking on me or apologizing, you fire me and kick me out of my home?!"

"That was an accident and you know it!"

"But are you not concerned about how I'm doing!? I'm pregnant!"

"You must be okay if you're on this phone yelling at me, and I don't care about that baby! You ain't got no business getting pregnant by him anyway!"

"Boogie! What's wrong with you?! You're acting like a man I dumped instead of my son!"

"Ain't nothing wrong with me but the fact that you won't do what I tell you. Maybe now you'll see I'm not playing! Maybe you'll leave him alone before he hurts you!"

"The only person hurting me is you!"

His response was to hang up on me.

A few seconds later, my mother's number popped up on my phone. I ignored her call and slid down in the bed. I didn't cry, couldn't cry. I just lay there with my eyes on the ceiling.

When Leland made it home and saw me lying in bed in a ball, he climbed in with me and asked, "You and the baby okay?"

I nodded.

"You talked to your son?"

I nodded again.

"You wanna talk about it?"

I shook my head.

He reached for me and I shook my head again. "I just need to be alone," I said.

"No, you don't. You need me to hold you. Just…let me hold you, baby."

When he pulled me into his arms, I didn't resist him. Instead, I closed my eyes and leaned into him, letting him rock me to sleep.

# 30

# Leland

After I convinced her to get out of bed that afternoon and eat the
pizza I'd ordered, she finally told me about her conversation with
Daniels and all the shit he'd done. To be honest, I was relieved. He'd
just taken himself out of the picture in a major way and made room
for me to do what I'd been wanting to do all along—take care of her.

Of course she was upset about the situation, as hurt as any mother
would be, but she was also pissed that he thought taking things away
from her—her job, her home…hell, the nigga even had her car
towed out of the condo parking lot—would make her fall in line like
a kid, like he was her damn savior. I mean, if I hadn't thought to
grab her cell phone and her purse when the ambulance came, she
wouldn't have nothing but the clothes on her back and the few items
she'd left at my place. What kind of shit is that? I guess the
motherfucker thought I was broke or wouldn't take care of her. Well,
he had me fucked all the way up. The plan was for her to move her
stuff into my place anyway since we were married, but Daniels
struck before we had time to do it. It didn't matter. She'd get to
refurnish my condo if she wanted, and then I'd let her pick us a
house in St. Louis and in Houston and wherever else she wanted. I
had been wanting to buy her a car damn near since the first time I
touched her, already had one picked out. And she could max out all
my credit cards to fill up my closet. Nothing was too much for her. I
even told her I'd fund a foundation that she could run, her *own*
foundation, and thanks to her son, I didn't have to worry about her

refusing my gifts or fussing about me buying them anymore.

After we ate, I ran her some bath water, helped her climb in, and was planning to bathe her into some gentle sex—because I wasn't trying to hurt my baby. No more pussy smacking until my little one was out of there—when my phone started ringing and wouldn't stop. I sighed and told her I'd be right back. I would've let it ring, but it was always in the back of my mind that something could be going on with Aunt Ever, since she wasn't getting any younger and was non-compliant like a motherfucker when it came to handling her high blood pressure. Turned out, it was Kat, but that didn't ease my mind with the way her marriage was going.

I grabbed my phone from where I'd left it in the living room and sat on the couch as I answered it. "Yo!"

"The hell is going on?! You're married?!"

With my eyes stretched wide, I replied, "Damn, can you stop yelling?"

"Can you answer me, Leland Randall?!"

"Okay, *Juanita*. If you don't sound like Mama right now…"

"Leland!"

"Yeah, I'm married!"

"And she's pregnant?!"

What the fuck? "Wait a minute, how you find all this out?"

"No, the question is: why'd you keep this from me? Me?!"

"I was gonna tell you. We were gonna tell everyone…later."

"What kind of shit is that? I got why she wanted to keep things from her insane-ass son, but now she's making you hide stuff from your own family? I don't like this and I'm beginning not to like *her*!"

"Hold up a minute, now! She ain't never make me do shit! You know me better than that! I do what the fuck I want when I want!"

"Then why didn't you tell me?!"

"Dang, Kit-Kat! Look, I ain't even bought her a ring yet. It was my idea to wait to tell folks until after she had a ring. She didn't make the decision to keep it secret."

"What about the baby? Why didn't you tell me she was

pregnant?!'"

"I don't know. It's early. She just wanted to wait."

"Leland—"

"Kat, there is no anti-McClain conspiracy. It's just that everything happened fast. We ain't really used to none of this our self yet."

"You should've at least told me and Ev and the twins! Ev is hella pissed at you right now! You know he thinks he's your daddy!"

I sighed. "I know he's mad, gotta be. I'll talk to him, try to explain."

"You better."

"Yeah...so now you wanna tell me where you got your information?" I was sure Daniels wasn't spreading the news, so how did she know?

"It's all over social media. There's even a picture of y'all leaving the hospital. You can see the bandage on her head. What happened to her?"

"A picture?! Look, let me call you back." I didn't have time to explain what happened to her and perpetuate the lie Kim told the hospital about her injury.

"Okay—hey, can I ask you something?"

Shit, she was not going to let this go. "What?"

"Are you happy? Are you happy with her? Are you happy about the baby?"

"I'm very happy with her. I love her, Kat. And the baby was planned, so yeah, I'm happy about that, too."

"Good. If you're happy, then I'm happy for you, because you deserve to get what you want. You deserve your own family even though you used to swear you didn't want a wife and kids."

"I honestly thought I didn't, sis."

"But she changed all that, huh?"

"Yeah, she did."

"Well, I just hate that my family is falling apart at the same time."

"Y'all aren't gonna work things out?"

"No. I should've left years ago. I've wasted enough time trying to make something work that he doesn't care about—sixteen years. I gotta move on and try to make a better life for myself."

"You could always come here, make a fresh start. You can run your business from anywhere, and I could hire you to do something. Maybe you could be my assistant since Aunt Ever seems to think I need one, and honestly, I think so, too, with my career and all the business stuff I'm dealing with."

She chuckled into the phone. "Imagine that, me running your life."

I had to laugh at that, too. "Like you been tryna do for years."

"Yeah. Well, let me think about it."

"A'ight. I'll hit you back later."

"Okay."

After we hung up, I went to Instagram to see what she was talking about, and yeah, the news about us was all over the place. According to *Tea Steepers*, a hospital source said Kim came in for treatment after she suffered an accident at home. The source also said I was with her and had informed them that she was my wife and that she was pregnant. This was all true, so that meant some nurse or something had violated our privacy in a major way.

The photos that were posted were of us walking out of the hospital, getting in my truck on the hospital parking lot, and driving away. *Tea Steepers* posted one of them side by side with a picture of Kim and Armand, providing proof of my "mystery wife's" identity. My last IG post—a pic of me and Polo clowning around after a game—was full of comments either congratulating me on my new marriage and baby or congratulating me for getting the ultimate revenge on Daniels. Kim's account was private, so I didn't see too much activity on her posts, but I could imagine she had a million new follow requests.

I tapped out of the app, went and checked on Kim, who was still soaking in the tub, and then headed back to the living room to call my oldest brother and get that cursing over with. I'd call the twins and Aunt Ever later. I was pissed at the fact that the news was circulating without our consent, but glad everything was out in the open. We were finally free to be together on every level. The world knew I loved this woman, and there wasn't anything better than that.

# Kimberly

I was so proud of Zabrina, I thought I would explode! Well, either it was pride or the ten pounds I had gained two months into this pregnancy since Leland was under the impression that me going to my exercise class would hurt the baby. I wasn't showing, but my hips were getting embarrassingly wide, much to his delight. Anyway, Zabrina's six-week residency at Plush had become a full-time gig, and Leland and I were there to watch her perform and help her celebrate. After all that mess with Boogie, I needed this night. I needed to have fun.

Leland bought half the tables in the club so anyone else Zabrina wanted to invite to celebrate with her could, and since Zabrina wasn't quite the black sheep I was, it seemed she'd invited the whole damn family. Even my granny was there, a couple of tables over from where me, Leland, Zabrina, and her man sat.

"Come on, let's do another one," Leland said, wrapping his arm around my shoulders.

"You know what? I'm about tired of all these pictures," I protested.

"It's dark in here so the other ones weren't that good. I'ma use the flash this time."

"It's dark in here because we're in a nightclub, Leland."

"I know. Smile."

"Leland…"

"Do it for the 'Gram, baby."

I rolled my eyes and then leaned in close to Leland and smiled into the camera of his phone.

"Perfect! I'm about to post it now," he said.

I rolled my eyes again.

Leland chuckled and kissed my cheek. "Stop pouting."

"Girl, I cannot get over these rings. Damn, Mrs. McClain!" Zabrina shrieked, as she grabbed my hand and held it up to her face to get a closer look at the ridiculous diamond and platinum wedding set Leland bought me. "You walking 'round wearing these without a bodyguard?"

"Shiiid, who gon' fuck with her on my watch?" Leland asked.

"Damn, my bad," Zabrina said, giving me a look that said his words had turned her on as much as they had me. "So, y'all picked out any baby names yet?"

"Yeah, Leland Jr. and Lelandria," Leland said.

"I done told you *hell no* to naming my daughter that," I replied.

"Come on, baby. You already said we could only have one. Let me name it."

I leaned in, placed my hand on his hard thigh, and kissed his cheek. "Double hell no."

"You know what?"

"What?"

He answered me by grabbing the back of my head and sticking his tongue down my throat. For a second there, I forgot where we were. I was damn near in his lap when I heard, "Ain't that how you got pregnant in the first place?"

My mother.

I had hoped her miserable ass wouldn't show up, but there she was.

I broke away from Leland and sighed, looked around the table to see that Garner was gone—probably to the bar since I swear he was a borderline alcoholic, but he was good to Z, so whatever—and that Zabrina was gathering her purse. She didn't like my mother any more than I did.

"I got pregnant because I was *trying* to get pregnant," I said, my eyes narrowed at her.

"Um…hey, Aunt Diana!" Zabrina cut in. "Well, let me head on back to my dressing room to get ready. See y'all later."

I glared at her retreating back before returning my attention to my mother. Zabrina's mom, Lima, was a free spirit who couldn't sit still long enough to raise Zabrina, let alone terrorize her like her sister, my mom, did me. That's why Zabrina spent so much time at my grandmother's house back in the day. As a kid, I used to wish we could trade mothers. Hell, sometimes I wished I was a damn orphan.

As my chubby mother fell into Zabrina's abandoned seat with a grunt, she fixed her judgmental-ass eyes on me. "Kimberly, you gonna introduce me to this man you snuck off and married or what?"

I really despised her. Like, really.

"Leland, this is my mother, Diana. Mom, this is Leland," I mumbled, my eyes on the empty stage just a few feet in front of us.

I felt Leland lean forward. "Where?" he asked.

I turned to face him. "Huh?"

"Where's your mom, because I know this ain't her," he declared, his eyes wide as he stared at my mother.

She giggled, covering her mouth with her hand.

My. Mother. Giggled.

The hell?

"I *am* her mother!" she said, in this light voice I'd never heard her use before. What in the entire world was happening?

"No, ma'am. I don't believe that! I was just about to ask Kim why she didn't tell me she had a sister!"

This woman giggled *again* and batted her eyelashes coyly. "I really *am* her mother! She has a brother. No sisters."

"For real?!" He snaked his right arm around my shoulder and extended his left hand in front of me to my mom. When she took his hand, he leaned forward and kissed hers. "So glad I had this night off so I could meet you. Things with me and your daughter moved so fast, we haven't gotten around to meeting everyone in our families." That was a lie because I'd met his whole family in Texas, but I knew he was just trying to help me and I loved him for that.

"Oh, that's okay!"

Really? After all the voicemails she'd left cursing me out, telling me how I was further fucking my life up by marrying Leland and that he was going to first kick my ass all over the United States and then dump me *and* my baby, it was okay? After all the texts she'd sent asking me how I could betray Armand like this, it was okay? It was okay even after she told me I should call and apologize to my son who gave me an accidental concussion, fired me, locked me out of my home, and took my car?

Wow.

"I'm glad you came out tonight, Miss—hey, would you mind if I called you mom? I lost my mom when I was young and it'd be nice to be able to use that word again," Leland said.

With a big-ass grin on her face, my mother replied, "Noooo, I don't mind!"

Leland was laying it on thick as hell, and she was eating it all the way up.

Some song I barely paid attention to came on, and Leland asked, "Mom, would you like to dance?"

Her eyes were big as hell when she said, "Oh, I haven't danced in years. I just work and sleep."

Leland stood his big sexy ass up—for the first time ever, I was getting to see him in a whole suit—and walked around to my mother. "Well, I'm about to change that." He offered her a gigantic hand which she quickly took, and then she followed him the few inches to the dance floor that was partially covered with tables for Zabrina's impending show. I watched as my mom, in what looked like a funeral-ready black skirt suit, stepped with my towering husband in time to what I now recognized as Johnny Gill's *This One's for Me and You*. I loved how Plush kept the music grown and sexy.

"Gone, Di!" my feisty grandmother shouted, egging my mother on. The next thing I knew, she was out of her seat, following Zavier, Zabrina's brother, to the dance floor, and soon, the tiny space was full of my family members including my cousin Shelby, who'd been giving me the stink eye all evening because I actually *was* with

Leland after I'd spent months lying to her about it. I smiled, thinking about how I missed being around them—Shelby, included—especially my granny with whom I'd shared a special bond as a child, but I wasted so many years occupied with bad relationships that I'd distanced myself from everyone but Zabrina. Then I dove head first into raising Armand. I didn't regret that although I did a horrible job that landed us in a place where I hadn't spoken to him since the day he fired me. But I could see where putting all my energy into only one part of my life and neglecting the rest wasn't the right thing to do. I needed to fix that, starting by spending more time with my granny. I was blessed to still have her.

As I looked around, I realized my brother, Kent, wasn't there. He was guilty of the same thing I was. He'd blocked everyone out but our mother. But I could understand why. Growing up watching her live a life I would emulate wasn't easy for either of us. I made a mental note to reach out to him, too, even if he was a stuck-up asshole.

I was so deep in thought, I didn't notice Leland and my mother returning to the table and jumped a little when he tapped my shoulder. "Come on, baby. Dance with me," he said, with a beautiful smile on his face.

Once out on the floor, he pulled me into his arms and we swayed to Daniel Caesar's and H.E.R.'s *Best Part*. I closed my eyes and relaxed against him. He felt so good, as good as he always felt.

"I see you been replenishing your ho' gear. You look good, baby," he whispered in my ear, as he rubbed his hands over the purple waist beads hidden beneath my clothes.

I can't lie; I turned my own self on in the yellow baby doll romper I wore with brown Giuseppe Zanotti sandal heels, an outfit inspired by Mrs. Greer Hill and purchased thanks to the generosity of my husband who'd bought me a new wardrobe and an SUV in the weeks since my son cut me off. I had money saved up, but Leland damn near cursed me out when I tried to buy my own stuff.

"Well, you told me to take your card and get what I needed, so I figured that included ho' clothes," I said.

"You know it did. I'ma kind of tear your ass up when we get home."

"Kind of?"

"Yeah, I'ma fuck you, but I ain't gonna *fuck you* fuck you. Gotta take care of the baby."

"Leland, I told you, you're not gonna hurt little Harvey."

"Keep playing about my baby's name. Keep playing."

I rose up on my toes and kissed his juicy lips. "You have any idea how much I adore your crazy ass?"

He shrugged. "How can you not adore me when I got a big—"

"Dick and a long tongue. Yeah, yeah, yeah."

"Your ass ain't gon' be saying yeah, yeah, yeah later tonight."

"No, I'ma be saying *Leland...Leeeelaaaand...oh, Lelandddd...*"

"Keep on and we gonna get arrested for lewd conduct on this dancefloor," he murmured.

"Is that a promise?"

With narrowed eyes, he kissed me like there was no one in that club but the two of us.

A few minutes later, we were back at our table with my giddy mother and a proud Garner as Zabrina took the stage and ripped that motherfucker up!

# 31

# Leland

"You think there's a hot pot place in Sacramento?" Kim asked.

"Look at you. You acted a fool the first time I took you to get hot pot, and now that's all you want!"

"That's all *your baby* wants."

"That's because my baby has good taste like me."

As she rolled her eyes, my phone buzzed in my pocket. "Hello?" I answered.

"What-up-there-now, Nephew?"

"'Bout to head out. Got a flight to catch. 'Sup, Unc?"

"Put it on speaker," Kim whispered.

I covered the phone with my hand. "Hell, no! You ain't gonna be laughing at my uncle."

"Killjoy," she said, with a pout that I kissed. Then she zipped up her suitcase and sat on the side of the bed. Yeah, her ass was hitting the road with me. I didn't have time for her stupid-ass son to pop up starting shit, because if he ever laid another finger on her, I was going to body his ass. No questions asked.

"I was calling about Ever. She having some kind of surgery soon. She didn't want nobody to tell you, but I know you need to know. If something went wrong and you didn't know, your ass would have a damn fit."

"Sure would. Thanks for letting me know. I'ma call her now. I won't tell her where I got the information."

"Hell, you can tell her. I ain't her man; I ain't scared of Ever's big ass—what?! I'm on the phone with Leland! Damn, Lou! Don't start that shit with me right now!"

"Hey, Unc—"

"Gone and call her. Tell that pretty Kimmy I said hey."

I swear I was gonna have to put my foot up Uncle Lee's ass sooner or later.

"Your man said hey," I said to Kim as I grabbed our bags. "Come on. Let's go."

"Now you see how I feel about you and Little Kim."

Kim drove us to the airport so that I could call Aunt Ever and wouldn't kill us after hearing what was going on with her. I replied to her hello with, "So you keeping secrets from me now, huh?"

"That damn Lee Chester can't keep nothing! It's just a test, a dye test for my heart."

"And you thought I didn't need to know that?"

"I thought you had enough going on. New wife, baby on the way, basketball. You don't need to worry about me, Leland."

"You let me worry about what I need to worry about, woman. When is this test? I need to come down there for it?"

"In a few weeks, and no! Barbie's taking me, and Wyvetta's gonna be there."

"You sure?"

"Yes, baby."

"Well, you have Barbie text me the details so I can know everything."

"All right. Tell your wife I said hi."

"Hey, Aunt Ever. He's got you on speakerphone," Kim said.

"Hey, sweetie! Don't let that boy worry too much. I'ma be fine."

"Yes, ma'am."

After we hung up, I stared out the windshield and prayed my aunt was right. I didn't know what I'd do if something happened to her.

# Kimberly

"I know you're tired of me talking about it, but I just can't believe it!" Z gushed, as she took a bite of her hot dog. "Me? Singing in LA?"

"Believe it. Leland loved your show. I'm so happy for you, Z. I've never been to his club, but I hear it's really nice," I replied.

"You haven't been there? For real?"

"For real. I mean, I've been to his house. We were there a couple of weeks ago when he had that game, remember? But we didn't go to the club."

"Girl, that's your house, too, now!"

"I know. It's just hard to get used to the fact that what's his is mine. Still hasn't sunk in yet."

"Well, let it sink! His empire is your empire!"

"Empire? You're silly. But yeah, things have just moved so fast that I haven't had time to get adjusted. He's always so busy with everything, especially with all these games all over the place."

"And he's been dragging your pregnant ass with him."

"I know, right? I followed Armand around last season, but this is just…different."

"I know it is, because you ain't just following Leland around; you're also getting the shit screwed out of you in the process."

"Yep, and I love it."

"Hell, I know you do! So, you and Boogie still haven't made up?"

I sighed. "No, but I've been stalking his social media. I miss him, but he took things too far. In the past, I apologized and tried to mend things even when it was his fault that we were broken."

"Honestly, it was always his fault, Kim."

"No…the guys I dealt with, the poor decisions I made? That was me. But anyway, I can't be the one to fix us this time. Armand is gonna have to step up and own his shit. I can't do it for him."

"Good for you. I'm just glad you have Leland…and the fact that he's got money doesn't hurt."

"Okay?!"

We both laughed but were interrupted by the announcer. Our attention went to the floor as the lights in the arena dimmed, replaced by the flashing, spinning lights that were illuminating parts of the court and the crowd. I cheered when Polo's name was called and grinned at Kendra, who sat just behind me. She loved her some Polo but didn't trust him. I got it but hoped things would turn around for them. They were a good match, and after all, they'd been together forever.

When Leland's name was announced, I hopped to my feet even with my mile-wide hips and slight belly and screamed at the top of my lungs. I watched him do his new handshake which ended with him pointing me out in the crowd while Polo shaded his eyes like he was trying to find me, too. It was silly as hell, but I loved it.

And I loved him.

I loved him so much that I ignored the women a few rows above me who were screaming about how "motherfucking fine" he was.

The game was good, but there was so much on my mind, like how the Cyclones needed this win if they were going to make the playoffs and how badly Leland wanted that to happen. My mind also traveled to Armand and the fact that the Heat wouldn't be in the playoffs. I wondered who he was taking his anger over that out on and if it would land him in jail, because despite the state of our relationship, he was my son, my firstborn, and all I wanted was the absolute best for him. Then there was the fact that I'd be having a baby in five months, and since my husband had charmed my mother into being a halfway decent person, she was organizing a baby shower for me. That was nice, but it also meant she was calling me all the time, and even though she wasn't berating me anymore and had even tried to talk some sense into Armand, her being so…*involved* set my nerves on edge. But that might have also been due to her incessant mentioning of Leland in every conversation.

*"How does Leland feel about this?"*

*"What does Leland think about this?"*

*"What would Leland say about that?"*

Leland, Leland, Leland!

Hell, you'd think *he* was pregnant instead of me!

Or, that he was *her* man instead of mine.

I guess I should've been grateful for the change, but pregnancy hormones weren't having it. She was working my last, lonely nerve!

Despite all that was occupying my thoughts, I shifted my focus back to the action on the court where my man was showing completely out, and by the end of the game, the Cyclones had clinched their spot in the playoffs. I was on my feet again, cheering the victory as Leland and his teammates celebrated on the court. I knew the routine, knew it would be a while before I would leave the arena with him, and was preparing to wait with Kendra and the other wives and family members in our designated area when Leland climbed over the seats in front of me and grabbed me, lifting me off my feet and kissing me, the sweat from his face transferring to mine.

I was laughing, caught up in his euphoria as he placed me back on my feet and held my face in his hands.

"We did it, baby! We did it! Woo!" he shouted.

"Congratulations, baby!" I yelled in response, returning the kiss he'd given me.

In turn, he kissed me again, then bent over and planted a kiss on my stomach before leaving me to finish the post-game rituals.

"See, that's another reason why I can't marry Polo. He ain't never done nothing like that to me," Kendra said.

"Girl, I don't know what my cousin did to that man, but I'ma find out!" Zabrina declared.

"Besides giving him a hard time for months? I don't know what I did, either, but I'm glad I did it."

# 32

# Leland

"You played your heart out tonight and everyone could see it. What did making the playoffs with this young Cyclones team mean to you?" the reporter from the *Black Sports Now* network asked.

"It meant everything. I came here hoping for this, hoping I was joining a championship team, and now we're on our way there. I'm proud of all of us."

"So this is confirmation that your decision to leave the Heat was a good one."

"Definitely."

"So the beef with Armand Daniels turned out to be a good thing for you."

"I didn't leave over a beef with anyone. As I've stated many times before, there was never a beef on my end. Daniels is talented. I have nothing against him."

"Well, I guess you have to say that since he's now your family, right?"

This reporter was messy as hell. Most reporters had taken the high road when it came to my personal life, but this chick? Damn, was she with *Black Sports Now* or *Tea Steepers*?

"I have always had nothing but respect for him. Always," I responded.

"Hmm, well, this has been quite a season for you. New team, new wife, baby on the way…how are you handling everything?"

"All I can say is I'm blessed. I'm happy, and I couldn't ask for a better life right now."

"Okay, one last question: I hear you're a big Lil' Kim fan. Is that true?"

"I said it before and I'll say it again. I *Stan* for her. Ain't nothing changed."

"How does your wife feel about that?"

I smiled and winked at the camera, knowing Kim would watch this interview later like she did all my interviews. "She's cool with it."

\*\*\*\*\*

This was my favorite thing about Kim being in my life—having someone to chill with after a game. Having someone to hold as my body recovered from the abuse I put it through in order to make a living. Having soft lips to kiss and a soft body to wrap myself around. But most of all, knowing that the lips, the body, and the woman were mine and mine forever. Knowing that she loved me and allowed me to love her. I'd been missing that before, even though I thought I didn't need or want it, but I definitely needed and wanted her. And I loved her so much that the shit scared me. And my baby? Damn, I didn't know you could love a person who wasn't even born yet that much.

She leaned against me as we walked to my truck with the Cyclones security surrounding us, and as tired as I was, I didn't mind supporting her weight. I could smell her perfume in the night air, and although my stomach was rumbling, all I could think about was stripping her naked and taking both of us to Heaven as soon as we made it home.

"A'ight, ace! See you later!" Polo shouted, as he approached his ridiculously souped-up Denali which was a couple spaces over from my vehicle. *Flashy ass nigga…*

We were the last two team members to leave, which was the usual for us. "A'ight, man. Take it easy," I replied.

Kendra and Kim exchanged goodbyes, too, as we made it to my truck. I was opening the passenger door for Kim when I heard someone shout, "Aye, McClain!"

I watched Kim climb in and then turned my head to see who was calling me, thinking it was another one of my teammates since the Cyclones management didn't allow fans in this particular area. Maybe me and Polo weren't the last two to leave.

Not seeing anyone, I shrugged, closed Kim's door, and checked my phone when I heard it ding in my pocket. I'd received a text from my cousin, Barbie, about Aunt Ever, who'd had her appointment for her heart earlier that day and was evidently recovering well from getting a cardiac stent placed. Thank God.

"McClain!" the voice shouted again.

"Who dat?" I yelled in response, my face still in the phone.

"The motherfucker who's gon' end your punk ass!"

The shots rang out before I could react, hitting concrete and metal—*my truck*.

Kim.

I turned back to her but was yanked to the ground by someone. Security? I yelled for them to let me go, but whoever it was had a mean grip on me.

"Stay down!" I heard the person yell.

"My wife!" I countered.

Then there was more yelling, so much yelling and so many voices that I couldn't make sense of any of it. Yelling, gunshots, movement, rapid footfalls, more yelling, more gunshots, more feet beating the pavement. It was a confusing mixture of panicked sounds, and somewhere in the midst of it all, I could hear Kim screaming my name. Was she afraid for me or did she need me?

*Kim.*

*My baby.*

All I could think about was getting to her, to *them*. If I got shot, I got shot, but I had to get to her. I *had* to.

I wrestled myself free of whoever had me and hopped to my feet, bullets still pinging around me, voices still filling the air.

"I got him!" someone shouted.

*They got who?* I wondered, as I tried to orient myself to where I was. Whoever grabbed me had dragged me away from the truck, not too far, but far enough to confuse me, or maybe it was the melee around me that confused me—people running, other people shouting orders, someone on a phone, someone crying.

Someone crying?

I got my head right and rushed to my truck to see the passenger door laying open, glass from the windows littering the interior, and blood.

Not a lot of blood, but shit, it was *blood*.

Whose blood was it?

I spun on my heels, trying to figure out the direction of the crying, and realized it was coming from the back of my truck. Yanking the backdoor open, I found Kim lying on the floorboard rolled into a ball, shaking and crying. There was blood on her arms. Without thinking, I grabbed her, and she started yelling.

"It's me! It's me, baby! It's me!" I tried to reassure her.

She opened her eyes and wrinkled her eyebrows. "Leland?"

"Yeah, baby. I got you. I got you. Where are you hurt?"

"I-I don't know. I don't…I'm so sorry, Leland. This was my fault. I'm so sorry," she whispered, and then her eyes fluttered closed.

# 33

# Leland

The last thing I felt like doing was answering the phone, but since Everett had just recently stopped cursing me out for keeping my marriage and baby a secret from him, although months had passed, I accepted his call and leaned forward in the chair, my elbows on my knees, one hand holding the phone and the other holding my forehead. "Yo," I said, closing my eyes.

"You good, man? I heard some shit went down after the game. Tryna see if it's true."

"I'm fine. Scraped up from team security slamming me to the ground and dragging my big ass to safety, and the screen of my phone is cracked up to be damned from me dropping it. Other than that, I'm good."

"Good. Good. Kim? The baby?"

"Waiting to see."

"Okay...I'm on my way and I'm bringing Tommy with me. He's gonna hang with you, help you put a security team together. Him and Bridgette broke up, so he wants to get away for a minute anyway."

"Okay."

Silence from my big brother.

"What?" I asked, sitting up and letting my eyes round the filling ER waiting area. I hated hospitals. They reminded me too much of being eleven and losing my mom.

"You ain't gonna fight me on this?"

"Naw. Shit, you're right. You *been* right. If I'd had security, they could've protected Kim. I wanna be pissed at the team's security for leaving her hanging like that, but they were doing their job by protecting me. It was my job to protect her, and I failed. I failed like a mug, man."

"Don't do that to yourself, Leland. This ain't your fault."

"Yeah, it is. They got the guy and it turns out he's the stepdad of that kid I told you about from the basketball camp I volunteered at. The one at the center Kim used to run."

"The dude who was hitting on the little boy's mom? He's the shooter?"

"Yeah. I guess he's been pissed at me all this time for getting in his business and getting his ass arrested."

"The fuck he doing out of jail?"

"Cops said his girl wouldn't testify against him, so they couldn't hold him."

"Damn."

"I know."

A nurse called my name, so I said, "Gotta go, Ev. See you when you get here."

"A'ight, man."

I followed the nurse to the ER room where Kim lay in a bed, her head turned toward the wall. She'd given me an update on her condition and I couldn't believe what she'd told me, but now I was seeing it. I was seeing it with my own two eyes, but that didn't make it any easier to believe.

"Kim?" I said softly.

She turned her head and reached for me. I rushed to the side of her bed and pulled her to me, stroking the bandage on her arm where a bullet grazed it, then her hair, and letting my tears fall. She was okay, understandably shaken up, but okay. The blood was from cuts on her arms from the glass of the door windows and windshield that were shattered by the hail of bullets, and the one that grazed her. She was alive. She was still here, and for that, I was eternally grateful.

The first miracle I ever encountered was meeting and falling in love with Kim. The second and third were her agreeing to carry my child and become my wife. The fourth miracle was that despite that fool's best efforts, she was okay, and so was my baby.

*So was my baby.*

"I'm so glad you're okay," I said into her ear.

"Me, too. And the baby," she whimpered.

"Our baby is tough as hell," I replied.

She laughed against my shoulder. "Just like us, huh?"

"Just like *you*, baby."

"Hmmm, Leland, I need to tell you something."

"I already know."

Releasing me, she asked, "You already know what?"

"Who Shemar's stepdad is, who he was to you."

Her mouth dropped open. "H-how?"

"When I was talking to the police, they said his street name was Domo, but his government name is Andre Greene. I remembered the dude who choked you, the ex you said Daniels pulled off you was named Dre and how you reacted to seeing him and what he did to Shemar's mom, and I put two and two together, figured out it was the same dude."

Kim stared at me for so long that I asked, "I'm right...right?"

"Yes," she softly said. "I should've told you before. When I heard him call your name tonight, I recognized his voice, and I just knew he was going to hurt you and it'd be my fault."

"Naw, baby. What he did tonight had nothing to do with you. He never saw you that day at his house. *I* was his target."

"But he had to have seen us together on social media and stuff. He had to know I was your wife."

"He probably did, but his beef was with me, not you. If he was gonna come for you, he could've done that a long time ago. Your son might've beat his ass, but dude had a gun. Daniels couldn't do shit to stop a bullet."

"Maybe you're right."

"I know I am. Anyway, they got him and he's going down for real this time. He actually shot a couple members of the security team and there were plenty of witnesses."

"He did?! Are they okay?!"

"Yeah, they're good. Minor injuries."

"Good," she said through a sigh. "But I don't understand how he got so close. Isn't that area restricted?"

"Get this, the nigga works at the arena. Been working there for a while, since before I joined the team."

"Wow!"

"Yeah." I sat on the side of the small bed and grasped her hand. "Look, baby, this was on me, and I probably should say some shit like you'd be better off without me, but that'd be a lie."

"Wooooow."

I smiled at her. "Just saying. Anyway, we're gonna be fine. Ev is gonna help me hire some bodyguards, get a security team of my own together."

"Good! You've been needing one."

"It's for you, too, baby. I gotta take better care of you."

"You take the best care of me, Leland."

"Naw, I can do better. I should've been had you a bodyguard, but I'ma fix that. No more playing around with your safety."

"Okay, baby."

I was leaning in to kiss her when a knock sounded at the door. "Excuse me. Mrs. McClain, your son is here to see you."

I looked at her and she nodded.

"Okay, I'll go get him," I said.

She grabbed my arm before I could leave her bedside. "Leland—"

"If he behaves, so will I. Let me go get him."

She sighed and nodded again.

He was sitting in the waiting area, a few feet from where I'd been sitting before, but I knew he had to have arrived after I went back to see Kim, because I would've noticed him...I think. Shit, who knows? My mind was all tangled up, and when I wasn't sitting out there worried about my wife and child, I was dealing with calls from family members and Polo, who managed to pull out of the lot before the shooting started, team reps, and the team publicist. Hell, the damn cops had even questioned me there for a hot second, adding to their on-site interrogation. So yeah, I could've missed him, but I was pretty sure I didn't.

His head snapped up from where it'd been buried in his chest, and he looked up at me as if he sensed my presence. There was concern in his eyes, but that didn't mean anything to me. I had some stuff to get off my chest, and this seemed like as good a time as any.

Hopping to his feet, he moved closer to me. "I-I was at the game tonight, and after I left, I heard the news. How is my mama? I need to see her."

Shaking my head, I stuffed my hands in the pockets of my jogging pants. "We need to get some shit clear before you go see her."

"Look, McClain—"

"Naw, bruh...*you* look. That's my wife back there. *My wife.* Ain't shit I won't do for her and my baby. If you think I'ma let you go back there talking shit to her and upset her, you're out your damn mind. And if you lay a finger on her, accident or not, I'ma fuck you all the way up. I promise on my mama and my daddy, I will break your neck if you ever hurt her again. Matter of fact, your ass better not even flinch around her in my presence. Let me see you blink in her direction and I'ma—"

"Man, that's my mom! I just wanna see her. That's all!"

I stared at him, didn't move a muscle.

"Look, man...I ain't got no beef with you no more. I can see you ain't playing with her like I thought you were. I just..." At that moment, he broke down. I mean, tears and snot were going everywhere.

I was still ready to whoop his ass, though.

"I think it's good she found you. She seems happy in the pictures you been posting on IG. I just...I don't want her to get hurt. I thought you were gonna hurt her," he continued.

"Like you hurt her?"

"Like *everybody* hurt her."

"Well, I ain't everybody."

He nodded as he looked me in the eye. "Yeah, I can see that. She's happy. Never really seen her happy before."

We both stood there as I tried to decide if I believed him or not.

"I just wanna see my mom," he pleaded.

"Shit…come on, man. You can see her, but I'ma be right there."

He nodded.

# Kimberly

"Here's your phone. I forgot to give it to you," Leland said, when he returned. "I grabbed it from the truck."

"Thank you," I said, as I took the phone from him.

"I'll be right outside the door, okay?" He kissed me and left the room, leaving the door ajar.

My eyes settled on Armand, who stood just inside the room, his eyes on the floor.

"You scared to be close to me or something?" I asked, my words cutting through the tangible tension in the air.

I watched as he lifted his eyebrows and eyes, head still lowered, and dragged himself over to me, instantly putting me in the mind of a ten-year-old Boogie. Then I thought about him at three, always shaking his little booty to some song, earning his nickname.

He made it to the bedside and lifted his wet eyes to my face, speaking words through them that I knew were stuck somewhere behind his pride.

Resting my hand on top of his that was gripping the side rail, I assured him that, "Hey, I forgive you."

His eyes widened. "You do?"

I nodded and reached up to place my hand on his cheek. "Yep, and I've missed you. You been okay?"

He shook his head. "Been missing you, too."

"No need to. You can always call me."

"I was so worried when I heard about the shooting. I'm glad you're okay."

"Me, too." I watched him nod and took a deep breath. "Armand, I know how you feel about Leland, but I love him and I'm married to him and—"

"Look, Ma...I'm good with it now. I mean, I still don't like it or him, but I can see he loves you, so...I'ma let it go. Uh, I'm sorry for hurting you and taking your stuff. You can have your car back and I still own the condo so I can give you the key and you—"

"That's okay. I don't need anything."

"Yeah, I saw that Land Rover he got you. It's nice."

"Thanks. Armand...I wasn't your responsibility and I shouldn't have accepted that stuff from you in the first place, so—"

"But you're his responsibility?"

"He thinks so."

We were quiet until he asked, "Boy or a girl?"

I frowned, then rested my hand on my tummy. "Oh! We don't know. We want to be surprised."

"But you're happy, right? About the baby? And he's taking care of you?"

"I've never been so happy, Boogie. Leland is good to me, really good to me."

"Good."

My phone buzzed, and upon checking the screen, my eyes widened. "It's-it's my brother."

"Uncle Kent? Really?"

I nodded. I hadn't talked to him in years, literal years.

"I'ma let you get that. I'll talk to you later. Love you, Ma."

"Love you, too, Boogie."

Leland was back at my bedside when I said, "Hello," into the phone.

"Hey, sis. It's been a while, huh?"

# 34

## Kimberly

His huge hands gripped my hips as he plowed into me, his pace hectic but rhythmic as his big body crowded the back of mine.

"I will fuck up the world for you, you know that, baby? Ain't shit I wouldn't do for you."

"Ohhh, shit!" was my response, because he was rubbing and bumping up against all the right spots over and over again, sending me so close to the edge that I could peer over the cliff and see my destination perfectly.

His hand snaked its way under my dress and bra to my full breast. He palmed it, then squeezed it, still gripping my hip with the other hand. Then his hand slid up to the waist beads that had become a mandatory part of my wardrobe, according to my husband.

My *husband*

That was still unbelievable to me, had been since the day it happened. Never in a million years did I think I'd be someone's wife. Especially his wife. He was so good to—

"Oh, oh, ohhhhhhh!!" I gripped the edge of the vanity, bracing myself as I climaxed and Leland thrusted deeper, harder, faster.

"I love you, baby. I'ma always love you," he said into my ear.

"I love you, tooooo," I whimpered.

A few strokes later, he lost his rhythm, grunted, groaned, and collapsed onto my back. "Shit," he muttered. "I can't believe you made me do that."

Catching my breath, I replied, "It was only a suggestion."

"You saying, 'Why don't you find us somewhere to fuck because I'm horny as hell and my pussy is beating like an HBCU drumline,' was just a suggestion? Really?"

"Yeah."

He finally lifted from my back, and I could hear him behind me adjusting his clothes. "That wasn't no suggestion; it was a challenge, and you know I don't turn down challenges."

I was still bent over the vanity in the small restroom, trying to steady my shaky legs. "Oh, my bad. Well, it's your fault for having a big dick and a long tongue."

He smacked my exposed butt, then leaned in and whispered in my ear, "And you know this. Hey, you need help getting cleaned up?"

"Yeah. You?"

I finally stood upright and turned to face him. With a smirk, he asked, "Now, why would I wanna clean you off me?" Then he pulled me into a kiss that on any other occasion, would've ended in round two. But not tonight. Tonight, round two would have to wait. Tonight, we had some celebrating to do.

\*\*\*\*\*

I tried not to look embarrassed as we exited the restroom to find Tommy guarding the door, but hell, he had to be used to this by now. Leland was adventurous when it came to sex, and I wasn't much better. And we'd taken to "christening" nearly every venue we attended an event at. So the unbothered look on Tommy's face wasn't fake. Now Quezz, the bodyguard who stood on the other side of the door? He was new and looked majorly uncomfortable, but he'd get used to it, too. He'd have to.

Back at our table, Leland pulled my chair out for me, and as I wiggled into it, Zabrina smacked her lips, rolled her eyes, and said, "You gonna mess around and get pregnant again."

I gave her a wink and a shrug.

Her still-fiancé chuckled, and she rolled her eyes at him. "I can't believe y'all had your bodyguards turning people away from that restroom. Y'all need help," Zabrina continued.

"That's your cousin's fault. She been on fire since she had the baby," Leland said.

I turned to him with a lifted eyebrow. "As if you don't like it…"

He lifted both his eyebrows and leaned in close to me. "Did I say that?"

"Maybe pineapples are an aphrodisiac, because I swear that's all she ever eats these days," Zabrina mused.

"Hell, you better start eating them," I muttered.

"I told you, I don't like pineapples."

"And I told you, you better learn to like them."

"Whatever. Back to my little cousin. I can't wait for this shindig to be over so I can go to y'all's mausoleum and kiss his little cheeks!" Zabrina gushed.

"Girl, if you can pry him out of Kat's hands. She's supposed to be Leland's assistant, but you'd think she was Junior's nanny. And a mausoleum is a tomb, Z. My house is not a tomb," I replied.

"Aw, shit, girl…I thought a mausoleum was like a mansion or something."

"Then just say mansion, fool!"

"Well, I don't blame Kat. Little Leland is just so cute! Even Aunt Ever was willing to fly just to see him!" Jo chimed in from where she and Everett sat on the other side of Leland.

"Damn, Jo! You 'bout to pop, ain't you?" Leland virtually yelled as Jo stood, then reclaimed her seat, scooting closer to the table. The sight of the tiny woman in a short dress with her stomach protruding was definitely a spectacle, especially when she was standing next to Everett. He was only dwarfed by Leland and Polo, who was out on the dancefloor with Kendra.

"And I'm only five months! I'ma die!" she whined.

"No, you won't. You know what?" Everett said, then leaned in close to her and whispered something in her ear that made her grin. I knew that grin, because I'd worn it many times before myself. He'd said something nasty to her. Those McClain men were something else.

Letting my eyes roam the room, I saw Nolan in a corner talking to Jo's assistant, Bridgette, who did not look amused. Neil was sitting at a table next to ours nursing a drink. I started to feel bad about Kat missing out on the fun since she was at our house babysitting our three-month-old little boy, but it was actually her suggestion, and I wasn't going to fight her on it.

Leland's wannabe girlfriend, my mother, was having a ball at her table with my grandmother, brother, and some other family members. That's when my mind drifted to my older son. I wished he was there helping us celebrate, but although he was no longer threatening to kill my husband, things with him weren't perfect. I just counted it a blessing that we spoke on the phone every week and that he'd finally agreed to get some counseling.

When Leland rested a hand on my thigh, I turned and smiled at him as I gently tugged on his beard. "Thank you."

"For what? This party? You've been working hard taking care of Junior, following my ass around the world, helping me start my foundation, and I didn't give you a real wedding, so it was the least I could do to give you an anniversary party."

I rested my hand on top of his, rubbing my finger over his huge championship ring. "No, for loving me and giving me a second chance at…everything."

He blinked a couple of times then kissed me softly on the lips. "Thank you for letting me."

# 35

# Leland

"Look, Little Man…Daddy is going to change your diaper. I'm tired, had a game tonight, and I'ma need you to cooperate. Do not pee on Daddy this time, a'ight? The last time, you hit me in the nose, and that was mad disrespectful. I love you, even cried when you were born, and I gave you my good looks, so I'ma need you to do right by me. I been tryna convince your mama to give you a little brother or sister, but if you don't get this peeing situation under control, I'ma withdraw my request."

Junior stuffed his fist in his mouth and kicked his legs in response.

I unfastened the diaper, but held it over his little private parts, took a deep breath, and said, "A'ight, son, here we go."

As soon as I opened the diaper, pee shot up like a damn geyser, hitting me right on my beard. Damn, his stream was stronger than a motherfucker. It actually made me kind of proud.

As he smiled up at me and kicked his fat little legs, I grabbed a wet wipe to clean myself up. "Man, I thought we were better than that, Junior!"

That's when I heard giggling behind me. I didn't turn around as I continued to change him, and said, "You trained him to do this to me, didn't you?"

As she wrapped her arms around my waist and laid her head on my back, she said, "No, I think it's his way of bonding with you."

"Uh-huh, I'ma bond with your ass as soon as I put him down."

"Shit, you better."

I snapped Junior's onesie and picked him up, kissing his fat little chocolate cheek. "Your mama is so nasty and your daddy loooooves it."

"You better stop bad-mouthing me to my baby."

"And as soon as you go to sleep, I'ma tear her up. I sure aaaaam."

"Leland!"

"What?"

"I can't with you," she said, as she left the baby's room.

"But you're going to. Yes, you aaaaaare."

"Ugh!"

I chuckled as I nuzzled my son's neck, making him giggle. "My boy."

I held him close, walking down the hallway of our new St. Louis house. As I stepped over the threshold of my bedroom to see Kim sitting on the bed in her gown, waiting for me with a pout on her face, I smiled and whispered to myself, "My family."

A southern girl at heart, Alexandria House has an affinity for a good banana pudding, Neo Soul music, and tall black men in suits. When this fashionista is not shopping, she's writing steamy stories about real black love.

Connect with Alexandria!
Email: msalexhouse@gmail.com
Website: http://www.msalexhouse.com/
Newsletter: http://eepurl.com/cOUVg5
Blog: http://msalexhouse.blogspot.com/
Facebook: Alexandria House
Instagram: @msalexhouse
Twitter: @mzalexhouse

Also by Alexandria House:

*The McClain Brothers Series:*
Let Me Love You
Let Me Hold You

*The Strickland Sisters Series:*
Stay with Me
Believe in Me
Be with Me

*The Love After Series:*
Higher Love
Made to Love
Real Love

*Short Stories*
Merry Christmas, Baby
Baby, Be Mine

Made in the USA
Las Vegas, NV
09 February 2024

85563862R00148